I0760446

FAE'S PROMISE

QUEENS OF THE FAE: BOOK SIX

MELISSA A. CRAVEN
M. LYNN

Edited by Cindy Ray Hale
Proofread by Nic Page
Cover by Covers by Combs

For those who say LGBTQ+ characters don't belong in YA or clean fiction.

You won't like this one either.

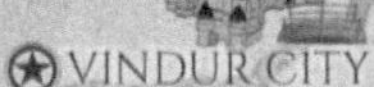
PRISON REALM
NORTHERN VATL
LOCH VILLANDI
FARGELSI KINGDOM
SOUTHERN VATL
DRAGUR FOREST
VINDUR CITY

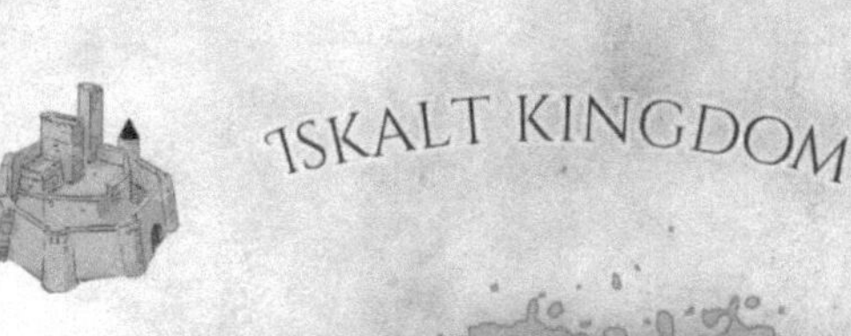
ISKALT KINGDOM

EASTERN VATLANDS
ELDFAL
SANDUR
SOL LOCH
UR KINGDOM
TEOTANN OASIS
ELDUR DESERT
H LANGT

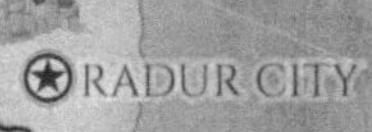
RADUR CITY

PROLOGUE

Toby

Fire ravaged the village, casting a wave of heat through the ranks of those begging for their lives.

Help us.

Please.

Stop!

Not my daughter!

Light Fae cowered as creatures they hadn't known existed tore through their homes. Homes that had once lain hidden safely behind the magic found in the book of power.

Tobias O'Shea skittered back, stumbling over something warm behind him. His eyes searched the square frantically until he saw what tripped him. A body. A young man lay at his feet, blood pooling in the grooves between cobblestones.

This was Aghadoon, the fae village his grandmother discovered in the human realm using the book's power.

The book.

Someone crashed into Tobias from behind, and he fell

forward, diving to the left to avoid the dead man. His knees hit the stones, sending pain rocketing through his body. His hands slammed down next, the shock reverberating up his arms.

Blood seeped through the cracks in the stones, its warmth soaking into Tobias' scratched palms.

He scrambled back until he hit the side of a building that didn't burn. Fire from surrounding surfaces licked at the walls, yet it remained intact.

Tobias pressed his back against the cracked wood of a door and drew his knees in to his chest, hearing the words his grandmother, Enis uttered to him only hours before.

It'll be okay, Toby.

This book can give you magic, the kind of power you've never seen.

All he wanted was his sister, his twin.

But Enis was right. It hadn't been the first time he held magic in his fingertips, but it was the first time the power belonged to *him.* His sister wasn't channeling power through him, he wasn't strengthening her magic. This was his magic.

Enis taught him how to use the book to awaken the O'Shea magic in his blood, the portal magic. And it led him here.

Tobias closed his eyes, wanting to pretend the world wasn't coming down around him, that every time he heard a body thump to the stones it wasn't his fault. He'd brought them here, the Dark Fae king and his army.

The innocents of this village had only ever wanted to protect the magic of the book.

"Tobias!" Someone screamed his name, but he couldn't find them amidst the cacophony. A creature King Egan had called an ogre ran across the square, each stomp shaking the structures nearby.

A Light Fae, who'd been a prisoner until weeks before, used

his magic, drawing power from the sun to keep the fires blazing. An Eldurian. He had to be.

Tobias knew the Eldurian queen. The future Eldurian rulers were his cousins since his mom and theirs called each other sister. It would hurt them to see their ancestral magic used for such evils.

There'd been a place for people who did evil things.

The prison realm.

But now...

"Tobias!"

He heard it louder that time, the voice. Uncurling himself, he searched for someone, anyone he knew.

A sword flashed, the sun glinting off its rusted blade, almost blinding Tobias as an unfamiliar fae ran for him.

He froze in the moment, wishing there was something else he could do. Tia would have had a plan. She'd have used her power to save the day.

But all he could do was open portals, though he'd only done it a total of once. He wasn't sure where to begin or if he could even manage it on his own a second time.

His eyelids slid shut. If he couldn't help Tia save the world from Egan Byrne, he'd rather not play a part in this war at all.

But the blow never came. Instead, warm droplets sprayed his face. He opened his eyes to find Riona kicking the slain fae off her sword. Her wings, a mixture of white and swirling black shadows, stretched out behind her, adding to the fear he already felt around her.

"Tobias." He recognized the voice. Had she been the one calling for him this entire time?

When Tobias didn't respond, Riona bent down to grab his arm and hauled him to his feet. She pushed him forward, kicking open a door as she did and shoving him inside before shutting out the battle ensuing outside. Her wings curled in, making her odd tattoos the only thing separating her from the Light Fae.

"Tobias." She shook him. "Toby, did you crack your skull?"

He shook his head.

"Then speak, child. Don't scare me like that again. I've been searching for you the entire fight. You ran from the king's side."

He had. When Egan killed the first fae, Tobias ran.

"You came for me?"

She nodded, the blood spattered on her dark skin giving her a harsh look. But if she wanted to protect him, did that mean she was still loyal to his Uncle Griff?

"The king would have my head if we let you get hurt. You're our way back to the fae realm, remember?"

His heart sank. Maybe she'd never been loyal to Griffin at all. Maybe it was all a plan to get here, where she could help the king find the power he sought.

Tobias couldn't look at her hard expression anymore. He breathed deeply, trying to get control of his heart the way Mom taught him. Mom. Tears welled in his eyes. What would she say when she found out what he helped the prison fae do?

He blinked away tears, hearing his sister's voice in his head. *Iskaltians don't cry, Toby. When we're hurt, we get back up again. We fight.*

She wouldn't have let anyone use her.

Wiping at his eyes, he scanned the room they'd entered. "Why isn't it on fire?" Everything else in this doomed village was.

Riona slid her sword into the sheath at her waist, her shoulders relaxing the tiniest bit as she glanced to the door. "Because it's been spelled."

Spelled? Tobias walked on shaky legs to one of the shelves

where ancient looking leather-bound books and scrolls were stacked in tight rows.

The twin Prince and Princess of Iskalt were no strangers to tragedy or danger. They'd spent months in the human realm with their evil Uncle Callum and lived. But they'd been together. Now, Tobias couldn't even feel his sister anymore.

Riona sighed as she blocked the door with a heavy wooden chair she wedged under the doorknob. "The king has given strict orders that no one is to enter the library. We won't be found until the slaughter is finished."

Tobias flinched at the word slaughter. An entire village of fae who just wanted to live their lives while providing a sacred service. They were gone.

Grainne's lineage had protected the spell book for so many years, and now it was snuffed out in a single day.

A library that didn't burn and was obviously important to the king? Tobias reached for one of the scrolls, but Riona's voice stopped him.

"I wouldn't do that if I were you."

Tobias curled his fingers in, despite her protest, making him more curious than ever. He'd never been one to act on curiosities. That was Tia's way.

Riona slumped onto a wooden chair in front of a long, cherry wood desk. "I never thought this was possible." She rubbed a hand over her face.

Tobias inched closer to the fearsome warrior. "What are you talking about?"

"From what I've been told, kid, your O'Shea magic would have woken years ago if you had any potential for magic." O'Shea power was different from the Iskaltian magic he didn't have. It didn't wait to fully manifest until one came of age.

"I'm only ten." He crossed his arms, unable to look at her.

"Yes, which is my only hope."

When he didn't respond, she continued. "The book woke your portal magic, but it's different from the other O'Sheas. Your father, your uncle... they struggle to take more than a few people through with them at a time. Yet you brought part of an army into the human realm on your first go. There's also the time skew. If Griffin leaves the fae realm at night, it's daytime in the human realm, rendering him powerless until the moon rises again. But you... despite the darkness and the full moon, it was day in the prison realm when we left. And now..."

"It's still day."

She nodded, giving him a weary sigh. "Did Callum bring you to the village?"

Tobias nodded.

"So, you knew where to portal, but I wonder if the power that book gives you would let you portal to places you've never seen before." She rested her arms on the desk and shook her head. "That book breaks all the rules."

Tobias didn't get a chance to find out if the fear he heard in her voice were true because a flash of light blasted through the door. It didn't burst inward like Tobias expected, but the chair blocking it exploded into a thousand tiny shards of wood.

The door opened, revealing King Egan flanked by two Light Fae with wicked smiles.

Riona rose to greet her king. "Egan, you should know nothing can destroy this library." She dipped her head in respect.

A wide smile spread across his face. "Just a test, darling."

She lifted a brow. "And that." She pointed out to the square where Tobias caught a glimpse of the carnage and turned away. "Is that a test?"

Egan walked forward and put an arm around Riona. "No, dear. That was a victory."

Enis followed him into the room, her eyes searching the

library before finally landing on Tobias. "Toby." For a moment, he wondered if the relief on her face was genuine, but as she wrapped him in a tight hug, he found he didn't care. His body shook in her arms, and he sent a silent apology to Tia, wherever she was.

It turned out, Iskaltians did cry.

At least this one did.

Griffin

Retreat.

It was a strange thought. The army pulled back from the battle they'd been fully engaged in, but it didn't lessen what they'd already lost. It didn't clear the rocky valley of the bodies of their fallen friends.

It didn't wash the blood from a warrior's hands.

Griffin O'Shea wasn't a man to back away from a fight, but even he'd known they couldn't defeat Egan's Dark Fae army who had defensive powers he'd never imagined they possessed, powers that kept the Light Fae from decimating them with magic.

For a seventh straight day since the battle, he stood looking at the bloodied rocks spanning the distance from the trees at his back to the prison realm at his front. There was no longer a barrier separating the two, no magic keeping him on opposite sides from his family.

He'd fought for them, battled against an army of people

who weren't altogether different from the ones he'd lived with for the last ten years, and yet suspicion followed him wherever he roamed among the Iskalt and Fargelsi camps.

The fae who remained, the ones who'd lived through the onslaught until Egan's army pulled back for a reason they couldn't understand. Their eyes held a wariness.

Griffin walked past the pyres that had burned for an entire day after the battle. He didn't let himself avert his eyes from those who suffered, the ones who'd come because of him. If he hadn't set out on that fateful mission for Egan to find the book of power, maybe none of this would have happened.

But his people would have still been trapped.

"Why hasn't Egan returned?" Griffin kicked over an empty pot, letting his irritation get the best of him. "Nothing makes sense." They couldn't leave the Myrkur border, couldn't provide Egan with a clear path into the three kingdoms. But there'd been no sight of his people since they attacked from both sky and land.

He'd told Lochlan everything he knew about the Dark Fae king, every strength, every weakness. Griffin wanted to lead the advanced Iskaltian and Fargelsian forces into the dark realm to meet the enemy forces head on before they could recover, but Lochlan refused, saying he wouldn't lead his people into a realm they did not know to fight a king they'd never heard of before a week ago.

In this war, Egan would have to make the next move.

"And why the heck is my brother a self-righteous jerk who has to be right all the time?" He imagined if they'd grown up together, Lochlan would have been their father's favorite, mastering his books and his magic in ways Griffin never could.

But they didn't grow up together, a fact that had never been more clear when recognition finally lit in Lochlan's eyes only hours before the battle, when he knew Griffin for what he was —or, at least, what he used to be.

"You going to burn the camp down?" Myles looked up from the book he was reading. "Yesterday I sat by Lochlan when he ranted and raved about you, and I swear he almost set me on fire."

"Since when do you read?" Griffin plucked the book from Myles' hands and looked down at the cover. "The mythical fae?"

Myles took it back. "The grumpier O'Shea took me into the human realm after you left for Myrkur—again—for a few of their books once he realized they knew more about our world than we did."

"It's just a book of myths."

Myles lifted a brow. "And you think their myths aren't rooted in fact? This book contains information about fae who live in the waters, in the skies." He shrugged. "Even ogres, though I'm still not sure I believe Shrek is out here running around."

Griffin sighed, lifting his eyes to the sea of tents winding through the thick forests in the mountains outside Myrkur. It was considerably less than it had been a week ago. He dropped to the ground next to Myles. "I don't know one named Shrek, but I've only met a few ogres."

Myles smiled in that human way he had whenever he thought fae were amusing for not understanding what he said. He closed his book. "Griff..."

"Spit it out, human." Griffin had never given Myles much thought after dragging him to the fae realm. He hadn't wondered where he was while Griffin spent ten years in the prison realm. Yet, he'd come to have a grudging fondness for the boy over the last few months.

"Are you okay? Like... really, really okay?"

"I don't look it?" He forced a smile, knowing how he must appear to those camped here, the ones who now remembered the stories of Griffin, the traitor, the Iskaltian prince who chose the wrong side.

"I mean... you always have that ugly mug... but lately it's been—"

"Uglier?"

Myles let out a humorless laugh. "I guess."

"I'm guessing the words are yours, but the question is not." He let his eyes follow the familiar trail to the tent belonging to the King and Queen of Iskalt. Queen Brea sat on a stump digging her hands into the bucket containing the day's washing. A servant stood by, horror plain on her face at the sight of the queen washing her own clothing.

Myles followed his gaze. "Is it wrong for her to be worried about you?"

"No. I feel it too." The worry, the remnants of a broken marriage bond that returned with the memories. It didn't return the love, exactly, but he was tied to her. A fact both she and her husband knew as well.

"I don't understand why you two can't just clear the air."

"Myles." Griffin shook his head as he pulled his knife free and reached for the stone he'd used to sharpen it. And sharpened it again. The steady sound of the blade kept him from focusing on the magic inside him.

"No." Myles rose up on his knees and inched closer. "Hear me out. Okay, so I know I'm like the only person in this entire camp who will talk to you."

"Not true."

"The only person who isn't a kid." He paused as if waiting for Griffin to contradict him.

But it was the truth. Griffin had been shut out of everything. Strategy sessions, war planning. Other than Myles, the only people in this camp who spent any time with him were Gulliver and Tia, the latter only because he didn't try to make her talk like Brea and Lochlan did.

"Go on." Griffin continued sharpening the already sharp blade.

"Like I said, I may be the only adult here who will talk to you, but I'm not the only one who cares about you. It's complicated, Griff. You have to understand that."

The truth was, he did.

"I need a walk." Or to hit something. Where was Egan and his army when he needed them?

After ten mostly peaceful years in Myrkur where they struggled to survive but didn't have to fight for their lives, he was back to his old self, yearning for a fight. Jumping to his feet, he ignored Myles' protests.

All Griffin had done for the last week was replay the events in his mind, talk to Myles, and sharpen his blade. He wasn't sure how much longer he could do it. He wound through rows of tents where Iskaltians and Fargelsians followed him with their eyes. He'd betrayed both peoples when sitting at Regan's side. Ten years didn't erase what he'd done.

Back then he'd longed to be known, to sit on a throne. And now... everyone knew him.

The smaller Fargelsian army and the advanced force Lochlan and Brea had led from Iskalt were bolstered just before the battle by the arrival of the rest of the Iskaltian army.

The remaining army of the three realms—the one loyal to Eldur, stayed back along the border of Iskalt and Eldur, a last defense if the Dark Fae broke through.

Griffin found Gulliver surrounded by a circle of soldiers who laughed and gaped at everything he could make his tail do. Seeing the soldiers laugh after the tough week they'd had was uplifting.

Tia leaned against a tree, keeping herself apart from the soldiers. She hugged her arms across her chest as if afraid someone would come along and rip her heart out. Maybe they already had. He knew the feeling.

"Hey, kiddo." She lifted dark eyes to his, and he wondered if he was mistaken at the relief on her face. Knowing she wouldn't respond, he didn't wait for an answer. He loved how much she liked human terms and belongings. She was as fascinated by the other world as Gulliver was. During the battle, Gulliver had named himself her protector—along with a guard her mother assigned—and he hadn't left her side.

Griffin tried not to think too much about the similarities he might share with Tia, not now that he knew a truth no one else did.

Other than Riona.

Pushing her betrayal from his mind, he wrapped an arm around Tia's shoulders. "How about you and I go find some quiet?"

She nodded, the brightness she once held in her eyes gone. He jerked his head toward the path they'd taken many times over the last few days. It twisted through the trees before bringing them to the edge of camp, where a small clearing let them escape without drifting too far from the safety of the army.

He saw Lochlan standing with two of his generals and pulled his arm back from Tia's shoulders. Still, she followed him.

He pushed through a curtain of branches and leaves, creating an opening for Tia.

They sat side by side on the bright green carpet of tall grasses. Above, the trees shielded them from the sun.

Tia lay back, her hands resting on her stomach.

Griffin watched her, not saying a word. It wasn't that he

didn't know what to say, just that there was no reason to speak because he knew this girl had the same emotions rolling through her. It was like half of her was taken right along with Tobias.

Just like Riona.

And his mother.

The difference was Tobias never chose to leave her.

Griffin reached out, folding one of her tiny hands in his larger one. He didn't know if Tia would ever find out he was her father, but he wasn't sure he wanted that—to completely upend her world. To take that away from Lochlan—even if Lochlan was currently not on team Griffin.

Griffin didn't know how long they lay there before Gulliver's shouting broke their peace. He pushed through the opening to the clearing, his chest heaving.

Releasing Tia, Griffin jumped to his feet. "What's wrong?"

Gulliver's haunted eyes flicked from Tia to Griffin, and he swallowed. "I need to tell you something—"

Tia's scream cut him off as she pressed her hands to the side of her head and rocked from side to side. "Toby, no!"

Tears streamed down her face, and Gulliver dropped to his knees at her side, pulling her up to look at him. "Tia... what is it?"

More tears. Seeing Tia cry was such a rare sight, Griffin watched her carefully.

Gulliver dipped his head to meet her gaze. "Is it Toby?"

She nodded. "I see..." She couldn't finish.

Gulliver gripped her hands. "He's in the human realm, isn't he?"

How? Griffin watched them, not quite sure what was going on. Egan didn't have an O'Shea with magic with him. They couldn't get to the human realm.

Gulliver looked to Griffin. "You can't ask me how I know,

Griff. I won't tell you. But Enis used the book to awaken Toby's O'Shea magic. I think that's what she's seeing. Egan's army has destroyed Aghadoon, leaving only the library intact."

That wasn't possible.

But with the book of power in the mix, he still believed it. "I need to get to Lochlan. We have to march into Myrkur now." There were too many people he cared about still in there to forsake it. He had to make his brother see that. "Can you get Tia to her guard?"

Gulliver nodded. "Make him listen, Griff."

When Griffin pushed through the branches back into camp, he froze. Soldiers who'd been sitting idly by their tents on his way through now scrambled to don their armor and wield their weapons as brigadier generals shouted orders.

Griffin had to find Lochlan. He pushed through the hordes of men and women preparing for another battle, reaching the command tent as fast as he could. Shoving past the guard outside, he pushed his way in.

Lochlan stopped mid-sentence as his advisors turned to look at Griffin, not a single one hiding their disdain.

"Shouldn't you be preparing to run to the enemy, brother?" Lochlan didn't even bother looking up from his maps.

Griffin's jaw clenched. "I didn't deserve that after fighting Egan with you, but I don't care. Right now, you need to listen to me. Enis has used the book to awaken Toby's O'Shea magic."

"That is Prince Tobias to you," one of the advisors snarled.

"Enough. I *will* speak with my brother on this matter." Griffin wished he could call on his magic, but the sun prevented it from flooding into his arms. Still, he clenched his fists as if holding it back. "Egan has destroyed Aghadoon."

No one even blinked.

"Destroyed what?" one of the men near Lochlan asked.

Lochlan crossed his arms. "The village that once protected the book. Why is it of importance now?"

"You have no idea how this book works, do you?" Griffin would never forget what he'd read in it. He only understood pieces of the whole, but he couldn't ignore it for the tool it was. "The village... the book is the key to accessing every spell, every history, every piece of magic housed in the Aghadoon library, the most dangerous and powerful magic the realms have ever known."

"If Egan has the book, why does he need the library?" Lochlan asked.

There was no time for this. "Because a spell does not exist in the book if it is not in that library. When one has the book, they see what the book allows them to see. But in the library, there is no limitation."

No one spoke for a long moment as they stared at each other in confusion. A voice came from the doorway. "Is my son okay?"

Griffin closed his eyes at the sound of Brea's voice.

Lochlan cleared his throat. "The best way to save Toby is to meet this army head on."

"What army?" It made sense now why the soldiers were preparing to march.

"The one full of Dark Fae who just marched over the border where the barrier once stood. We fought them before, we've been preparing to do it again. This king has sent a much smaller force this time."

"No, that doesn't make sense. Egan's units retreated. If they come for another fight, they will lead with an air strike first."

Lochlan nodded to a guard. "Get my brother out of here and inform the rest of the generals we are prepared to march."

The guard grabbed Griffin's arm, but he jerked away and stormed from the tent to find Gulliver waiting. "Come on, Gullie.

We need to find out what's happening before my brother leads us into ruin." Egan wouldn't risk one part of his army unless he needed to hide what the rest was doing—like Griffin suspected he'd done with the first battle, the one Egan didn't fight in, the one Riona retreated from in the midst of chaos. Was that when he'd left for the human world? He'd sent his army to fight as cover, hadn't he?

But now... why would he send a small force now?

"It can't be Egan, Griff." Gulliver's tail flicked in agitation. "They're still in Aghadoon. I'm sure of it."

At some point, Griffin would demand to know how he knew. But there was no time.

He didn't realize they'd been followed until he heard soft footsteps behind him. Turning on his heel, he prepared for a fight only to come face to face with Brea. The magic inside tugged at him, wanting him to move closer.

He refused to obey it. "Here to make sure I don't interfere with your husband's war?" The words came out harsher than he'd intended.

Brea didn't even flinch. Her eyes hardened. "Lochlan is a stubborn man. I know you, Griffin O'Shea. Something isn't right here."

He met her eyes for a brief moment. "You used to know me, Brea. But I'm not that man anymore. I have more people I'm fighting for than you and your husband."

"Your brother."

Griffin didn't give that a response. When Lochlan hadn't remembered him, he'd hoped they could be true brothers. But he realized now that was just a dream, a delusion. There were people trapped behind Egan's forces whose fates were unknown. They needed him, and he needed to remember who he was fighting for.

Hector... *he* was Griffin's brother. Shauna, his best friend.

And Nessa. He worried for her like Brea worried for Toby, like a parent.

He stopped, facing Brea, as a horn sounded, calling all their forces to the front. "If you want to help, Brea, command one of your men to give me their horse."

Her eyes searched the camp full of soldiers leading their horses to the lines of cavalry. "Benjamin," she called.

The young soldier approached. "Yes, your Majesty?"

"Griffin needs your horse."

"My horse, Majesty?" The boy's ears turned pink with indecision.

"Yes. The king will not like it, but I trust Griffin. I will take any blame that comes your way."

The soldier bowed his head. "Of course, Majesty." He handed the reins to Griffin without hesitation. Griffin wondered if Brea was loved everywhere she went. First in Fargelsi, then Eldur, and finally she thawed the cold hearts of Iskalt.

Benjamin gave her one more long look before running to join the lines of foot soldiers.

"Thank you." Griffin took the reins.

"Don't let me down, Griff."

He wouldn't. Not this time. Pulling himself into the saddle, he looked down at Gulliver. "Stay with the queen. Keep her safe."

He didn't stick around to see the scowl he knew those words would bring to Brea's face. Digging his heels in, he snapped the reins and galloped through the crowded camp, forcing soldiers to jump out of the way as he approached the troops preparing to march out.

Breaking through the Iskalt line, he ignored the shouts from the generals as he raced through the trees and along the narrow mountain pass, determined to catch sight of this enemy army, to find out if it was a trap.

He rounded a bend and pulled up on the reins, a smile stretching across his face.

Griffin rode at the head of the army approaching the Iskalt forces. He waved a white flag high over his head. The sun sank on the horizon, meaning Iskalt would soon be at full power.

And Griffin had to make them see reason first. Lochlan sat atop his dark steed, ready to lead his army. "I'll go talk to him," Griffin shouted over his shoulder. "Stay here."

As he neared his brother, he wondered which family mattered more. The one at his front or the one at his back?

Lochlan tried to remain stone-faced, but Griffin caught the terrified glances toward the other fae. They'd seen what an army of Dark Fae could do.

"Joined the enemy again, brother?" Lochlan sneered.

Griffin sat ramrod straight atop his borrowed horse. "They are no more my enemy than you, Loch. These fae are from Myrkur, but they pledge no allegiance to Egan. In fact, they'd like to help us defeat him." Griffin glanced back over his shoulder, catching sight of a few Slyph flying above the army to intimidate the Light Fae.

He waved their leader forward.

"This is Hector." Hector stepped up to Griffin's side. "He's my brother." Griffin hadn't gotten the chance to tell Hector how much it meant to see him here.

Lochlan's stony expression cracked at that. "How did your force get past Egan, Hector?" Suspicion rang in his tone.

"Egan is gone." Hector's tone was flat.

Lochlan sat up straighter. "What?"

"Egan is no longer in Myrkur. A few of my people witnessed the army disappear, but I'm not quite sure how the magic works."

Griffin knew exactly where they'd gone.

Lochlan visibly paled. "Toby," he muttered, seeing the truth in Hector's words. He steeled himself and yelled to his people. "There will be no fight today. We are among friends."

As Hector's small army joined the ranks of the Light Fae, the two sides didn't mix, but there were furtive glances both ways. Lochlan's lines broke, allowing the new allies into camp.

Griffin barely noticed Brea ordering food to be made for Hector and his people as they tried to determine what was next. Instead, he jumped from his horse and ran through crowds looking for a few distinct faces.

Gulliver found them first, coming out of nowhere to cut in front of Griffin and barrel into Nessa, lifting her in a crushing hug. Griffin did the same to Shauna, pressing her so close their hearts beat in time with each other. A tear slipped down his cheek as he thought of the months since he'd seen them last, when he'd wondered if Egan had killed them.

But he hadn't, and they were right here.

Gulliver and Nessa joined their hug, and a hole in the center of his chest filled. His family was okay.

The four of them cried as they clung together, no shame too great to stop them.

They didn't break apart until a horse thundered into the camp, looking like it had been running for days. A haggard messenger stumbled from the horse, dropping to her knees, weary eyes lifting to the crowd of soldiers still recovering from the almost fight.

"She's wearing Eldur colors," someone murmured.

"Bailey!" Brea ran forward, Neeve at her side. They helped the young messenger to her feet and murmured in low tones.

Griffin inched closer, trying to figure out what was going on, why this girl would almost kill herself riding into their camp.

Her cracked lips parted. "Majesties. I have dire news," she said, her voice growing stronger with the message. "Eldur has fallen."

Riona

Riona followed the narrow stone path along the Dalur River through Raudur City. Even after weeks of occupying the city, she still couldn't get used to the exotic people of Eldur with their spicy food and robust personalities. Or the infernal blazing hot sun.

In Eldur, clear sunny skies were a daily occurrence—not even a cloud to offer a respite from the heat and endless bright light that still hurt her eyes.

Sliding her sunglasses back in place, she followed the directions Rowena had given her to the marketplace.

Rowena. Now there was a fae she wouldn't mind helping escape the Eldur Palace. Maybe then the woman would finally stop trying to be her *lady's maid.* In all her life, Riona had never known what it was like to be waited upon. Not until she arrived in Eldur with Egan's army and watched as he laid waste to the beautiful city, taking it for himself. He'd moved Riona into what Rowena said were Brea's old rooms and set the servant on her, saying the old woman was his gift to her for showing her loyalty by returning to his side.

At first, she thought she might like having a servant, but she found out rather quickly that lady's maids were an opinionated lot, and she avoided hers as much as possible.

Riona picked up her pace, feeling the fine hairs on the back of her neck and wings stand up straight, like she was being watched. The boarded-up windows and soot-covered mounds of rubble were a sorry sight to behold of the once beautiful city. Riona had never seen anything like it. Even in its current war-torn state, the city was incredible, carved right out of the canyon walls far above the Dalur River. She imagined crowds of Eldurians must have filled the narrow streets before the Dark Fae arrived. Now only the bravest of souls—or the most desperate—ventured out of their hiding places.

Taking a turn down a dark alley, Riona checked her directions again. She wasn't looking for just any marketplace. The mainstream market was all but closed these days, anyway. She was looking for someone with special skills. She just hoped they would be willing to help her.

She pushed through the screen door and stepped into the dark shop.

"Can I help you?" A kind voice met her in the cool darkness.

"Yes, please." She took her sunglasses off and approached the counter of the apothecary. It wasn't the usual shop. That was destroyed in the battle. This was the temporary shop the local apothecary set up to help the Eldurian people get through this difficult time with the essentials that could still be had. It was supposed to be a secret shop.

"You're one of them." The man's previous kind tone disappeared as soon as he caught sight of her wings. "We do not serve dark beasts in this establishment."

The cutting remark hurt, just as it was intended to, though the Dark Fae *had* destroyed their city. She'd heard all sorts of insults since her arrival in Eldur. She shrugged it off. If nothing else, Riona Nieland had a thick skin. "I have coin to spend. Coin I would rather see put to good use in this city than spend it in the human realm acquiring what I need."

"You have access to the human realm?" The tall, thin man stared down his crooked nose at her. "You're the one in charge here?"

"Yes. And as I said, I have coin to spend. I would see it used to help your people."

The man gave a doubtful snort before he approached her at the counter. "What do you need?"

Riona took her sunglasses out of her pocket. "I was told you might have the skills to create something like this."

The shopkeeper picked up the glasses, examining the dark lenses and their unusual construction.

"You want me to make dark glasses for your beast brethren? So they can see better to kill more fae?" He placed the glasses back in her hand. "Not interested."

"We are all fae," Riona said softly. "Light and Dark Fae."

"You are killers, Madame. All of you."

"By that logic, am I to believe all Light Fae are exactly the same? You are all good and kind creatures of magic who have never waged war against your brothers, usurped thrones from young princes, or imprisoned an entire nation of fae?"

The man met her gaze and shook his head. "You may have a point, my dear, but I cannot—will not help you."

"There is an entire army of Dark Fae fighting alongside the leaders of Fargelsi and Iskalt this very minute. They need the protection these glasses can give them. Not to fight against you, but to fight with you."

"I'd like to believe that, but it is difficult to trust such a thing."

"What if I hire you to make the glasses, but you can deliver them to one of your own kind? A friend of mine who works with this army will take delivery of the glasses, and he can vouch for their use." At least she hoped they were still friends.

"You will pay up front," the man relented. "I can make the dark lenses, but I will need a smithy to make the frames. How many do you need?"

"As many as you can make, sir. And the lenses as dark as you can make them."

"Evan." He held out his hand. "I hope I don't live to regret this."

"Thank you, Evan." Riona shook his hand. "You have my word, you will not regret this. Send word to Rowena at the palace when you have them ready."

Is operation 'make it stop' a go?

Riona rolled her eyes as she stared down at her journal. The boy had spent far too much time with Myles, and he had a fondness for talking like a human, but his idea for the sunglasses was a good one.

Yes, I found someone who has agreed to make them. You may tell Hector he can stop complaining about the blasted sunlight very soon.

You should also warn him, the light here in Eldur is more miserable than anything he's seen of this land so far.

I'll just let him find out that for himself. Gulliver's neat handwriting shot across the page. It was a lot more fun talking to him through the journals than it was when King Egan had the mate to hers.

How is your journey?

Awful. We've been riding forever, and we still haven't reached Eldur. We are out of the mountains now. Lochlan says we will reach the border soon, but then the journey across Eldur is a long one and very hot. He won't tell me what a desert is. Says I complain too much, and I should talk less.

Riona snorted a laugh at the thought of the icy King of Iskalt up against Gulliver's curious mind.

Give the poor man a break, he misses Toby.

How is Toby? I hope he isn't as bad as Tia. She won't talk much. She misses him something awful.

He is about the same. Riona cast a glance across the sitting room where Tobias sat looking out the window at the courtyard below. He sat there most days when the king didn't have need of him. Riona thought he intended to sit there and watch until his sister arrived.

"Toby?" Riona called. "Do you want to send Tia a message?"

"She knows I miss her." Toby didn't glance her way. He just kept staring at the palace gates across the courtyard as if he expected his sister to walk through them any moment.

"What about your parents? Do you want Gulliver to tell them anything?"

"No. I'll see them soon." His voice was so small and distant it broke her heart to hear the pain he fought to hide. He was a lot like Griffin in that way. A little softer and a great deal kinder, but that was likely Brea's influence. There was something about Toby that reminded her so much of Griffin it almost hurt to look at him sometimes.

She glanced back down at the book on the table in front of

her. Gulliver's scrawl appearing on the page. *You know you can ask me about him, Riona.*

She knew she could. And she knew Gulliver would tell her. But she wasn't sure she wanted to know. Not yet.

I know. She wrote. *I'll ask you about Griffin soon. I promise.*

Where is Egan? Gulliver asked instead. The kid was good at not pushing her to talk about things she wasn't ready to talk about. He was wise beyond his years.

He is here in Eldur at the moment, gathering information from his generals. But he remains in the human realm with Enis at Aghadoon most of the time. I believe they are searching for ways to fight against the Light Fae, but Enis assures me, she will not show him anything of value. Riona wasn't sure how much she could trust that woman. She went wherever the book of power went. Right now, Egan had it and the library that contained knowledge of all magic.

And when he's gone, you're in charge of Eldur? Gulliver asked.

Yes. It wasn't something she was proud of.

Then why don't you just take control of his army and come join us when he's gone and can't do anything about it? His army will go where the money and the food is. And I'm guessing there's a lot of both of those in the palace.

Because when the king leaves Eldur for Aghadoon, he takes Tobias with him to open portals for him, and I will not leave without Toby. That was why she was here. For Toby. For Griffin's son. As much as she might want to leave, she refused to turn against Egan when he had Toby O'Shea under his thumb.

Griff's yelling at me. Gotta run, TTYL.

Riona didn't know what that last part meant, but she wiped her hand across the page, letting the book's magic recognize her touch before their words faded away. She shut the book, hiding it in a secret compartment she'd discovered in the table beside the settee. Her journal could not fall into the wrong hands. It was her lifeline to Gulliver, and through him, Griffin too. It was the only thing keeping her sane.

"Tobias?" She crossed the room to sit on the empty chair beside him. The warm breeze blowing in through the open balcony doors was soothing. This oasis city was so beautiful, she could almost see herself living here if the world wasn't such a giant mess right now. War was coming for them all. She couldn't think beyond that. "Would you like some tea?" Rowena seemed to think tea was the answer to everything.

"No, thank you," Toby murmured.

"You want to go visit Logan and Darra? Your cousins might like to have someone to play with. Especially Logan, I hear he's pretty bored with just his baby sister keeping him company." Unfortunately, Riona could do nothing for the young Prince and Princess of Eldur, left behind with their grandmother, Faolan in the absence of their parents. Egan was all too eager to take the royal family as prisoners upon his victory over Raudur City.

"Maybe later." He turned toward her, his glassy eyes almost looking right through her. "I'm okay, Riona."

She sighed, sitting back in her chair. "I just can't believe that, Toby. Not when you look so sad."

"I'll be okay ... I think."

"Why don't you tell me what's on your mind? Maybe it will help."

Toby turned his sad eyes on her. "Do you think my papa will be mad?"

"Mad? At you?"

Toby nodded, his eyes misting over.

Riona leaned in closer. "Your papa could never be mad at you, Toby. Nothing that has happened is your fault."

"I led the king's army into that village through my portal. They killed all those people. It's all my fault." His lip trembled, and she was terrified he was going to cry. Riona never knew what to do with crying children. She found herself wishing for Rowena to return. The grandmotherly woman would know just what to say to make Toby feel better.

Riona took his hand in hers. She sympathized with the boy more than he would ever know. "That wasn't your fault, Toby. Sometimes when we're forced to do things we would never willingly do, it can feel like we've done a bad thing. But the responsibility for those things does not fall to us. You didn't kill all those people. Egan did. And he will pay dearly for all the wrong he has done. Trust me, your mother and father know exactly who is at fault for the destruction of Aghadoon and the sack of Eldur. They will never think badly of you for doing what you had to do to survive."

Toby leaned over and wrapped his gangly arms around her, nestling his face against her neck. "Thank you, Riona. I'm glad you're here with me."

CHAPTER THREE

Griffin

"My bum hurts."

Griffin ignored Gulliver's complaining as he focused on the feel of the horse beneath him. It was a stronger beast than any he'd seen in Myrkur, one that had done Griffin well in battle.

When he was fighting against the people he felt should be his.

"I'm tired."

Griffin glanced at Gulliver out of the corner of his eye but didn't respond. He had too much on his mind.

Like Riona who hadn't fired a single arrow in the battle weeks ago. He still couldn't get the image of her among the Slyph forces, turning to fly back into Myrkur for reasons he couldn't fathom.

"I'm hungry."

Griffin turned in his saddle to give Gulliver a scathing look. "Really? Is that all that's wrong with you? You're in pain, tired, and hungry? What about the heat? Would you like me to shield you from that too? Is the vast expanse of Eldurian desert not to your liking?"

"Griff." The disappointment in Brea's voice cut him, but he couldn't call the words back. He closed his eyes and released a breath.

"I'm sorry, Gullie." His eyes slid open to the stricken face of the boy.

Gulliver gripped the reins of his horse and pulled them back to slow. "I'm going to ride with Tia. She might not talk, but at least she won't yell at me."

Griffin sighed as he watched Gulliver ride toward Tia.

"We're all a little on edge." Brea sidled up next to him, her white mount keeping pace with his.

"So, we're talking now?" Over the weeks of their long ride through the Northern Vatlands and across Eldur, Griffin mostly avoided Lochlan and Brea. He'd fought Egan's army beside them, but none of them had known what to say next and the silence grew between them.

With Lochlan, it was deliberate. He hated Griffin. Griffin could see it in his eyes. But Brea... hers was born more out of mourning the loss of her son rather than regretting the return of her memories.

Griffin's hands clenched around the reins. "I'm sorry. I'm just..."

"Tired." She gave him a weak smile. "Griffin, you're preaching to the choir here. I'm riding alongside my ex-husband—something that doesn't exist among the fae—to the kingdom that became my first true home. Since the moment we learned of Egan's capture of the palace, I have spent every moment terrified for my people, but not only them. Egan now has more than my son."

Griffin hated himself for not considering how hard this was for her. Alona, the Queen of Eldur, was a sister to Brea. Finn, the king consort was Lochlan's best friend. Both were poised to fight Egan and terrified for their children's lives inside the palace.

Brea was quiet for a long moment. "I don't know this Dark Fae king or his people, but Griff, I need you to tell me... do you think my mother is alive?" Her steely eyes met his.

Griffin wanted to give her the hope she so desperately sought. He wanted to tell her Egan probably let Faolan dine on fine food and spend her time in the gardens. But he'd seen what the king did to amuse himself. His eyes caught on Shauna. Nessa rode in the saddle in front of her, not because she wasn't big enough to ride on her own, but because her sister wouldn't let her go far. Both of them sported lasting scars thanks to Egan.

Brea nodded as if his silence was the answer she needed. "Griff, you and I have never been exactly honest with each other. Our history is fraught with lies and deceptions, but also more. I remember every moment we spent together before you went to the prison realm, but I also have the more recent memories. You saved my daughter. Her dreams... they were about you, weren't they?"

He nodded. They had to be. Tia dreamed of the prison realm before she'd seen it, of a man saving her from it. Griffin.

Her father.

He shook his head to clear it of that thought. The long ride gave him a lot of time to think. Brea and Lochlan could never find out. They'd raised Tia, and she loved them. He wouldn't do anything to interfere. Instead, he'd be her uncle, her friend, and still get to love her.

Brea's lips pursed, and it was such a familiar look on her face a laugh rolled out of Griffin.

"What?" Her brow scrunched.

He fixed his eyes on anywhere but her, looking from the

dusty desert road to the army surrounding them. "You just look like the girl I remember."

An errant strand of hair fell in her face, and she tucked it behind her ear. "I'm not that girl."

At the words, the magic that wanted him to love her sparked to life. "You'll always be the human farm girl I saved from Lochlan in the human realm."

One corner of her mouth quirked up. "You didn't save me from Lochlan. He broke me out of jail and wanted to take me to my real mother. You..." She shook her head. "You took me from him and brought me to Fargelsi where I was Regan's prisoner."

"You make me sound so evil."

She laughed, and the sound soothed something inside him. He'd longed to hear Brea's laughter since the moment he crossed into Myrkur.

"Well, you weren't exactly a good guy." Her laughter died. "But you are now, aren't you? We're finally on the same side."

"Your husband doesn't think so."

She glanced back over her shoulder to where Lochlan glared at them from atop his horse. "Well, you know Lochlan. He's kind of a grumpy gus."

Griffin couldn't help smiling at that. "I missed your odd human phrases."

Brea's smile dropped, and she looked toward the horizon where the sun had started to rise. Once they'd crossed into Eldur, they traveled at night to avoid moving their army in the heat of the desert sun. "I missed *you,* Griff. I didn't know that's what the feeling was, but for ten years it has felt like a part of our world was missing."

"I didn't deserve to be part of your world."

She shot him a scowl. "You're an idiot if you think that matters. You're family, Griff, whether my oaf of a husband will admit it or not. You and I weren't truly in love, but that doesn't mean I don't love you. I do. My daughter obviously does. For some reason, even Myles seems to think you've changed." She laughed. "That's probably one of the reasons Lochlan is so grumpy."

"Why?"

"Well, he and Myles have always had this bromance, but he wasn't able to go searching for our children with you, and now you return and Myles talks about the great Griffin O'Shea. Lochlan is probably jealous."

Griffin snorted. He doubted that had anything to do with Lochlan's anger. "Why now, Brea? Why have we waited two weeks for this conversation?"

She drew in a long breath. "My heart is broken, Griff. My son is a prisoner, and I just don't have the time to hold grudges anymore. I can barely think of anything else, but I'm not mad at you for what you did ten years ago. Our world has moved on. But... you didn't make me see. When you returned to Iskalt... we knew some of what you were to us, but you should have tried harder to make me see. There was a time you were all I had. You changed my life, and I *forgot* you. Why didn't you make me see?"

"I tried."

"I know." A tear rolled down her cheek. "But now I have two forms of marriage magic twisting inside me. I never wanted to star in my own reverse harem, Griffin!" Her voice grew so loud the fae surrounding them glanced their way.

"Um." Griffin lifted a brow. "A reverse what-now?"

"Nothing. Just another of my stupid human sayings. Ignore me."

He couldn't ignore her if he tried, but Queen Neeve's voice lifted through the riding party telling them it was time to set up camp, and Brea rode to join her sister. There was no tree cover nearby now that they were deep in the Eldurian desert so they'd have to rely on their tents to protect them.

There was a reason Griffin opted to brave Loch Villandi to get to Iskalt instead of going through Eldur.

The Iskalt and Fargelsian armies made camp together. Hector's Dark Fae separated themselves to set up their tents. They struggled during the day more than anyone.

Griffin remained atop his horse watching Lochlan lift Tia down and cradle her against his chest before Brea joined him. He watched Neeve help Myles down—being that she was stronger than him.

Around him, soldiers made camp, prepared to spend another day avoiding the sun before marching toward an inevitable battle in Eldur, ready to fight for a cause they believed in.

This truly was a new fae world, one in which the three kingdoms protected each other. Sliding down, he handed off his reins to Lochlan's groom who traveled with them and insisted on serving both O'Shea brothers.

Lochlan may hate him, but he'd still assigned a servant to help Griffin set up his own camp among the Iskaltians. Yet, Griffin couldn't fathom sitting in a sea of people he didn't know, people who didn't trust him.

He found Gulliver laying against his pack outside Tia's tent, a notebook in his lap. "What are you doing?"

Gulliver jumped at the sound of Griffin's voice and slammed the book shut. "Nothing. Just waiting on you." He leaped to his feet and tucked the book in his bag. "Is it finally time to eat?"

Griffin laughed. "They'll have the cook fires going soon. Look... I'm sorry I was—"

"A douche?"

"Myles," Griffin grumbled. "Stop listening to his human words."

Gulliver shrugged. "It's okay, Griff. It's not exactly the first time you've yelled at me, and it won't be the last. I figured you enjoy it, so I may as well let you."

Griffin stared at him for a moment before laughing and swinging an arm over the kid's shoulders, hugging him to his side. "I do love you, Gullie. No matter what I say."

Tia waved to them as she ducked into her tent.

Gulliver's cheeks heated. "Griff," he whined. "Let me go."

"Sure, sure." He ruffled his hair. "I think I'm going to find some friends to eat with if you want to join me."

He shook his head. "I have to stay near Tia, remember? You told me to protect her."

"In the battle, Gulliver."

"Well, the battles aren't over. Plus, I think she needs me more than you do right now. Is that okay?"

Griffin looked toward Tia's tent, knowing Gulliver was right. "Of course it is." He wanted to tell him how proud he was of him, but he thought that would embarrass Gulliver, so he stepped back.

"Tell everyone I said hi."

Griffin nodded. "I will. See you tonight when we leave? We should only have another day of hard riding."

"Sure, Griff. See you then." Gulliver ducked into the tent, and moments later Griffin heard Tia's soft voice. She wouldn't speak to anyone else, but Gulliver got her words. Griffin was glad she had him.

He started off through camp, planning to leave the Iskaltians and Fargelsians behind in favor of his family. The sound of two horses nearing camp had him walking in Lochlan and Neeve's direction instead. The two royals met the messengers at the edge of camp.

An older man slid down first. "I have an update from Iskalt."

"What's happening in Iskalt?" Griffin asked.

Neither royal questioned his presence, but only Neeve spoke. "Brea has messengers keeping her up to date on her children's safety as do I." She pointed to where Brea spoke with Myles, and the messenger headed that direction.

The second messenger jumped down, her sprightly move a surprise to Griffin. She pushed back her chain mail hood, and he realized she was even younger than he'd realized.

"I come from Queen Alona of Eldur."

"Go on." Lochlan urged her to speak.

"The Eldurian forces were camped on the border of Iskalt and Eldur when the palace and city were taken. The queen now has us north of the palace and patrolling the area. We've managed to get some news from inside. The old Queen Faolan is alive. We know that much. As are the Prince and Princess of Eldur."

Lochlan's shoulders dipped the slightest bit. He didn't show his relief most of the time, but Griffin could see it in him. He loved Faolan. She was more a mother to him than their own.

The messenger continued. "Both Queen Alona and King Finn are with the army, so they are safe. She will be relieved that I found Iskalt and Fargelsi so close."

"What of the city?" Lochlan asked.

The messenger's face fell. "It's been sacked."

That couldn't be true. Raudur City was the grandest city in the fae realm. Every kingdom aspired to create such a marvel.

It was no longer there...

"I'm sure you're tired." Lochlan rubbed the back of his neck. "And hungry. Eat and rest before returning to Queen Alona. I'm sure Queen Brea will want to speak with you."

Griffin drifted away from them, his steps dragging as he made his way through camp. This was real. Everything was real.

Egan truly held the crown jewel of Eldur.

By the time Griffin crossed the sandy clearing between the Iskalt camp and Hector's camp, he was ready to collapse. Until he caught sight of a number of fires the Dark Fae cooked over and Hector's people—Griffin's people—collected in one giant group, gathering their strength.

These fae were the reason he was here. They'd made the impossible decision to fight those like them, to do what was right after hard lives with bleak futures. Now, their future held too much bloodshed and uncertainty.

Yet, they were still here.

"Griff." Shauna's smile was exactly what he needed to soothe the turmoil inside.

"Hey, everyone."

Many of them shouted greetings to Griffin, welcoming him despite the fact he wasn't truly one of them. There was a royal meal waiting for him back with Brea and Myles, comfortable tents and servants.

But here there was family. No matter what Brea said, he'd never found this anywhere else. He lowered himself to Shauna's side and accepted a bowl of stew from Hector who was cooking it himself.

Nessa scooted toward him and curled up against his other side. Shauna looped her arm through his and leaned her head on his shoulder.

"Gulliver said to tell you all hi," Griffin started. "But he probably just meant it for Nessa."

They all laughed.

He closed his eyes, soaking in the sound, the feel of his people surrounding him. They didn't look like him with their horns, wings or their many other features. But they knew him, every part that mattered.

Every step that brought the two armies closer to Eldur was another move toward war. The battle of Myrkur was only the beginning, a distraction while Egan took a bigger prize. If he remained in control of the desert kingdom and the powerful book, the fae world would be divided like it was ten years ago by Regan and Callum.

This time, Griffin wouldn't let that happen.

He stood at the front of the armies with Hector to his right, watching smoke rise up from the city in the distance.

Two Slyph men glided through the morning haze, touching down in front of Griffin. They didn't have tattoos stretching across their skin like Riona, but there were other similarities to her. One of them had stark white wings while the other's were more of a dusty brown.

"Kristjan." Hector greeted the first before turning to the second. "Theo. What news have you brought to us?"

Kristjan stepped forward, his wings stretching wide as he pushed thick black curls out of his eyes. "We got past the guards into the city, but couldn't get far. Egan's soldiers patrol the streets. The Slyph were nowhere to be seen, but the ogres and Asrai were out in force."

"And the city?" Griffin asked.

Theo ducked his head, a sadness in his gaze. "It did not fare well. We only managed to get past some of the rubble before having to return, but the people who remain are shut inside their homes, not venturing into the city."

Hector put a hand on his shoulder. "You did well. Thank

you. Go get your breakfast. We do not know what the next few days will bring and may have need of you yet."

Lochlan stormed toward them, ignoring the Slyph going the other way. "You sent spies into the city?"

Griffin sighed as he turned to face him. They'd sent Kristjan and Theo after the camp quieted for a reason.

Lochlan had barely spoken to Griffin in weeks, but now Griffin didn't have time to deal with an irate king. "How else did you expect to get information?"

"Egan could know we're here because of your stupidity."

Brea ran toward them, Queen Neeve at her heels. "Lochlan, stop."

Griffin crossed his arms. "We didn't send any of your people. Ours can blend in."

"Your people?" Lochlan scoffed.

Hector took a step toward Lochlan, ready to defend Griffin, but Griffin held him back.

Brea reached them and stepped in front of Lochlan. "Neeve approved it."

Some of the red receded from his face. The Fargelsian queen had just as much authority as he did.

Lochlan turned to Neeve. "Why wasn't this discussed with me?"

It was Brea who answered. "Because you're blind where Griffin is concerned. We knew you wouldn't like the idea since it came from him. Now, stop being a scorned brother. You are a king, Lochlan O'Shea. It's time to act like it. Our son's life may very well depend on us all working together."

That seemed to deflate Lochlan's anger.

Neeve, ever the calm ruler, turned to Griffin and Hector. "I take it the news isn't good from your expressions?"

Hector heaved a sigh. "I'm sorry, Majesty. Raudur City appears lost. Our men tell us some of what they saw is in ruin.

The people are hiding from the Dark Fae patrolling their streets."

Her face remained an emotionless mask as she contemplated the words. "Thank you for asking your people to take the risk, Hector." She sent Lochlan a look. "We appreciate it and recognize the bravery your people exhibit by not joining Egan. It is always harder to do the right thing."

"Thank you," Lochlan grumbled, thoroughly shamed.

Neeve turned on her heel. "We must come up with a plan to meet Egan's forces, but also to make contact with Queen Alona again and maybe get someone inside the palace. Lochlan, you and I will confer with our advisors." Her next words appeared for Lochlan alone. "Hector and Griffin are welcome to join us, and their ideas will be considered." She marched away with a shake of her head.

Brea slipped her hand into Lochlan's and pulled him after her sister.

Hector let out a low whistle. "You said she was once a servant?"

Griffin nodded. He'd known Neeve most of his life. She had as much reason to hate him as anyone. While he'd lived in Regan's luxury, she'd been helping fae escape through the Vatlands to get away from Regan's influence.

Yet, she treated him as she would any new advisor, like someone who hadn't yet lost their last chance.

He looked to Hector. "She was never just a servant. Neeve has always fought for her people. But I think growing up in the lower class is what makes her such a good queen."

Patting Hector on the back, he realized it was the same thing that made Hector such a good resistance leader. He'd never given up on the good in his people despite living in Fela where every day was a struggle. It started with protecting his mother and sisters.

Now, he protected the idea that the Dark Fae could be good, that they too could live in peace.

"Come on." Griffin jerked his head toward where the others had gone. "When a queen invites you into the important discussions, you never say no."

Hector gave him a bewildered look like he wasn't sure he belonged among such royalty.

But when Griffin started toward Neeve's tent, Hector followed. It was the first step toward full cooperation between Light and Dark Fae. A peaceful future outside the prison realm had always been just a dream, but maybe one day it could truly join reality.

Riona

"The Eldurians certainly know how to build a palace." Egan gave a low whistle at the opulent gardens built at the apex of the palace grounds above the canyon city below. From here they could see for miles across the green oasis to the desert sands, illumined in the russet colors of the setting sun.

Where Egan's eyes fell to the beauty of the Eldur Palace, Riona's attention went to the endless sea of soldiers and tents reaching out to meet the horizon. The Iskalt and Fargelsi armies had the city surrounded to the south and east, but Egan didn't even flinch at the sight of their unified forces. As long as he had Tobias O'Shea in his grasp, he could evade his enemies with a simple portal.

But Riona was certain the Eldurian army, camped to the north of the city and isolated from the other armies would make a move to take back their city. And the Eldurian heirs Egan had taken prisoner.

"The flowers are beautiful here, are they not? Such rich colors."

"Yes, sire. They are lovely." Riona followed Egan around the winding paths of the exotic tiered garden.

"We shall hold a celebration here to reward our faithful soldiers for their hard work."

Riona nodded absently. No doubt the Dark Fae army would destroy this lovely place in their enthusiasm for celebration and too much wine and ale.

"And what of our next steps, sire?" Riona paced beside him with her hands clasped behind her back, just under her wings.

"We have everything we could possibly need, Riona." Egan turned to face her in the fading light. Evening would be upon them soon. That always made her feel better, just knowing Griffin was out there with the full use of his magic.

"What will we do concerning the siege, my Lord?" She gestured at the surrounding armies.

"They can't touch us, dear girl. They will tire of this eventually and return to their kingdoms."

"And you will keep Eldur for yourself?"

"For now." She didn't miss his evasive tone. "With the discovery of the Dark Fae's defensive magic, the Light Fae have no way to resist us. Their magic can hurt us, but not without great physical cost to them."

It was true, their magic could breach the Dark Fae's natural defenses, but it took great effort on their part. "We should not forget their swords can still damage us, sire."

"I have the book, Toby, and the library. Even Enis remains at my side to study the secrets of magic only I control."

"Toby."

Egan frowned at her.

"The boy's name is Toby."

Egan shrugged. "This army is nothing but a show of force. These Light Fae may try to intimidate us, but they are weak, and they will grow weaker still as they lie in wait. They rely too much on their magic, and magic can't help them now. Once I have found the right war spells, we will deal with this nuisance, and then I will take Iskalt and Fargelsi too. It is time all fae were united under one king."

"And what of the Eldurian heirs, my lord?" Princess Darra was only four years old, and her brother, Prince Logan was eight.

"They're more of a nuisance than an asset," Egan muttered.

"Perhaps we could use them to negotiate the surrender of the Eldurian monarchs?" Riona suggested. She hoped it wouldn't come to that, but for the time being, she wanted Egan to think of them as bargaining chips rather than something useless to cast aside.

"We don't need their surrender, and we don't need their children either." A vicious smile spread across Egan's face. "Perhaps what we need to lessen the boredom of a siege is a little demonstration? Have them bound and whipped at the city gates at sunrise. That should show them what we think of heirs around here. Throw the old queen in too."

Riona took a deep breath to steady her nerve. "Very well, my Lord." She nodded. In trying to make things better, she'd made them so much worse. "I shall see to it at once." Riona left him to marvel at the flowers.

Returning to her rooms in the palace, Riona groaned to find that woman rooting through her things again.

"What are you doing?" She snatched her undergarments from Rowena's aged hands.

"It's called laundry," Rowena snapped, jerking the dirty clothes from Riona's grasp.

"I can wash my own things."

Rowena turned to the washroom and scooped up the

clothes Riona had discarded there. "A lady should never do her own washing."

"Good thing I'm not a lady," Riona called over her shoulder.

"I've heard that one before." Rowena shuffled around the bedroom and the sitting room, gathering items of clothing to be washed when they weren't even properly dirty yet. "I won't bother trying to get you into a dress for your king's grand dinner this evening. Even though you have a wardrobe full of beautiful dresses that dreadful king of yours ordered for you." She paused to dust a perfectly clean table. "They've even been altered to accommodate your lovely wings too. Pity they shall go to waste."

"I would gladly put on a dress if it would get you to leave."

"And then who would see to your ladyship?" Rowena moved back into the washroom.

"I've lived a very long time seeing to myself, Rowena," Riona called over her shoulder as she sat in the chair under the window, searching the side table for her journal. The nosey maid was into everything. She wouldn't be surprised if Rowena had found it in the false bottom of the drawer.

Breathing a sigh of relief at the sight of it still where she'd left it last, Riona sat back against the chair, kicking her boots off and taking up her journal and inkless quill.

The young prince and princess were being held in the palace nursery, and there was simply no way Riona could allow them to be punished as Egan had suggested. She needed to get them out of the palace.

How is the siege going from the other side? Riona scrawled the quick note to Gulliver. *I sure could use someone with your skills here on the inside.*

The rush of water brought her out of her thoughts. "What are you doing now, woman?" Riona rolled her eyes at the racket coming from the room with the enormous swimming pool that woman insisted was a bathtub. She stashed the journal into its hiding place just as Rowena marched back into the room.

"It's time you wash, my lady. I won't hear another word of protest. This has gone on long enough." Rowena tapped her foot against the brightly colored rug beneath her feet.

"I know you aren't suggesting I don't have enough sense to wash myself regularly." Riona scowled at the old fae woman.

"Bathing from a basin is not enough in this climate for a lady of your stature. You've been out in the hot sun, baking in those leathers you insist on wearing. You need a proper bath. Now march." Rowena pointed to the washroom. "I will get you in that bath one way or another."

"I'd like to see you try, old woman." Riona narrowed her eyes.

Rowena gave a knowing smile. "A servant to the queen's household is privy to many secrets." She placed her hands on her ample hips. "Secrets an enemy of that vile king would find useful. Especially an enemy he keeps right under his nose. One he doesn't yet realize is working against him."

"What do you think you know?" Riona's shoulders tensed. Had she been too careless and let something slip around this cursed woman?

"I am an old woman, child. I have served four queens, and I've learned much from observing among the shadows. You have no loyalty to the king you profess to serve. Your loyalty is to that boy you protect. The Iskalt prince is the only reason you are still here. Now, get in that bath."

"And you expect to trade this bath for what?" Riona stood, an amused smirk tugging at her mouth.

"Information, child." Rowena swatted her with a linen drying sheet.

"And what information do you believe you can share with

me? Information important enough to warrant that bath?" She stepped into the washroom and folded her arms across her chest.

"A servant moves about the palace without notice, my lady." Rowena turned to toss a handful of dried flowers into the steaming bathtub built into the floor. She added several sprinkles of fragrant oil to the water too. "We have our own ways of coming and going so we never run into the royals or their court as we go about our work."

Riona shed her vest and belt. "Meaning the servants have their own hallways and stairways behind the scenes?"

"I am sure your king's palace is much the same." Rowena moved to help Riona out of her shirt, but Riona was quick to slap her hands away.

"Egan's castle is nothing like this. The servants frequently pass him in the halls." Riona chewed on her bottom lip. "He certainly wouldn't expect there to be passages and stairs meant for the servants alone." She slipped out of her leggings.

"To my knowledge, the Dark Fae king still loses his way around the palace, though he has yet to see much of it." Rowena placed a drying sheet along the edge of the bathtub as Riona took the first step down into the depths of the pool.

"Rowena, can you tell me how to get inside the royal nursery?" Riona sank down on her knees, letting the hot, sweet smelling water engulf her.

"I can, my lady." Rowena smiled. "I would be happy to show you where you might visit them this evening."

"Perhaps late this evening. After the king and his men are deep into their drink?"

"My thoughts exactly." Rowena moved faster than an old woman should and the next thing Riona knew, she was under water and the cursed woman was scrubbing her hair.

Riona moved slowly through the dark palace. It was late, but Egan and his court of favorites were still celebrating in the great dining hall. They'd gotten into the queen's special stash of sweet fae wine that was far more intoxicating than anything the Dark Fae had ever had the pleasure of drinking.

She was certain the king hadn't even missed her when she finally slipped away.

Smoothing her hand down over the rich fabric of the golden gown Rowena had chosen for her, Riona picked up her pace, her wings fluttering behind her like shadows. The few guards she'd passed in the courtyard were either snoring or carousing with their own small celebrations. No one noticed her. She was counting on that luck to stay with her throughout the night.

"Rowena, we must—" Riona nearly shrieked and reached for the dagger sheathed at her waist when she found someone waiting in her room. Someone who was not Rowena.

"The food here is way better than the crap we're eating at camp." Gulliver reached for a pastry stacked on a silver tray. With one hand he stuffed his face, and with the other, he drank down a mug of sweet cold cider, using the flat of his tail to dab at his mouth.

Riona let out a strangled sigh, resting her hands on her hips. "What are you doing here, Gullie? And how have you gotten Rowena to feed you?"

"You said you needed me, so I came. And the lady maid is nice."

"Lady's maid." Riona pinched the bridge of her nose.

Gulliver snorted a laugh. "Are you a lady?"

"No. But you need to tell me how you got into the palace. Hopefully without being seen."

"Who do you think you're talking to, lady?" Gullie crossed his arms over his chest. "No one saw me, promise."

"Mr. Gulliver." Rowena swept into the sitting room with a tray full of meat pies.

"Don't wait on him, Rowena." Riona snatched up a pie for herself. She hadn't eaten a thing at dinner. "This one will have you running to the kitchens all night."

"The poor dear was so hungry. I don't think they were feeding him enough. Conditions with the siege must be dire."

"Probably not." Riona crossed the room to pull Gulliver into a hug. "This one is just a bottomless pit."

"You look beautiful, Riona." Gulliver chomped down on a pie. "I've never seen you in such a fine dress."

"You saw me in Fargelsi in that awful blue dress."

"That was not a pretty dress. The gold suits you."

"Well don't get used to it." Riona headed for the bedroom to change into her leathers.

"What do you need my help with?" Gulliver flopped onto the settee and put his feet up on the table beside his meat pies.

"Feet off the table, young sir." Rowena rapped his ankles with the end of her duster.

"Ow, that hurt." Gulliver rubbed his ankle.

"We have some children to rescue." Riona returned, munching on the last of her pie.

"Toby?" Gulliver turned to her with wide eyes.

"No, I'm afraid we can't reach Toby. Egan keeps him close and under guard. But there may be a few others we can help tonight. Rowena will show us the way."

"I have drawn you a map to the nursery." Rowena waved them over to the low table in front of the settee. "It will raise more suspicion if I escort you than if you go alone, presumably on the king's orders."

"Very well." Riona nodded and bent to look at the map.

"I'm afraid I won't be of much use in getting them out." Rowena twisted her hands nervously.

"That's what I'm here for." Gulliver popped half a meat pie into his mouth and dusted the crumbs off his tunic. "Let's do this." He reached out a fist for Riona to bump.

Riona tapped her fist against his. "You were in the human realm for such a short time, how did so much of it rub off on you?"

"What can I say? I really liked Television." Gulliver followed her to the door. "Thank you for the food, ma'am. It was the best I've eaten in weeks."

"Any time, dearie." Rowena's cheeks flushed pink. "Be very careful you two."

"We've totally got this."

"This boy sounds just like my Brea." Rowena chuckled as they stepped into the empty hall. Rowena rushed off back to the servant's quarters, and Riona and Gulliver made their way to the back halls the maid sketched for them.

It was a maze of dark narrow corridors, twisting and turning until they reached the first set of stairs that would take them closer to the queen's household.

Riona almost stopped breathing when they encountered a few servants running off to deliver late night snacks and drinks to whoever they were attending. But none of them paid her or Gulliver any mind.

The second set of stairs took them deep into the queen's quarters, ending with a short hallway with a single door at the end of it. Peeking out, Riona noted the rich plum colored carpet and the dim lighting of the royal residence where Egan himself was staying when he deigned to spend any time in Eldur away from his precious library.

Three guards stood outside the nursery doors as Riona and Gulliver approached. She could see it in their faces, her reputation preceded her. She was still known as the king's favorite and his most skilled warrior.

"Stand aside, the king has orders for the young prince and princess. They are to be whipped at dawn, and I must make them ready."

The guards shared a look and then stepped aside, not sparing a second glance for Gulliver who slipped into the room behind her.

The children slept soundly, and she wasn't sure how she was going to get them up and ready. Children were not her forte.

"Who are you?" A jeweled knife appeared at her throat.

Riona swallowed, uneasy with the knife pressing into her skin. "A friend, your Majesty." She took a hesitant breath. "I am here to take the children to Brea O'Shea." She knew it was a name that would get the knife removed from her throat.

"Brea is here?" The former Queen of Eldur stepped into the dim light of the moon sweeping into the room through the huge windows.

"There is a siege, my Lady."

"You are Egan's woman." She stared down her long nose at Riona's wings.

"I am loyal to Griffin O'Shea, not the king."

"Griffin? Lochlan's brother from the prison realm?" Faolan sat down on a stool beside her granddaughter's bed.

"Yes. I am only here to remain close to Prince Tobias. I cannot rescue him, but I may be able to help you and your other grandchildren."

"Why would you risk it?" Faolan swept a hand over Princess Darra's blond hair.

"Egan means to have you and the children flogged before the Fargelsi and Iskalt armies in just a few hours. I won't let that happen." She'd seen young children suffer at the end of

Egan's whip many times, but she would tolerate it no more. Over the last weeks, Egan trusted Eldur to her while he was away in the human realm at Aghadoon. She'd regained his trust. He would never suspect her.

"Then we must get them ready to leave at once."

"You too, your Majesty," Gulliver said. "We cannot leave you here. Brea would have a fit if she knew we were here and didn't rescue you."

Faolan smiled at him. "It restores my soul to see Dark Fae working against this man who calls himself your king."

"He is not my king, your ladyship." Gulliver bowed at the waist.

"I must stay here with my people." Faolan moved to wake the prince. "I cannot leave them to the whims of Egan. I may not be able to do much for them, but I will stand with them." She lifted the sleepy princess from her bed and handed her to an equally sleepy prince.

"What's happening Grandmother?" Logan blinked his bleary eyes.

"You're going with Riona and her friend here." Faolan stooped to Logan's level. "She's going to take you to see Aunt Brea."

Logan's eyes widened in surprise. "Truly?"

"Truly." Faolan smoothed a weathered hand over the boy's brow. "I will see you again soon, but you must go now, darlings. Tell Aunt Brea and Uncle Lochlan I love them."

"Come with us, Grandmother? Please?" Logan shifted under the weight of his sister.

"We'll come back for your grandmother soon." Gulliver reached to take the princess from the small prince, settling her in his arms. She went right back to sleep, murmuring against his coat as his tail moved to stroke her hair. Gulliver took Logan's hand and had them moving toward the nursery door.

"Riona's a nice lady. And she has the prettiest wings," Gulliver said to the young prince. "But she's going to have to pretend to be mean until we can get you back with your aunt and uncle. And if you're scared, it's okay to cry."

Logan nodded, his eyes already bright with tears he was working very hard not to shed.

Riona stepped into the hall first. "Come, quickly, my patience is running thin." She let her voice take on an angry tone as she ushered the children down the hall. "And stop your sniveling." She yanked on the door to the stairway that would lead them back into the servant's halls.

Once away from the guards, they moved quickly down the stairs, retracing Rowena's directions until they were back on the main floor.

"This way." Gulliver crept down the corridor toward the kitchens.

"How did you make it all the way to my rooms without being caught?" Riona followed him, keeping the prince between them.

"Most people just don't see me. I'm nobody, so I can go anywhere and no one questions if I belong there are not. As long as I keep to the shadows."

"You clearly have a talent for it." She followed him past the kitchens to the rear of the palace to yet another set of winding stairs that seemed to go on forever. As Gulliver guided them through a heavy wooden door, they were suddenly outside, far above the canyon city.

"Where are we?" Riona glanced around at the empty yard. The sun would be up soon, and they needed to be far away from the palace by then.

"There's an orchard up this path. Just don't touch the trees, they're wicked hot."

"Fire nut trees," Logan murmured. "They get hot when the

nuts are nearly ripe." Logan seemed to relax now that they were outside. He lifted his face to the sky, breathing in the fresh air. Taking his sister from Gulliver's arms, he nodded. "We should hurry."

Soon they were deep into the smoke-filled orchard, moving quickly toward the field lined with tents. Riona spotted Iskalt soldiers and slowed to a stop.

"This is where I leave you." She pulled Gulliver into a hug. "You're a good man, Gullie. Thank you for coming to help, but don't ever do that again. It's too dangerous. Let's keep our talks to the book."

"Well, I can't guarantee it. If I get hungry again, I might have to come pay you and Rowena a visit." Gulliver flashed her a smile and waved. "Love you, Riona. It'll be your turn next."

"Love you too, kid," she murmured with a wave as she watched them approach the soldiers who would take them back to their king and queen. The sky was just beginning to lighten, and she needed to get back to her rooms before the palace began to wake for the day. She would pay dearly for this if Egan ever found out, but it was worth it.

CHAPTER FIVE

Griffin

"Where is that kid?" Griffin paced back and forth. He'd recieved a message from a Fargelsian soldier come to tell him Gulliver was seen sneaking out of camp in the middle of the night and still hadn't returned.

"He's probably fine." Shauna sounded like the words were for herself more than Griffin.

He turned to her. "Really? You remember what happened the last time he ran from us? He found his way into the stores of one of the most dangerous men in Myrkur who came back to capture him. I almost had to trade my life for his. If it wasn't for Ri..." He didn't want to say her name. It physically hurt.

And now Gulliver was gone.

Griffin started pacing again as Hector ducked out of a tent and joined them where Shauna had started a small fire—more to have something to do than of necessity.

Dark Fae roamed the camp, staying clear of the agitated Griffin. The night time hours made those of Myrkur more comfortable, allowing them to sleep in their tents during the day to avoid the Eldurian sun.

Across the sands, the Iskalt army remained in a similar state of unrest as they took power from the moon. The Fargelsian camp was far quieter, which was why Gulliver chose that route as his point of exit. He hadn't wanted to be stopped.

"Griffin?" Hector crossed his arms.

Griffin didn't respond as his mind ran through a thousand wild scenarios of what could have happened to Gulliver.

"Griff." Hector jerked his head to something behind them, and Griffin turned.

Tia stood at the edge of their camp, her eyes wide as she stared at the Dark Fae. Griffin didn't blame her hesitation after Egan held her captive. She'd met few Dark Fae who treated her well.

Griffin reached her in a few strides. "Tia, are you okay?" She was probably upset about Gulliver leaving her.

Her mouth opened like she wanted to say something, but the only person she'd spoken to since her brother was taken was Gulliver.

Griffin glanced at the fae behind him. Hector joined Shauna in front of the fire while Nessa dozed in Shauna's lap. They too were grieving. Everyone was. Shauna hadn't mention Sinead, but her loss was felt by them all. Yet none of them had been as profoundly impacted as the little girl in front of him.

A tear slipped down Tia's cheek as her mouth opened again.

A thought came to Griffin. Gulliver wasn't exactly secretive, and if he'd tell anyone, it would probably be Tia.

Griffin put a hand on each of her shoulders and dipped his head to meet her glassy eyes, so different from the confident, trouble-making girl he'd first met in Iskalt. "Tia, if you know where my son is, you need to figure out a way to tell me."

She hiccupped back a sob and nodded. "Uncle Griff." The words burst out of her as if forced, like a dam finally breaking free. "He went to the palace."

Fear ripped through Griffin. Lifting his eyes to the sandstone structure across the expansive canyon, he imagined Gulliver skulking about the halls avoiding Egan or Riona's detection.

Griffin had to believe Riona wouldn't hurt him.

He slid an arm around Tia's shoulders and looked back at his family. "We'll get him back." It was a promise to himself as much as them. He refused to lose that boy. "Tia, have you told your parents?"

She shook her head.

"Have you talked to them at all?"

One of her shoulders lifted in a shrug.

"Okay, come with me." He marched Tia toward the orderly rows of dusty gray Iskalt tents. Soldiers looked up as he passed, a weariness on their faces despite the newness of the war. The Light Fae had no taste for siege or battles after so many years of peace. Griffin could see it in their passionless expressions. In contrast, the force of Dark Fae Hector led had known nothing but struggle. This war was supposed to be the end of that.

Lochlan sat with Myles in front of his tent, a wry smile on his face—the kind of expression Griffin remembered from when Lochlan didn't know him, yet treated him as a brother, anyway. Just like Hector was Griffin's brother, Myles and Finn were Lochlan's. The three kings were family.

Myles saw Griffin and Tia approaching before Lochlan did, and his smile widened. "Yo, Griff! Here I thought you forgot we totally became friends before everyone else remembered you too. You here to wish me happy birthday?"

"It's your birthday?" He didn't claim they weren't friends

because whether he wanted it or not, Myles was right. "That's human name days, right?"

"You're catching on, buddy." He gestured to the fire in front of them. "Take a load off." His eyes bounced from Griffin to Lochlan and back. "Unless you two would rather battle it out."

Lochlan, ignoring Griffin, reached a hand out to his daughter, a sight that made Griffin look away. "Hey, baby girl. Come here." Tia folded herself into her dad's lap. Lochlan and Myles were so different from the kings that came before them.

"I couldn't imagine Regan ever sitting on the ground."

Lochlan didn't look at him, instead resting his chin on Tia's head and staring into the flames.

Myles released a dramatic sigh. "You two make my head hurt. Griffin, is there a reason you came to see this lump of a king beside me? Lochlan won't ever say it, but he's happy you're free of the prison realm and helping us set the world right. Oh, but he also wants you to know that no matter how close you guys get once he gets over himself you'll never replace me in his heart."

Griffin would have laughed if it wasn't for the scowl on his brother's face and the heaviness created by Gulliver's absence.

"Oh." Myles wasn't done. "Also, Lochlan is the one who sent the Fargelsian to alert you about Gulliver because he cares about you, and Gulliver is practically his nephew."

Lochlan shot Myles a scowl.

Myles lifted both hands. "Don't shoot the messenger, dude."

"While this is entertaining, Myles, my son is out trying to get into the heavily guarded Eldurian palace for reasons I doubt anyone knows." A thought occurred to him, and he looked to Tia. "Unless someone does know why he went."

Lochlan looked down at Tia. "She doesn't know anything,

Griff. Don't even think about questioning her."

Griffin crossed his arms over his chest. "How do you think I know he went to the palace?"

"She..." Lochlan finally met his gaze. "*Spoke* to you? You?"

Griffin had never wanted to deflate Lochlan more than in that moment, but still, he couldn't reveal his true connection to the girl. "Does that matter right now? I want your permission to take a small force after Gulliver."

"Why mine? Hector could give you the soldiers."

Griffin shook his head. "Hector loves Gulliver, and he'd risk his own life for him, but he knows this siege is not his. He won't do this without your permission. I won't lie, we could all be captured. But I can't sit here and do nothing."

Lochlan started to say something but commotion at the edge of camp stole their attention.

"She's just a kid," someone said.

Lochlan pushed to his feet and set Tia down, taking her hand. "I'll be right back."

Griffin couldn't stay behind and wait, so he went after him with Myles behind him.

Before they reached the camp boundary where guards were spaced evenly apart, Brea ran past him.

"Darra?" she yelled, gaining speed.

Griffin didn't know who Darra was, but he kept going until he saw a little girl stumble and fall to her knees. Brea pushed past everyone and dropped at her side. "Darra? Can you speak? How did you get here?"

She coughed. "We... walked."

"From the palace? That's at least an hour." Under normal circumstances, an hour's walk wouldn't be a struggle. In Myrkur, that was an easy trek. But here in the deserts of Eldur, even without the blazing sun, the heat made any travel on foot difficult for fully grown fae, let alone a child.

"There's someone else coming!" a guard yelled.

The shout had Griffin peering into the dark to make out another figure making his way toward camp carrying a young boy in his arms.

"Logan." Lochlan ran forward to lift the boy into his arms, but Griffin couldn't take his eyes from the remaining figure, the one who left camp many hours ago and now returned breathing heavily, but alive.

Tia broke away from her dad and ran to Gulliver, wrapping her little arms around his middle.

"Gullie," Griffin whispered, watching the crowd engulf him.

Pushing his way through soldiers throwing questions at Gulliver, Griffin reached him. They stared at each other for a long moment before Griffin crushed him to his chest.

"Don't scare me like that again." Griffin couldn't let go.

"Let's be honest, I probably will."

A laugh wound through Griffin as he finally pulled away. "Make me understand this."

Gulliver shrugged. "A friend needed my help. That's what we do, isn't it?"

"You know these children?"

"They aren't the friend I meant, but they are important, Griff."

Brea backed away from the little girl to let one of the camp healers give her water and make sure she was okay. "He's right." She turned to Griffin. "This kid of yours just saved the Prince and Princess of Eldur."

Alona's kids. The number one reason the Light Fae armies hadn't been able to storm the palace. Griffin didn't know what to say, so he pulled Gulliver into another hug. "I'm so proud of you."

"A minute ago you were telling me not to do this again."

Griffin shook his head as he released him. "We will only beat Egan with bravery, and you, kid, are the bravest fae I know."

Red crept up Gulliver's neck. "I'm a thief. I just figured maybe it was time I stole something more important than hams."

Brea laughed as a tear tracked down her face. "In the human realm, stealing people is bad. But you did good, kid."

"Auntie Brea?" Logan wiped water from his lips and sat up.

"I'm here, honey." She shooed the healers away, reaching a hand to each of the kids.

Lochlan stepped up to Gulliver's side. "They look malnourished."

Gulliver issued a sad sigh. "They are. Egan kept them away from anyone else with their grandmother."

"Faolan?" Lochlan turned to him. "You saw her?"

Brea looked to them. "Where is my mother?"

"She wouldn't come." Gulliver's shoulders fell. "We tried to convince her, but she said her people needed her."

"That sounds like her." Lochlan took on a look of pride and love, the kind of look Griffin had never worn for Regan. He'd respected her, loved her even, but he'd never been proud of her.

The day Regan was chosen to raise Griffin and Faolan was chosen for Lochlan was the day their fates were sealed.

Darra crawled toward her brother, sobs racking her tiny body.

Brea gathered them both against her. "You're okay now." She tilted their chins to look at her. "Your parents are on the other side of the palace. They're so worried about you. Lochlan?"

"I know." He met her gaze, only hesitating a moment before turning to Griffin. "I need one of your winged fae again. It's the only way we'll get news of this rescue to the Eldurian army. Alona and Finn must know they're safe."

"Of course. I'll take care of it." He gripped Gulliver's elbow. "Come with me. I'm not letting you out of my sight."

Tia pushed her way forward, gesturing to Gulliver and then to herself. She turned hard eyes on her father and sucked in a breath. "I'm going with Gulliver."

He looked so stunned to hear her speak, he nodded.

As Griffin turned away, Lochlan called to him. "Take care of her."

Griffin met Lochlan's gaze over his shoulder, knowing it took everything Lochlan had to let his daughter go with him. "Always."

He didn't care if he embarrassed Gulliver when he took his hand. Gulliver in turn slid his free hand into Tia's and the three of them crossed from the Iskalt camp to return to their people.

Hector shot to his feet as soon as he saw them and yanked Gulliver forward, wrapping him in a strong hug. "You scared us, kid."

"That's what Griff said, but I saved a prince and princess. It was awesome. You have no idea how cool the Eldurian palace is. It has all these secret stairwells and hallways. It's like a thief's dream. But the only thing I stole was people, and Queen Brea told me that was okay. Well, I suppose I nicked a few pies while I was there."

Hector looked to Griffin for confirmation, and Griffin nodded. "It's true. The prince and princess of Eldur are now safe because of Gullie here. We need to get a message to the Eldurian queen. Can you send a Slyph with the news that we have her children, but the queen mother remained behind?"

"Sure, I'll assign someone the task myself." Hector looked to Gulliver once more. "Glad you're okay."

Gulliver grinned. "I'm always okay, Hector. Myles says

surviving is like my superpower—whatever that means. But it sounds cool."

Shauna and Nessa approached next and Gulliver fell into their embrace.

When Gulliver pulled back, a grin stretched across his face. "You should have seen me." He tugged Tia forward to stand at his side as he regaled them with stories of his epic adventures right under Egan's nose.

But one thing was missing.

Gulliver said a friend needed him, but there were only a few people he could have known in that palace. Egan, Toby, Enis, and... Could that be it? Was Riona the part of the story Gulliver left out?

He didn't know how long they'd relaxed by the fire-- Gulliver tired from his adventure and Griffin exhausted from the worry. The girls dozed off, leaving only Griffin and Gulliver. A comfortable silence stretched between them as they looked to the stars, the same ones shining over Myrkur.

"Griff, do you regret it? Helping to figure out how to take the magic down? We unleashed all of this on peaceful kingdoms."

Griffin had asked himself that question too many times. Did he regret his own actions that led to war? Again.

He leaned back on his elbows, his eyes falling on Tia and Nessa, one a princess of said peaceful realms and the other the product of a hard life in Myrkur. Yet, as they slept, they both looked like little girls, few differences between them. That was what they were fighting for.

For the Dark Fae of Myrkur to be able to live full, happy lives. For them to be seen as equals among the fae who didn't even know they existed. Yes, most of the Dark Fae fought with Egan, but at the root of it, they wanted the same thing.

To be seen.

To be known.

For the world to remember they were here.

"No, Gullie." The sun was just beginning to peek over the horizon, and Griffin's Iskalt magic faded away with the night, but the Dark Fae would still be who they were. Neither the sun nor the moon controlled them. They had no words of magic.

Their magic was inherent in who they were, integral to their very being. It wasn't meant to cause harm. That was the beauty of it. Defensive magic kept them safe, a noble goal. They weren't weapons.

His eyes drifted from the stars to Gulliver. "I don't regret it." For once in his life, he knew what he did was right. "No matter what happens in these battles, the Dark Fae didn't deserve to be kept separate from the world. When something is wrong, Gullie, it is our duty to fight for change."

"I know." Gulliver failed to suppress a smile as the glow of the fire flickered across his face. "We have to do the right thing. I learned that from you."

Griffin never imagined in his life that he'd inspire someone to do good, that they'd look at him as the example for how to live their lives, how to fight. When he'd first entered the prison realm, he hadn't known who he was anymore. Redemption hadn't seemed possible, so he didn't try. That first year, he spent most of his time feeling sorry for himself.

Until Gulliver... until this kid made him want to be better, to be worthy of remembrance.

"Gullie..." Griffin rubbed a hand over his face, wishing whatever secret Gulliver held didn't have to be pried out of him. "This friend you have in the palace—"

"Riona." The name burst out of him. "It's Riona." Gulliver collapsed onto his back, staring into the dark sky. "I'm sorry, Griff. I should have told you, but she didn't want me to."

Griffin released a breath. He'd suspected, but the confirmation struck him like a bludgeon. "Why couldn't you tell me?"

He sat up. "I don't know. Honestly. Riona... she's not with Egan. She's still on our side, and she misses you so much she can't bring herself to ask about you. I know she does. But I think she's afraid she'll let you down, and it's easier if you don't know she's still doing what you asked."

Griffin rubbed the back of his neck. "What I asked?"

Gulliver met his gaze, lowering his voice to a whisper. "She's protecting your son."

At the words, Griffin's gaze darted to Tia, making sure she still slept. Her eyes remained closed, but Shauna's eyes slid open, locking onto him. Griffin would have some explaining to do, but now was not the time.

"How are you communicating with her?" He turned to Gulliver.

"The books she used with Egan. I managed to steal his. She has great ideas, Griff. She's having an Eldurian smith make some of those human sunglasses for the Dark Fae in our army."

"Did she ask you to come tonight?" He couldn't imagine Riona putting Gulliver in that much danger, but if she had...

"Not exactly. She just said she wished I was there to help her. Egan was going to have Darra and Logan whipped in front of all of us today. We had to get them out of there. Darra is only four, and Logan is Nessa's age. If I hadn't gone, they'd probably end up dead. You love Brea, right?"

"Well," Griffin sputtered, the marriage magic pulling tight. "In a healthy, non-romantic, she's-married-to-my-brother kind of way."

"Well, duh. How else would you love her?"

"Don't say duh."

"Why?" Gulliver's brow furrowed.

"It's too human." He put a hand on Gulliver's arm. "I

understand. You were needed, and you went." He'd have done the same thing if Riona needed him, if he'd known she was still on their side.

That knowledge lifted a weight from his shoulders, and his heart came alive inside his chest once more. She hadn't betrayed him. She'd chosen differently than he had all those years ago when he went into the crumbling Fargelsi palace for Regan.

"Riona is stronger than me."

Gulliver pursed his lips as his tail curled around into his lap. "No, Griff. She just loves you. Yeah, I'm sure she also wants to do what's right, but she's in the enemy's camp because *you* asked something of her. She's staying for Toby, for you."

A choice he hadn't made for Brea even when the marriage magic tied them together. Sure, he'd gotten her to safety, to Lochlan, but he'd returned to the evil queen he called his mother.

Maybe Riona was right. Maybe he'd never truly loved Brea in that way. He'd wanted her, sure. He'd liked her a heck of a lot, but love? That was staying with a dangerous man and working against him. Letting others think you betrayed them.

It was Riona.

"Gulliver, take me to your journal. Please."

Gulliver pushed himself to his feet. "Should we wake the girls?"

Shauna's voice joined in. "I'll put them to sleep in my tent. You two go."

"Thanks, Shauna." Griffin looked from Shauna to Nessa and Tia, knowing she'd keep his daughter safe.

Gulliver started walking toward the Iskalt camp. "So, I've been sleeping outside Tia's tent. She lets me keep my stuff with hers."

"Tia's tent? You mean—"

"The journal is in the mean Iskalt king's tent. That a problem?"

"No, Gulliver. Not a problem." He didn't care where he had to go to get the journal. He needed to speak with Riona.

Griffin leaned against a rock on the outskirts of the Iskalt camp with the journal in his lap. Gulliver left to seek a bed as the sun rose on the horizon.

The book sat in his lap open to the page Griffin had written a single word on. *Riona...* He hadn't known what else to say.

So, he waited. And no response came.

"Griff." Lochlan's grunt came as no surprise. Griffin had seen him approaching.

"Don't worry, I'm going back to my camp soon." He hadn't returned to Shauna, knowing he'd have a lot of explaining to do.

"You are of Iskalt. This is your camp too."

Griffin snorted, not taking his eyes from the page. "Sure, Lochlan." He expected his brother to walk away like he had so many times before, but instead, Lochlan lowered himself to the ground, kicking one leg out in front of him and bending the other.

Griffin tore his eyes from the book. "What do you want? I'm too tired to handle your scorn right now."

Lochlan gestured to the book. "Myles tells me that journal is supposed to contain messages from someone inside the palace."

Of course Myles had known about Gulliver and Riona before Griffin had. "It contains nothing except a lame attempt for me to contact Riona."

Understanding lit in Lochlan's eyes. "You know, I never

really believed she'd changed sides."

"Lochlan, you hated her. Even when you didn't remember me, you didn't trust her."

"At first, I didn't. But neither did you. I saw it in your face when you looked at her. She was loyal to Egan. But she changed, didn't she? Just like you did."

"Is there a point to this conversation? You've refused to say more than a few words to me for weeks. And right now, I'm a little busy waiting for Riona to write back."

"You're in love with her."

Griffin pushed out a breath. "Of course I'm bloody in love with her, you oaf. She's tried to kill me... a few times... and she yells at me a lot. We don't really get along, actually. But I love her so much I hate myself for doubting her. And now... she's in that palace because of me."

"I'm sure it's not—"

"I asked her to protect Toby." Griffin pounded a fist into the book. "Before Tia destroyed the magic, they sent Toby to a different section of the barrier. I stayed to protect Tia, and Riona promised she'd protect Toby. I didn't expect that promise to take her onto the enemy's side."

Lochlan didn't respond for a long moment. "Brea thinks I've avoided you because of the partial marriage bond returning between you, but I can see you don't love her. Not now. But you and she were together, Griff. None of us remembered it, we didn't know she'd been married before when she announced she was pregnant."

He rested his arm on his knee and looked away. "We thought our kids were early. Twins often come a bit early. It was expected."

Griffin shook his head, wanting to deny it, to pretend Lochlan wasn't coming to the realization Griffin feared.

Lochlan sighed. "I don't know what the truth is, Griff. We

will probably never know for certain, but even the possibility... I haven't been able to look at you."

Griffin could have told him what he knew, but the words clogged in his throat.

Lochlan went on. "Your Gulliver may have saved us tonight. We can now attack without worrying for the prince and princess. Alona may even forgive you for kidnapping her all those years ago."

"Yeah, I sort of did that a lot, didn't I?" Griffin looked down at his hands resting against the open journal in his lap. Words appeared on the page.

Lochlan stood. "I just... I don't know what I wanted. Maybe... Brea has been saying it's time I stop hating you. Maybe she's right." He looked like he had more to say, but he only nodded and walked away.

Griffin stared after him before looking back to the book.

This isn't Gullie, is it?

He smiled at the words. She could tell it was him based on one word. He dragged the inkless quill across the page. *It's me.*

Griffin.

He smiled, hearing her say his name in his mind. *Gulliver returned with the Eldurian prince and princess.*

That's good, Griff. Really good.

He released a sigh and closed his eyes, picturing her sitting next to him. *I doubted you.*

I figured you would.

She'd always been perceptive. *I'm sorry,* he wrote.

It took a moment for her response to appear. *I know. I'm keeping my promise to you, Griff. Toby is under guard when he's here, but I'm staying close.*

When he was there? Griffin knew exactly what she wasn't saying. If Egan had taken Aghadoon, he and Toby spent time going back and forth. *Thank you for keeping him safe.* There was so much else he wanted to say to her. He missed her. He wished he could see her, feel her. But he couldn't find the words.

Instead, he did what he always did. He focused on the problem at hand. *Are you with him now?*

Her response was immediate. *I am. I have this servant who knows how to get to places unseen. I came to check on him and have been sitting by his bed for a while.*

Griffin released a breath. Talking to Riona made him feel closer to getting Toby home, back to his family. *Can you wake him? Someone here needs to know he's okay.*

Give me a moment.

Griffin pushed himself to his feet and trudged back to the Myrkur camp where he found Shauna watching over Nessa and Tia inside her tent.

"Hey." Griffin poked his head in the tent.

Shauna smiled. "I still have a hard time believing Nessa is safe. Makes it hard to sleep."

He understood exactly what she meant. He found himself watching Shauna and Nessa and Tia whenever they were near, unable to clear his mind of their imprisonment in the Myrkur palace.

"Wake Tia. There's someone she needs to talk to." He handed her the book. "Tell her to wait for her brother's words to appear and write back to him."

"Where are you going?"

His eyes found Tia once more, her angelic face relaxed in sleep. "They aren't mine, Shauna. And right now, my brother needs to know his son is okay."

By the time he reached Lochlan's tent once more, the sun already blazed hot against the dry cracked ground. His Iskalt magic no longer gave him strength, but he didn't need it.

Not this time.

Riona

Without the Eldurian kids to make an example of, Egan strapped Faolan Cahill to a post at the city's edge and gave her thirty lashes himself. By the final strike, blood poured from her wounds, and her head lolled forward.

Afterward, Riona sat by her bed. This woman was once the Queen of Eldur before abdicating for her adopted human daughter. She was the mother of two queens, a woman who hadn't ruled in ten years, yet there was a quiet strength within her.

A smile curved Faolan's cracked lips as her eyes slid open to find Riona.

"I'm sorry." Riona hadn't been able to stop it. She couldn't prevent Egan from hurting anyone. There was a profound powerlessness in her situation.

"My grandchildren?" Faolan wheezed.

"They're safe." Riona nodded as she tried to hold back her tears. "They made it to Brea and Lochlan." To Griffin.

Faolan's entire body relaxed at the news. "Thank you for saving them."

"I wish you'd have gone with them."

She gave a small shake of her head. "My job isn't finished here. This palace is full of those who've served my family faithfully. They never abandoned us. I must not abandon them now."

"He's probably going to kill you. Egan... he's dangerous." A tear slid down her cheek.

"I have lived a beautiful life, my dear. Do not cry for me. I have raised two wonderful children in Alona and Lochlan. My daughter, Brea, came back to me many years ago, and I've had the joy of loving her. I am a grandmother many times over. And the love of my life, the woman I never wanted to live without, died fighting Queen Regan. So, my dear, save your tears for those who've never known my happiness. Whatever Egan does to me, it is okay because my family is safe."

Despite Faolan telling her not to cry, Riona couldn't help it. She'd never had anything close to a mother, but she could imagine what it was to be connected to someone so fully.

The door to the infirmary burst open, and Egan marched in, flanked by two Slyph. "Riona, you are spending too much time in this palace with these people." He stalked forward and reached out to clamp his fingers around her arm. The tattoos squirmed under the pressure, and she bit back a growl of pain. "I do not know how the children disappeared, but you do not want to see me question the old queen." He bared his teeth at Faolan. "It will not be pleasant. I'm sending you to Aghadoon. When we first attacked, we were able to use the book to allow us to see it temporarily, but we've been working on a permanent spell, and Enis has finally worked it out. So, you'll be able to see the village for good now. And I want you there permanently."

Riona tried to take a step back, but he didn't let her go. "Permanently, sire? You need me here." She needed to be here. With Toby and Faolan. There was so much to do to ensure Egan didn't win.

"I can spare you. The protection of that library is our top priority. The armies outside the city are merely a distraction. Pack your belongings. I'll retrieve the boy to open a portal."

Aghadoon looked different than Riona remembered. Egan didn't allow Toby to join her, forcing her to say goodbye to him in Eldur after he opened a portal, realizing she would never be able to keep her promise to Griffin.

Egan would always win.

The portal snapped shut behind her, and she stared at the village that looked like it hadn't faced a destructive battle. The destroyed homes and shops had been repaired, but that wasn't possible after so little time.

Dark Fae patrolled the streets, but they let her pass, her reputation preceding her.

She stopped outside the library, peering in but not crossing the threshold. Enis sat at a table in the center hunched over an ancient looking scroll.

Gone was the harsh sun of Eldur. Instead, rain drizzled from a gray sky. A chilled wind pushed the braids from her shoulders, sending a shiver down her spine.

Her pack hung heavy against her back, but there was one thing she needed to do before she could rest.

A grassy square stood in the center of the village. Black numbers were burned into the stone, changing each time the village moved.

Black numbers that could be the key to everything.

Pulling out her journal, Riona wrote the numbers across a worn yellow page. There was no other message, but Griffin would understand.

She thought her only purpose was to keep Toby safe.

But Egan had handed her another weapon.

Aghadoon.

They came two days later in the early morning. On this day, the rain didn't drizzle, it poured down as if the very skies wept at the battle of the fae world spilling into the human lands. Again.

Riona stood outside the village in a field awaiting the portal that would bring her closer to getting back to Griffin.

It opened in a flash of violet magic that was now so familiar to her. Dark Fae spilled through the portal with Hector at their lead. Griffin appeared last, shutting them away from the fae world.

"Are you ready for this, Riona?" Griffin stopped in front of her, his eyes skimming over her face like he wanted to see everything. But they had a mission. This wasn't a time for reunions.

She nodded. "Aghadoon is just now waking up. There will be guards patrolling the streets. The only fae remaining belong to Egan."

"Does everyone see it?" Griffin asked, looking to Hector.

"Of course we do." Hector lifted one brow. "It's a village. They don't just disappear. Fae! With me!" He took off running, his broad head bent to display his sharpened bull horns, and his thick legs thundered toward the village. Slyph jumped into the air, zooming ahead, their bowstrings drawn. Others with tails and horns and a myriad of other features joined in a battle cry, their voices rising together as one. It wasn't the full army Toby had managed to bring through before, but maybe it would be enough.

These people of Myrkur were united—not like Egan's army where each race kept to their own lines and units.

Riona didn't fly, choosing instead to keep pace at Griffin's side. Drawing her sword, she crashed into the village, slamming into the first guard she saw. Her sword sliced through him, and she moved on to the next.

Blood sprayed her face, feeling like warm tears on her cheeks before the rain washed it away. Griffin shot her a grin, his hair dripping, as he dove into the fight, and it gave her the strength to keep going, to fight fae she'd claimed to be allied with, the ones she was supposed to lead in Aghadoon.

Some stared at her in shock as she cut them down, others ran for their lives in the face of the onslaught.

The battle wouldn't last long as Egan's soldiers rose from their beds to fight for their lives. All Riona could focus on was her next move and the man at her side.

Griffin didn't leave her, and she stayed with him as they worked together to clear a path toward the library. Unlike when Egan took the village, Hector ordered his fae not to burn the village or destroy what they'd come to take.

Riona's chest heaved as she dodged an arrow from an airborne Slyph. The flying fae drew another, and Riona watched as the arrow sailed through space, aiming for Griffin's back.

Running toward him, Riona slammed into Griffin, shoving him as hard as she could into the open doorway of the empty library. They both lost their balance and fell to the ground.

Riona recovered first, jumping to her feet to close the door. It brought back the memory of hiding in the library with Toby as Egan took the village. Only this time, the right side would come out victorious.

Griffin rose to his knees, clutching his side.

"Are you okay?" Riona stepped toward him.

He nodded. "I took the hilt of a sword to my ribs, but I've felt worse." Pain flashed across his face as he got to his feet. The sounds of battle drifted into their sanctuary, swords clanging, soldiers yelling.

It had to be almost over by now.

Riona and Griffin stared at each other for a long moment, both sucking wind. She didn't know who moved first or which one of them was faster as they collided in a searing kiss that sent warmth racing through her limbs, despite the rain-soaked clothing clinging to her skin and water dripping from her wings.

Griffin's kiss was as good as she remembered, as she'd dreamed about. For this small moment in time, he filled her mind, chasing away thoughts of a queen who might not be alive any longer, a king trying to destroy the fae kingdoms, and the battle they'd achieved a momentary escape from.

But one never forgot the impact reverberating in their bones of their sword making the killing blow.

"Griffin," she whispered against his lips.

His hands wiped the rain from her cheeks, and she met his dark gaze. "I missed you. The magic inside me is saying this is wrong, that I need to obey the shreds of the marriage bond that returned with the memories, but still, Riona, I missed you. No magic could make me stop."

Her brow furrowed. Those words weren't the ones she wanted when she knew this moment of theirs couldn't last. "Kiss me again."

He didn't hesitate, but this time he went slow, as if savoring every second of their connection. His touch burned into her, reminding her this time didn't belong to them, that their mission was bigger than anything they felt for each other.

Griffin pressed his forehead against hers. "I know we have to get back out there. But first, where is Toby?"

"Egan kept him in Eldur. He's supposed to return here when Egan wants me to come back."

His eyes searched hers. "What you did here, Riona... we'll control this library now. The magic in the book is all from here. With this power, we can win."

A smile tilted her lips as her wings wrapped around them, enclosing them in a cocoon. "You will. I believe that. Egan must be stopped."

He sighed. "You're returning to him, aren't you?"

"I have to. He still has Toby. I have to find a way to contact Toby for a portal. As soon as I do, you need to move the location of the village. There's a spell kept under the stones in the square where the coordinates appear."

He smoothed a hand over her hair and pulled her into a hug. "Riona, I l—" The door flew open, and Riona pushed away from Griffin, cutting off whatever he wanted to say.

"You can't keep me here," she yelled, reaching for the sword that had fallen when she'd tumbled to the ground.

Enis stood in the doorway, the book clutched to her chest. "Riona, leave him. We have to go."

Riona wished she didn't see the hurt in Griffin's eyes at his mother's callousness. For Toby, she told herself. And Faolan and every other Eldurian in the palace. She had to go back.

Giving Griffin one final look, she followed Enis out into the rain.

"I contacted Egan." She started running, using the buildings to hide from Hector and his soldiers who dragged corpses from the village, the battle over.

"How?" Riona chased after her. She didn't know they'd been in contact.

"I copied the spell that created your journals. It's a rudimentary version, but it works for emergencies. We need to get to the edge of the village before they change the location."

The ground rumbled beneath their feet, and an unnatural fog rolled across the village. Griffin had found the spell, and he didn't require the Iskalt magic he didn't currently have, not with the Fargelsian words. Magic zipped through the air, tingling along her skin and forcing her defensive magic to the surface.

"Come on," Enis yelled.

The cobblestone streets heaved under foot, rattling against each other. Riona turned the corner, running for the road out of the village.

"Jump." Enis hurled her body through the ancient pillars that served as the village boundary.

Riona lunged after her, her shoulder slamming into the stone as the village shook and disappeared behind them.

A laugh escaped Enis. "We made it."

Riona watched the empty field where the village was only a moment before, unable to help feeling like everything she truly wanted just vanished.

Before she could think much about it, a violet portal, looking very similar to the ones Griffin created, opened, and Toby stepped through followed by Egan.

Egan stared at the empty field, his face red as a scream escaped his throat.

Someone would pay dearly for losing Aghadoon.

And Riona suspected that someone would be her.

Chapter Seven

Griffin

Griffin stumbled from his tent after a few hours of much needed sleep, but he still felt like something was off.

In some ways he was almost happy, knowing Alona's children were safe, his brother might not hate him after all, his Dark Fae family was back together, Aghadoon was safely moved to a location at the center of the army encampment, well beyond Egan's reach, Riona hadn't betrayed him, and he was pretty sure she was in love with him. Despite the imminent war, things were going great for Griffin O'Shea.

But something kept him on edge all morning as he joined his family for breakfast over the remnants of last night's fire. He wasn't sure if he was waiting for the inevitable bad news to tear his world apart again, or if he simply wasn't used to having good things happen.

"What is with you today?" Shauna nudged him to still his fidgeting.

"I don't know. Something's ... not right, but I can't put my finger on it."

"Griffin!" Lochlan's gruff voice was laced with panic. "What magic is this?"

"What's wrong?" Griffin stood to greet his brother as he rushed across the clearing between their camps. "Is it Tia? News of Toby?"

Lochlan's face grew hard as stone as he stared at his brother in surprise. "Tell me, Brother, did you not notice the sun failed to rise this morning?" He cast a glance around the Dark Fae camp. "Did none of you notice? Sunrise should have occurred more than an hour ago, and still the moon sits high in the sky as if it were midnight."

That was it. The thing that felt off. Griffin stared up at the unnaturally dark sky hanging over the palace and the army camped outside it. "I spent ten years under such darkness, Loch. It feels more natural to me than the sun."

"You really didn't notice?" Lochlan shook his head, running his hand through his hair. "This is magic like none we've ever seen before. Everything is twisted. My magic hasn't faded, and we received a frantic message from the Eldurians. They are beside themselves because they are powerless under this veil of darkness."

"It's Egan's doing." Griffin frowned. There was something too familiar about this particular darkness. Too convenient. "With the knowledge contained in the book of power, it's like he has gained a kind of power we don't understand, but a bit of darkness won't hurt us, Loch. It's just an adjustment we will have to make."

"It's not just darkness, Griff." Lochlan turned, pacing back toward him. "This magic, whatever it is, we cannot break through it. It is like a ... shield keeping us out of Raudur City. We can't attack."

"Then we will have to break through the magic keeping us out. We need to find the spell he's using. The one Enis is performing for him. Then maybe we can reverse it."

"I don't have the patience or the desire to figure out what Mother is up to in all of this nonsense." Lochlan tried to hide the pain it caused him, knowing his own mother was working against them, but Griffin felt the same pain. There was no hiding it for either of them.

"She goes wherever that book goes, and as long as Egan has it, she will be his puppet." Griffin shook his head. "We need to find the spell in the library."

"Neeve and Myles are already there with Brea, trying to learn what they can, but Myles is asking for you. He says you have more experience with the village and the book."

"They are almost the same thing." Griffin turned to wave to Shauna and Nessa before he followed his brother back to the center of the huge camp. Aghadoon stood in the middle of the sprawling army camp, but Brea managed to find the spell that would conceal it from their enemies. Neeve performed the spell the moment they moved the village from the human realm to Eldur. Even if Egan managed to defeat them, he would never find the library perched right at his doorstep.

"How?" Lochlan scratched his head.

"The book contains everything the library contains. It is a key with severe limitations. It will only show the reader what pertains to them. Or what it thinks they need to know. I believe the book shows the reader certain magic that is needed for current events. In the future when this war is won and a new conflict arises, the book of power will show its reader contents we've yet to see from it. But the library holds the secrets of all magic, we just have to look for it."

"I don't like it. A book should not have the power to make decisions." Lochlan charged through the crowds of Iskalt soldiers brimming with magic that should have faded hours ago. Griffin wondered how they would fare throughout the day. Would they grow weary, or would it become too much for them to bear, holding on to more magic than they could reasonably contain? He remembered well what it felt like to have his magic in a kingdom that saw no light, but before getting his power back, his body had been used to the constant darkness. Did that mean he could handle it more?

"I agree. The book cannot be trusted when its source is unknown. We don't know who created it or why." Griffin and Lochlan stepped through the crumbling pillars that had become familiar to Griffin during his visits to Aghadoon. The streets and homes were filled with women and children from all the kingdoms who had accompanied the armies. Brea and Lochlan had decided the invisible village that could be moved at a moment's notice was the safest place for them.

Tia made her way through a group of young girls, her eyes round and bloodshot from lack of sleep.

"She's having nightmares," Lochlan explained, scooping her up into his arms when she came to greet them. She still wasn't talking much, but as she laid her head on her father's shoulder, she reached a hand out for Griffin.

"Thank you for letting me talk to Toby in the magic book again, Uncle Griff."

"You're welcome, sweetheart." Griffin smoothed a hand over her strawberry blond hair that was a perfect blend of his auburn hair and Lochlan's blond hair. "Riona is taking good care of him."

Lochlan grunted as they approached the library, setting Tia back down. "Why don't you go find Gulliver, and try to get some rest, baby girl? I know you must be tired."

"I'll try, Papa." Tia left them to find her way back to the cabin where some of the other children were playing.

"Loch, get in here!" Brea called from inside the library.

"I take it you found something?" Lochlan raised his brow at her tone.

"Oh good, you brought Griff." She waved them over to the long table where she and Myles had a sea of books opened and scattered across the surface.

"Have you found anything useful yet?"

"Useful" Three pairs of eyes turned toward the King of Iskalt. Neeve stood on a ladder between two bookshelves that reached the ceiling.

"Lochlan O'Shea, this library is nothing short of enlightening," Neeve said, her tone one of reverence.

"For a Gelsi magic wielder, I suppose it is." Lochlan moved to sit at the table.

"No, Loch, that's not it at all," Brea said. "This place holds more than just Fargelsian spells. There are references and lesson books for Iskaltian magic I've never seen before, Eldurian too. And it's not just a catalogue of magic. The history of our world is right here. Histories we've lost. It's incredible."

"This library is priceless, Loch," Myles said, pulling his nose out of a book reluctantly. "We could study these books for the rest of our lives and never learn everything Aghadoon has to teach us. It's like ... finding the complete contents of the library at Alexandria."

"While that is exciting," Griffin interjected before someone else could sing the praises of the Aghadoon library. "Have you found anything that will help us defeat Egan?"

"We have discovered something." Brea picked up a book of Iskaltian magic for beginners. "See this instruction on how to use night magic to create a small cyclone of wind?"

"Most kids learn how to do that sort of thing when they first come into their power." Lochlan pulled the book closer to him. "And this method is convoluted."

"Do it." Brea said. "Just like the book says."

Lochlan read over the instructions with a scowl. "There's a much easier way to do this, Brea."

"Not the point, Loch." She sighed with impatience. Griffin knew that sigh well. And apparently, so did Lochlan.

The blue light of his magic flickered across his palms as Lochlan formed the small, slow moving cyclone, setting it free to circle about the room.

"Now watch this." Brea ripped the page from the book. "*Dóiteán,*" she whispered the Gelsi word for fire and the page went up in flames.

"Nothing happened." Griffin watched the lazy cyclone circle around them.

"It means there is another record of this magic here." Brea reached for a heavy volume on Iskalt wind magic and flipped to the page she'd marked with a piece of paper. Tracing a finger over the lines of the spell, she spoke the word for heat, letting the lines of the page smolder and darken under the heat of her finger. When the last of the instructions were destroyed, the cyclone stumbled and collapsed.

"You destroyed the records of the magic." Griffin's voice rose in excitement as he realized what this meant.

"What am I missing?" Lochlan frowned.

"Try to do it again from memory," Brea said.

Lochlan's magic sparked to his fingertips, but the cyclone didn't form.

"Destroy the record, and you destroy the magic." Lochlan stood, staring around the large room with shelf after shelf of books and scrolls covering every available surface. "This is a record of all magic."

"It's the source of everything we can do," Brea said in a breathless voice.

"But the book is a duplicate, isn't it?" Myles asked, sitting back in his chair, running a weary hand over his eyes.

"Think of it like an iPad." Brea turned toward her human friend. "It can access anything on the internet, but it doesn't contain all the knowledge found on the internet."

"The library is the internet, and the book is just a window that shows you what's here." Myles shot up from his seat. "So, if it's destroyed here, then the book can't access it."

"Exactly."

"Care to dumb that down for us non-humans over here?" Lochlan asked.

"We destroy the records of the bad magic Egan is doing to make it dark and keep us out of the city, then that magic will fail just like that little cyclone failed."

"Wait." Griffin dropped into a chair next to his brother. "Are you saying all we had to do to destroy the prison barrier was burn a page in a book here?"

"Yes." Brea's shoulders stiffened. "If we'd known that, we'd have saved my children a lot of heartache they're far too young to have endured. But I can't think about that, or I'll go crazy. Right now, we need to find the records of this awful magic and destroy it. That's something tangible we can actually do to help bring Toby home. So, that's what we're going to do."

Brea sat down and pulled a stack of books toward her. She would exhaust herself sorting through all these books, looking for any reference to a spell that would cause permanent night.

"I'll help." Griffin picked up a large volume on Iskalt air magic. "Wait." He put the book down. "The only person Egan trusts who can perform this complex level of magic is Enis." He refused to call her mother. "The Light Fae under his control are much too new at magic to possibly execute such difficult spell work."

"Yes, she would be the one responsible for this current mess." Lochlan scowled at the mention of their mother's name.

"She can no longer wield Iskalt magic. She was never very good at it because her family ties to Iskalt weren't strong. She only has Gelsi magic."

"Which means we need to be looking for a Fargelsian spell book." Brea sorted through her stack of books, handing more than half of them off to Neeve to return to the shelves. "That just narrowed it down by a lot."

"We've got this, Brea." Myles and Neeve set off to the back of the library to search for more advanced books containing Gelsi magic.

"You need to rest, Brea." Lochlan leaned over her shoulder. She moved to place her book on top of another open book in front of her.

"I will, I promise. I just want to finish searching this book, and I'll go take a break to check on Tia. I promise I'll take a nap."

"Griff, make sure she actually does that," Lochlan said, turning toward him. "I need to make my rounds at the front and see to our soldiers, but I'll be back soon to help with the search, though my knowledge of the language of power is minimal at best."

"We can handle this part, Loch." Brea assured him. "Go do your kingy things." She leaned up to kiss his cheek.

"We've been over this, Brea. *Kingy* is not a word I'm willing to recognize."

"Love you," she called over her shoulder as she scanned the page in front of her.

Griffin smiled at their easy banter even in the midst of so much heartache. They were good together. The remnants of the marriage bond didn't like that thought, but he couldn't deny that things had worked out for the best for the two of them.

"This book isn't nearly advanced enough." She slammed the leather volume shut. "It will be an excellent tool for Tia, though. She's far beyond the spell work of a typical student her age. This is more intermediate magic that actually might interest her. She likes nothing more than a challenge, but I'd prefer she tackle some of the fun stuff in this book than take on destroying a three-hundred-year-old barrier spell all by herself."

"You'd have been so proud of her, Brea." Griffin said. "She was so strong and brave. It scared me to death to see her do it, but I don't think anyone else could have. She's special. She and Toby both."

Brea forced a smile as she stood. "All my babies are special," she managed to say over the tears that threatened to spill. "I'm just going to go find another book." She darted down an aisle, and Griffin could hear her sobs as she tried to stifle them. Marriage magic or not, it killed him to see her so distraught over her children.

Griffin sifted through the books still left on the table, sorting them by their root magic, Iskalt, Eldur and Fargelsi magic. He pulled the last book closer to him. The one Brea had shielded from Lochlan when he leaned over her. And Griffin could see why she had.

He studied the chart that traced the lineage of the O'Rourke Queens, ending with Brea O'Rourke-O'Shea and her four children. Just as in the book of power, Kayleigh and Ciara's names connected with Brea and Lochlan's names. But Tierney and Toby O'Shea were connected with their father's name, Griffin O'Shea.

He wasn't sure how he felt about Brea knowing the truth. He would have spared her that heartache if he could have. The fact that some fragment of their marriage bond had survived was more than enough for her to be dealing with. As Griffin looked around the library, he wondered if there might be a way to permanently break their bond. If it was possible, the way to do it could be found somewhere within these walls. He could do that much for her at the very least.

"Griffin!" Brea raced back to the table with a scroll clutched in her hands. "O'Shea magic." Her hands trembled as she set the scroll down.

"What about it?" Griffin moved to her side to help her spread the ancient-looking scroll across the table.

"This is it. The record of your family's signature magic. It was granted to your ancestors eons ago. It's rooted in Fargelsian magic." She traced the fine print with her fingertips. "This is how Enis was able to awaken Toby's portal magic when it never showed in him."

"He should have inherited the O'Shea magic when his sister did. I can't imagine how he's creating such powerful portals at his age."

"This is how." Brea's eyes flew across the parchment. "She's enhanced his natural ability using the source magic to ... essentially redesign it to be stronger."

"That sounds dangerous." Griffin would gladly throttle his own mother the next time he saw her for daring to tamper with his son's magic.

"From what I can tell, it's not exactly dangerous, but there are consequences for abusing the power. He shouldn't be traveling as often as Egan is forcing him. Especially, because he is so young. Too young to be wielding such magic when he's never shown any signs of having magic at all." Brea's tone grew angrier as she read the complicated spell work that went into enhancing her son's dormant magic.

"We have to rescue him, Griff." She reached out and gripped his hand. "If he keeps this up, his magic is going to fall out of balance. He will fall ill with a fever that can't be controlled. He could have hallucinations and struggle to get the rest he needs to recover. Griff." Brea looked up at him with terror in her eyes. "This could kill him. Toby needs to find a balance with his portal magic. He can't keep creating these massive portals to move Egan's army between the worlds."

"We're running out of time." Griffin pulled her into his arms as she sobbed. "We have to find that record and burn it. We have to get into Raudur City and bring Toby home to his parents and his sisters. He needs you both, Brea." It was as much as he could bring himself to say, but he saw the recognition in her eyes. She knew he was trying to tell her. Lochlan was Toby and Tia's father in all the ways that mattered.

Riona

Riona's eyes snapped open. It was the middle of the night, but shouting from the halls outside her door had her leaping out of bed and reaching for her sword before she was fully awake.

"Riona!" The pitiful wail shot right through her.

"Toby." She rushed from her bedroom and across the sitting room, not bothering to grab a robe to cover the ridiculous sleeping gown Rowena made her wear.

Riona darted into the hall, fully expecting to see another battle between Dark and Light Fae. For the last few weeks, Egan sent portions of his army to attack the Light Fae camps surrounding the palace. It was only a matter of time before Griffin and his brother found a way through the magic protecting Raudur City from the invasion they were all waiting for.

"The snakes! They're coming!" Toby screamed, writhing in the Asrai soldier's arms.

"For the last time, there aren't any snakes in the palace."

"Unhand him." Riona drew her blade along the Dark Fae's throat. He was Egan's man, but if he harmed a hair on Toby's head, she would kill him without blinking.

"He escaped his rooms again," the soldier hissed in the creepy way of the Asrai who normally resided at the bottom of the Black Sea of Myrkur.

"Can't you see he isn't well?" Riona reached for Toby as the soldier released him.

"The snakes, Riona, they're everywhere." Toby turned his bloodshot eyes on her, his face flushed with fever.

She wrapped her arm around his shoulders and steered him toward her room. "He will stay with me for the rest of the night. His hallucinations are getting worse."

"Very well." The soldier relented and skulked away with two of his brethren. Asrai were the last creatures that should be guarding the boy. Some were acclimated to the land and its customs, but others were the stuff of nightmares. Egan must be desperate to keep his hold on Tobias.

"The snakes." Toby's bottom lip trembled.

"It's okay, Toby. There aren't any snakes in my room. We'll stay here for the rest of the night." She guided him into her rooms and closed the door behind them. Toby turned and threw his arms around her waist and burst into tears.

"I want to go home, Riona." He shook in her arms.

"I promise, I will get you home to your parents, Toby." She smoothed her hand over his dark curls, so like his mother's. He couldn't last much longer. Egan was abusing Toby's magic, and it was taking a toll on him.

"I heard the commotion." Rowena let herself into the room without knocking, balancing a tea tray with two steaming mugs. "Eldur Blossom tea. It will help you both sleep a nice dreamless rest." She pressed a mug into Toby's hands.

Riona helped herself to the other mug of sweet smelling tea. She could do with a nice dreamless rest herself.

Rowena soon had them both tucked into bed, and Toby was finally calm, curled up beside Riona.

"We have to get him out soon," Riona whispered. "It will throw us all into the war we'd all like to avoid, but it's time."

"We've fought wars before, and we likely will again." Rowena sighed. "I can't think of a better reason to fight a war than for the safety of an innocent child."

"Especially this child." Riona's eyes drooped from the effects of Rowena's tea. "He reminds me of his father."

"Where is that worthless brat?" Egan kicked in the door of Riona's bedroom. "I will not lose this war because of a stupid useless child." He dragged Toby from Riona's bed.

"Your Majesty." Riona scrambled to her feet. "He was ill. Out of his head with fever. I thought it best to keep him here where I could see to his care."

"He looks fine to me."

"He is feverish."

"All children are feverish."

"I'm afraid his magic is too erratic. It's making him sick, my Lord. We must be careful—"

Egan's fist shot out, striking her with a bruising blow to her jaw.

Riona stumbled but managed to keep her balance, dropping her head with a show of remorse. "I am sorry, your Majesty. I overstepped."

"It is not for you to tell me what must be done."

"Of course, your Majesty." She made a show of groveling—the one thing that was sure to please him the most.

"Come, boy. You will open a portal for my troops."

"My Lord, if I may?" Riona put herself between Egan and Toby. "I agree, the boy's portals are vital to your strategy, but I fear it is too much for him, portaling to the human realm so often, and with such large numbers, and immediately portaling back to Eldur."

"How else are we to lead an attack on the Light Fae?" Egan rounded on her, and she feared he might strike her again.

"You remember what Griffin said about Tia's magic? She and her brother are very young. They are powerful, each in their own ways, but they haven't come of age yet. Think of how useful Toby will be to you when he's older and more capable of welding his portal magic? I fear—if he uses his O'Shea magic too often, it could kill him, sire. And I would hate to see you lose such an important tool."

"Perhaps." Egan shrugged. "But perhaps his death will buy me a victory. Come boy. We have a battle to wage." Egan shoved Toby from the room, sending him with his soldiers to the courtyard where he frequently made his portals.

For nearly two weeks, Egan launched surprise attacks on the Eldurian camp closest to the palace grounds where those of Iskalt and Fargelsi couldn't help them. The Dark Fae's defensive magic put them on an even playing field, and the Eldurians couldn't use their magic in the perpetual night. The two sides clashed in bloody battles almost daily now. The Eldurians were skilled with their weapons and their battle tactics. But the Dark Fae were fast and their brute strength made them formidable foes. Riona shuddered to think of what this war could turn into if it went on much longer.

Making her way along the servant's halls to the dowager queen's rooms, Riona was determined to get them all out of the palace as soon as possible. It was time. She'd done what she'd set out to do. Protect Toby and keep Egan from destroying this world. But he wasn't listening to her anymore, and if she wasn't careful, she'd be the one under guard before much longer.

"Any progress?" Riona asked as she closed the queen's door behind her. It was getting harder to talk her way past the guards.

"Nothing." Enis paced the length of the queen's sitting room, wringing her hands together. "Egan won't let me take the book to study on my own anymore, so I have to be careful when I'm searching the book for answers. He's losing faith in me."

They all were. Riona was never sure where Enis' loyalties lay. She was faithful to Egan, for now, but she worried for her grandson. "Have you considered that maybe magic isn't the answer to everything?" Riona asked. "Maybe what Toby needs is an absence of magic. He is the boy who was born without it, after all."

Enis stared at her like she'd suggested the boy should visit a human doctor to treat his symptoms.

"It is time to make our move, ladies," Faolan said, wincing in pain. "Toby's health isn't improving. His mental state is getting worse with every portal the king forces him to open. The poor child blames himself for all the Fae who have died or been injured in battle. A thing like that weighs heavily on a grown man, but he's just a little boy."

"Will you go with us, your Majesty?" Riona asked, but she knew the answer already. Faolan would never leave her people.

"I must stay."

"I don't understand what you can do for your people cooped up in this room." Riona shook her head.

"It's the simple fact that they know she is here," Enis said. "They are trapped within the city, and the one thing that gives them hope is knowing their queen's mother is right there with them. If she abandoned them, it would kill their spirit."

"So I must stay." Faolan nodded. "But you three must go."

"I will help Riona get our grandson to safety," Enis said. "But I must return—"

"For the book." Riona finished for her. "The book Egan wouldn't know what to do with if you weren't here to interpret it for him."

"I fear he would destroy it if I left. The book of power must be preserved." Enis continued her nervous pacing. "But not at the cost of my grandson's life."

"Perhaps you should have thought about that before you awakened O'Shea magic that he'd shown no ability to wield." Faolan glared daggers at the woman who gave birth to the son she raised in her stead.

"I had little choice."

"Maybe you shouldn't tell Egan everything you discover in that book," Faolan shot back.

"Enough." Riona moved between the two former queens. "We will get him out tonight."

"Get him out of here." Egan kicked Toby's chair away from the high table in what Egan was referring to as the King's Hall.

The chair tipped over, and Toby went sprawling to the ground, shrieking about snakes and writhing on the floor like a madman with tears running down his gaunt cheeks.

"My patience grows thin with his childish lunacy." Egan tipped his wine glass and drained its contents. "I've a mind to toss him into the canyon and be done with him."

"I will escort him away from your presence, your Majesty."

Riona jumped at the opening Egan gave her. It was just what she was waiting for. With the king sufficiently drunk, there was a chance she could get Toby to safety before Egan suspected anything.

"Thank you, my dear." Egan reached for her hand. "You are the only one I can count on not to disappoint me."

"It is my honor to serve you, my Lord." Riona dipped her head toward the man who had raised her to be his greatest weapon. She longed for the day when she would never have to lay eyes on him again.

"The snakes!" Toby screamed, his eyes wild with fright. "Riona, they're everywhere. They want to destroy the king." He scrambled to her side, kneeling before her, he wrapped his bony arms around her knees. "Can you hear them whispering?"

"Get up." She jerked him to his feet, hating herself for treating him so roughly. "The king has no need of your antics tonight, boy." She marched him from the great hall toward the inner sanctum of the palace and the rooms where Egan kept the boy imprisoned.

Once in the shadows of the dimly lit corridors, Riona crouched in front of Toby, running her hand over his forehead. He was blazing hot with fever. "It will be okay, Toby. The snakes won't bother you anymore."

"Did it work?" He quirked a mischievous smile at her. One she'd seen often from Griffin.

Riona stared at him in awe. "You were faking it?"

"Grandmother Enis said I should be extra irritating tonight."

"You did good, kid. Now let's get you out of here." Riona took his hand, clammy with sweat, and steered him toward her rooms. She wasn't sure she could risk escaping with Toby the same way Gulliver had with Logan and Darra. She had half a mind to walk through the front door and dare anyone to stop her. But she couldn't take such a big risk with Griffin's son.

In the quiet corridor outside her rooms, the outrageous fountains trickled and gurgled. The whole palace was ostentatious, but those fountains were ... extra, as Gulliver would say. She wished he were here. That kid knew how to sneak around better than anyone, and she caught herself asking, *what would Gullie do*?

She glanced at the winding stairs that led up, all the way to the highest points in the palace. Gulliver might not walk out the front door, but he would use the quickest means of getting where he needed to go and then take that route like he owned it.

"This way." Riona led Toby toward the stairs. "And if we run into anyone along the way, do exactly what you did for the king just now."

"Yes, ma'am." Toby gripped her hand as they climbed the steep stone steps. There were hundreds of them, winding in an endless loop, all the way to the top of the tiered gardens that sat above the canyon.

Toby grew weary quickly, sweat trickling down his face. Riona had to carry him the last several flights, and even she was panting by the time they stepped into the cool night air. Toby groaned as she set him back on his feet.

"Quiet, Toby," Riona hushed him as she took his hand in hers. "Can you walk?"

He nodded, his eyes bright with fever in the moonlight.

"Wait here one second while I check for guards." Riona left him in the shadows, searching the garden pathway for sentries. They were posted at the base of the pyramid-like structure at the main entrance, but no one guarded the path that led to the stables and the myriad of pathways that wound back to the city streets. That was their way out. They just had to avoid the soldiers near the stables and make their way to the canyon road that led to the Eldurian army camp.

"Who's there?" a slurred voice called in the darkness that was like home to Riona and her kind. The soldier peered at her through a haze of drink.

"I am on the king's business." She lifted her head at the Light Fae sizing her up.

"Yeah? And what business is that?"

"Nothing that concerns you." Riona grabbed her knife from the sheath at her waist and hit him over the head with the hilt before he could gather his wits about him.

He sank like a stone to the ground in a puddle of wine.

Riona took up his cloak, wrapping it around her shoulders to conceal her wings. Pulling the hood down low, she returned to Toby.

"Riona?" His voice quavered. "Is he ... dead?"

"No, but he'll probably wish he were come morning. Let's go." She reached for his hand, and they set off through the shadows to the lowest tier of the garden. Once through the rear gate, they crouched in the tall grass where Egan's soldiers not welcome in the palace made their camp nearest the stables. The hour grew late, and the men were deep in their cups beside the warmth of their fires by now. But they weren't safe yet. And they wouldn't be until they found the Eldur camp.

With the solid stone of the city streets beneath them, Riona moved more confidently, one hand on her sword, and the other gripping Toby's hand.

Few roamed the streets at night, but with a soldier's cloak on her back, no one questioned her presence. Riona didn't know Raudur City well enough to navigate it in the dark, but she was determined to leave it behind, once and for all. Once Toby was safe, she had no need to return to Egan's side.

They walked quickly along a winding pathway at the cliff's

edge. Much of the city lay sprawled out beneath them, but she was searching for a route that would lead them up and away from the canyon roads. The longer they walked, the fewer soldiers they saw, but destruction blocked their path.

"I'm tired, Riona." Toby's voice was soft, and his breath was shallow. This kid needed a healer. And soon.

"We're nearly there." She bent to pull him into her arms, wrapping his gangly legs around her waist. He was too old to carry, but he'd lost weight in his time with Egan, and Riona was determined to get him out of this city one way or another, even if she had to carry him the rest of the way.

Her legs shook with the effort, but she kept walking for miles over mounds of rubble and around deep holes in the ground. Magic and weeks of battle had destroyed this end of the city.

Crouching low, Riona studied the lines of tents and smoldering fires that belonged to Egan's front-line soldiers. The ones keeping the Eldurians out of their city. But Riona knew a thing or two about these soldiers. They were nothing more than mercenaries. Soldiers here for a full belly and their fair share of wine and ale, and the spoils of war. They had no real loyalty to Egan or any king. That kind of army wasn't exactly diligent in their watch, and she was counting on their preference for a warm fire and a cup of ale to get her through the lines.

Toby's hot breath against her neck alarmed her. She wasn't entirely sure if he was sleeping, or if he'd passed out from the illness that plagued him.

Riona made a wide berth of the camp as it gave way to the lush forest of the oasis surrounding Raudur City. Under the cover of trees, she moved faster, her chest burning with the effort of carrying Toby. Part of her wanted to take to the skies and stretch her wings, but that was a good way to get shot. Her defensive magic would shield her from magical attack, but that would leave Toby vulnerable.

She walked all night along the aimless paths through the forest and grassy meadows until she reached the desert sands. Tattered tents stretched out before her as the moon settled along the horizon. It was morning.

Riona felt them before she saw them as they moved on silent feet.

Eldurian soldiers swarmed the area, their weapons at the ready.

"Who is the child?" a gruff voice asked.

"I am a friend," she gasped as she fell to her knees, dropping Toby onto the sandy ground.

"Dark Fae are no friends of ours." A soldier flicked his sword at her wings fanned out behind her under the cloak she wore.

"I am not your enemy." Her voice was like sandpaper in her throat. She was so tired and so thirsty. "I've brought—"

"Stand aside." A woman's weary voice joined those of her soldiers. "Tobias?" The Eldurian queen fell to her knees in front of her nephew.

"He is ill." Riona tried to swallow.

"Who are you?" Alona demanded as she reached for the boy. "Toby." She patted his flushed face. "Finn!"

"Your Majesty, we should send this woman and her child back where she came from."

Alona stood to her full height, which was somehow still intimidating, though she wasn't very tall—and she was human. "Soldier, that child is my nephew and the Prince of Iskalt."

"Alona, what's going on? Is that..." Her husband and King Consort of Eldur came to her side and quickly bent to lift Toby into his arms. "He's burning up."

"He needs a healer." Riona tried to stand, but with a dozen swords pointed at her, she decided to stay where she was.

"What's wrong with him?" Alona looked from Toby to Riona.

"His magic, it's making him sick." The look in the human queen's eyes sent a shiver of fear through her. She was as fierce as any fae.

"Take this woman to the queen's tent and give her whatever she needs," Queen Alona ordered. "She's just saved my nephew's life."

CHAPTER NINE

Griffin

Aghadoon sat in the middle of the army camp, yet walking from the village into the sea of tents felt like taking a long journey, leaving Griffin tired and wanting to seek his bed.

They'd seen no sun for a week now as reports came to them of attacks on the Eldurians to the north. Without their day magic, the army couldn't use magic to defend themselves.

And his Iskalt magic… During his time in Myrkur, he'd longed to feel it buzzing underneath his skin, the warmth when it pooled in his fingertips. But his body wasn't meant to hold magic for such a continuous period.

Griffin stumbled toward the Dark Fae camp, wanting nothing more than to collapse where he stood. His fellow Iskalt soldiers lazed around their tents, unable to rise while their Fargelsian counterparts cooked the day's first meal. There was a reason their magic was so much weaker than any other type of fae's. Because it was always there, always ready to funnel into their spells. If it wasn't weak, their bodies would break down.

Before he could escape the depressing Iskalt camp, he noticed a crowd of people near Brea and Lochlan's tent. With a sigh, he changed direction, trying to remain upright for just a little longer.

He'd left Brea, Neeve, and Myles in the library, searching for the spell creating the endless night. They said he was needed in camp, but he wasn't sure about that. As his legs weakened beneath him, he wondered if he was really worth anything at all at the moment.

Lochlan stood in front of his tent, his face an ashy gray. His body swayed like he too struggled to remain standing. Beside him, Hector looked like the symbol of health, and Griffin almost hated him for it. A few other Iskaltians stood nearby, also looking close to death.

Lochlan saw Griffin first, his expression not changing as he moved aside to reveal the fae he'd been speaking to.

Steps faltering, Griffin thought he imagined her at first. Riona.

A smile curved her lips when she saw him, but Griffin didn't understand. She wasn't supposed to be here. Fear wound through him. Had something happen to Toby?

He forced his legs forward, pushing the questions to the back of his mind because she was here. Riona stood in front of him, weary with dark circles under her eyes, but otherwise seemingly okay. And with Lochlan, of all people. Griffin swayed on his feet, unsure if he was dreaming.

"Riona?" Griffin only had to say her name once for her to rush toward him, concern in her eyes.

"You shouldn't be standing." She reached him, neither of them touching the other as their gazes connected.

"You shouldn't be here."

Her lips curved up again. "I am done fighting for Egan, Griff. I need to be on the right side in this, your side."

He reached a tentative hand out, letting the tips of his fingers trail over her dark skin. "Toby?"

Lochlan was the one who answered, pushing back the flap of his tent to reveal two sleeping children curled around each other. Tia and Toby should never be pried apart again.

"He was able to muster enough strength to portal us to the human realm and then to here," Riona whispered. "You should be proud of him."

He was. Griffin couldn't have been more proud of the boy sitting on the ground in front of him if he tried.

This was the missing piece, the last thing they needed before attacking Egan. He couldn't take his eyes from Toby as the remaining energy drained from his body. He didn't feel himself falling before his knees hit the ground. And when he crumpled forward, the only thought on his mind was that at least all of his kids were safe.

A damp cloth wiped sweat from Griffin's face as his eyes slid open to find the most beautiful face he'd ever seen hovering over him.

"Hi." Riona smiled in the way he'd so rarely seen. "You slept longer than I did." It hadn't been a dream. She was safe and here, just like Toby.

"You saved him." It was all he could think to say.

"I promised you I'd protect him." She pulled the cloth away and sat back on her heels. "I've broken a lot of promises in my life, done a lot of bad, but that was good. I like this feeling."

"What feeling is that?"

"Like we have something to fight for, something good to protect."

"Me too." He sat up with no difficulty and looked around the tent he recognized as his own. "Why don't I feel sick?" Had they found the magic that created the perpetual night? Did Brea burn the spell and bring back the sun?

Crawling to the doorway, he pushed aside the hanging canvas and peered out, surprised to see darkness still covering the land.

"Brea is kind of amazing, isn't she?" Riona crawled to his side.

"What?" He lifted a brow as he looked to her.

"They found a spell in the library, one that Lochlan tried to keep her from performing. It's pretty dark stuff and not altogether different from the prison magic."

Griffin sat back, finding her face in the dark. "What do you mean?" He didn't like the sound of this.

"They're still searching for the magic to destroy the darkness, but once they do, we can't attack Egan with a half-dead army."

"Riona, what did Brea do?" He got the feeling she didn't want to tell him.

"She found a spell similar to the one that infused the prison barrier with the magic of those who crossed." Griffin didn't need her to explain any longer. He pushed to his feet and darted out into the dark camp, winding through rows of tents to reach the Iskalt camp where soldiers looked to be regaining their strength. He sprinted for the village, not noticing when the sand turned to stone underneath his feet.

He burst into the library to find the table pushed against the shelves in the back and two fae laying in the center of the library.

"What did you do?" he murmured.

Brea and Tia clasped hands, holding tightly to each other as something lit their skin from beneath.

"I tried to stop her."

Griffin turned at the sound of Myles' voice. He sat in the dark corner of the room, a sword across his lap as if he, a human, was their protection.

Myles rubbed his eyes, not looking up when Riona entered behind Griffin. "She waited until Neeve left, knowing her sister wouldn't approve. But me... I'm just Brea's goofy best friend. The human. She didn't listen to me. And then Tia found her trying to perform the spell." He lifted bloodshot eyes to Griffin. "Brea was the most powerful magic wielder this world knew... until her daughter. She couldn't do this on her own, and Tia was so adamant about lending her strength." He shook his head.

Griffin took a tentative step toward the girls to stare down into their open eyes. "They took all the Iskalt magic into them, didn't they? What were they thinking?"

An irrational anger rose within him. Brea wasn't only risking herself, but his daughter's life was on the line too. No one knew the risks of such magic.

Riona crossed her arms over her chest. "They did it for all of *you*, for Lochlan. The two of you should be ashamed for doubting them after everything that has happened. Griff, you collapsed in front of me almost two *days* ago. Iskaltians were all on the brink of death. You think we could have fought Egan with a large part of the army dead from exhaustion before the battle even started?"

"It's only temporary." Myles pushed to his feet and set the sword on the table. "That's what Brea said. She needed to let the Iskaltians recover just until the spell to end the darkness was found. Then, when their magic returned, they could fight."

Griffin couldn't deny how horrible he'd felt and the strength that now coursed through him. He lifted a hand, testing his magic. The Iskaltian power didn't come, but he felt his O'Shea portal magic within his reach. Brea was right. The Iskaltian army would have been destroyed.

And if she could risk everything for this—even her own daughter—he could fight for it too.

The door burst open once more, and Lochlan ran in, his chest heaving. He took one look at his wife and daughter and advanced on Myles. "You let her do this?"

"You think I could stop her?"

"Lochlan." Neeve walked in behind him and froze, her gaze going to Brea. She didn't voice her thoughts on the matter as she turned to Myles. "I promised I'd bring help, and I have." Her eyes flicked to Brea once more. "We will find the spell we need so we can bring Brea and Tia back to us."

Griffin looked to his brother. "They can find the spell. You and I must prepare for the battle that will come when they do." He stepped forward and put a hand on Lochlan's shoulder. "Do you have your portal magic?"

Lochlan nodded.

"Then it is time we bring the three kingdoms together."

Griffin and Lochlan chose not to use the magic they'd found that enhanced one's ability to travel through portals. Instead, they worked together as neither of them had ever dreamed they would, to bring the bedraggled Eldurian army into the Iskaltian camp, using Toby to direct their portals to the Eldurian camp. They might not have had their Iskaltian magic, but the O'Shea power still bent to their will.

The usual time skew between the fae world and the human world didn't occur because of the endless night, allowing the O'Shea brothers—and son—to make their jumps quickly.

For weeks, the Eldurians had fought small skirmishes with parts of Egan's army as he tested their magic and attacked during the night when they had none. He probably assumed they were the weaker force being led by a human queen, but he didn't know Alona.

She'd stayed behind, letting each of her people go through the portals before her. Griffin and Lochlan couldn't take entire armies like Toby had been able to, so it was slow going. They refused to let Toby open his super portals—for lack of a better word—he could only help direct theirs.

As the brothers had prepared for their first portals, Toby came to them, steel in his gaze.

"I want to help."

Less than two days ago, he'd been at Egan's side. There was no way Griffin wanted him to become involved in the very thing that was draining his own energy.

"Okay." Lochlan had walked toward his son.

Griffin shook his head. "Lochlan, no."

They both knew at this point Griffin was Toby's biological father, but this wasn't his choice. Lochlan's hard gaze told him that.

"Brea and Tia are lying at the center of that library holding the magic of an entire army. You and I are shuttling the Eldurians here while Neeve and her people search for a way to end this night. And *my* son has more reason to fight than any single fae. He deserves to be in this just as much as his sister."

Toby's eyes had glassed over as he stared at his dad. Growing up without magic, Griffin could only imagine how useless he'd felt in the fae realm. But now they could give him the chance to do something good.

"We are O'Sheas." Griffin had stepped toward them, completing their triangle. "We do this together."

Toby's magic appeared first, a violet rift in the fabric of the world. Griffin's matching power opened a portal. Before he stepped through, he caught sight of the icy blue O'Shea magic escaping Lochlan. The whole of Iskalt magic might be inside Brea and Tia right now, but their family power, their heritage, had bonded the three of them together, giving Griffin the strength he needed for a few final portals.

Now, here they were six portals deep and exhausted.

They only stayed in the field outside Brea's family home in the human realm long enough to catch their breath before portaling into the center of what Toby said was the Eldurian camp.

At the edges of camp, ditches had been dug as a defensive measure that wouldn't have been effective against sylph.

A breath rushed out of Alona the moment she saw the three of them. The remaining force protecting her and her husband rose to their feet.

Lochlan stepped forward and folded the Eldurian queen into his arms. "Now, we fight together."

When Griffin used to think of Lochlan with Alona and Finn, jealousy overcame him. He'd been raised alone while Lochlan grew up with the eventual Eldurian royals. They were more siblings than Griffin had ever been.

Yet now, he saw what he had with Shauna and Hector, a bond that didn't exist purely because of the blood in his veins, a family that chose each other.

Finn lifted Toby in a hug before patting Griffin on the shoulder in an awkward "I remember you now" meeting.

"We should go." Griffin looked toward the smoke rising from Raudur City.

Alona ran a hand through her tangled blond hair and offered him a nod. "You're right." She turned to her remaining people. "Be prepared to enter the human realm before we make it to the Iskalt camp."

The moment they stepped through the final portal into their camp, Griffin's shoulders sagged, his magic retreating into him. Commotion sounded around them as Alona asked someone to take her to her children and walked off.

Lochlan kept a hand firmly on Toby's shoulder as Neeve rushed across the camp to him and murmured in a low voice. "That's good, Neeve. Are they... okay?"

She nodded. "I believe so. Brea took certain precautions according to Myles. She did not let Tia take the Iskalt magic into herself. That could have caused permanent damage before she is of age for her body to handle it. From what I can tell, Brea is simply drawing on Tia's strength. Tia was the only magic wielder strong enough to make sure we didn't lose Brea."

He rubbed a weary hand across his face. "When can we bring them out of the spell?"

"As soon as we find what we're looking for. We're close. You should prepare your soldiers to attack within the next six hours. I am going to do the same."

Finn sighed. "We'd hoped to rest our warriors, but Eldur will be ready as well. Though, we won't be much good without our magic."

"You will have it." With that, Neeve walked toward the Fargelsian camp.

Lochlan looked to Griffin and for once, there wasn't a hint of scorn or distrust in his gaze. "Will you help me, brother? We must convince our Iskalt brothers and sisters their magic will return before the fight."

Griffin wanted to say yes, to tell Lochlan he'd waited his entire life for someone to tell him the Iskalt people were truly his.

But what if they weren't?

Not anymore.

"I have to find my family." The words were only meant for

himself and not to hurt Lochlan, but he saw his brother's face fall. Was it possible that Lochlan spent his life wanting to be a true brother to Griffin as well? "Loch, I will fight beside you. You are my brother, and that will never change, but I need to find my son." His eyes fell on Toby and Lochlan's hand on his shoulder. It confirmed what he knew.

If a battle was coming for them, Griffin wanted to spend the last hours with the Dark Fae, with Gulliver and their family.

Lochlan gave him a nod before steering Toby to follow Finn. They too had to be with their family.

He found Gulliver sitting at the edge of Aghadoon, his shoulders slumped. He straightened when he saw Griffin. "You're back!"

"Stand up, Gulliver." Griffin stopped in front of him.

Gulliver jumped to his feet, his cat-eyes narrowing. "What's wrong? Are you mad I helped Tia get into the library to help her mom? I didn't mean to do anything wrong, I promise. Are you disappointed in me, Griff? Oh wow, you are, aren't you?" His eyes glassed over. "Please don't be. She asked me, and... then I couldn't leave the village, but Myles kicked me out of the library, waving a sword at me. So I've been sitting here. I don't want you to be mad at me."

Taking mercy on him, Griffin reached out and pulled him into a hug. "I'm not mad, Gullie. Not disappointed. You're everything I could ever want in a son."

"Whoa, I don't know what made you all sentimental, but this hug is kinda nice." Gulliver wrapped his arms around Griffin's waist.

Griffin laughed and pulled back. "I just wanted to see you. We're going into battle soon. When we do, I'm going to ask you to stay in Aghadoon."

Gulliver opened his mouth to protest but Griffin cut him

off. "Tia and Brea won't be in any shape to fight. You'll need to stay with them, to protect them."

That was the one thing that could keep Gulliver away from the fight. Protecting Tia.

"I won't let you down, Griff."

"I know you won't." Griffin slid an arm over his shoulders and steered him toward the Myrkur camp. "Until then, we should be with our family."

They found Hector speaking to some of his soldiers, having already been informed of the impending battle by an Iskalt general. Griffin smiled at the thought Lochlan considered this force a part of the true army.

There'd be no sleep tonight. Fires dotted the landscape, as soldiers waited for the sun to come—a sun they'd never imagined in all their years in Myrkur.

Griffin lowered himself between Shauna and Riona as they sat with a group of fae around a small cookfire that thankfully gave off light but little warmth. Hector's mom, Kiaran, smiled at him across the fire where she sat with her younger children.

Pressing a kiss to the side of Riona's head, he pulled her closer. A smile played on her lips as she relaxed against him.

Shauna knocked her shoulder into his. "We didn't know if you'd be with us tonight."

Hector joined them. "Of course he's here. Griffin is one of us." He winked at Gulliver. "We don't know what tomorrow will bring, but tonight we can give each other strength."

Griffin replayed Hector's words in his mind. *Griffin is one of us. One of us. One of us.* He wasn't Dark Fae. He'd been broken for so long. Yet these people had never once questioned his place among them since the moment Shauna found him. He never had to earn their affection.

And they'd taken Riona in as one of them despite her history. He'd always be grateful to them for that.

Wrapping one arm around Shauna and extending a hand to grip both Riona's and Gulliver's hands on his other side, he prepared himself mentally for the battle to come. His eyes fell to Nessa, curled up in Shauna's lap, the girl who'd started his adversarial relationship with Egan when he'd tried to save her.

And he was still trying to save them all.

Now, it was possible in a way it never had been before.

They spent most of the night talking in low tones, their laughter punctuating the darkness.

He didn't know how long he'd been there when a familiar buzz raced along his skin, his Iskalt and O'Shea powers curling together.

Lifting a hand, he watched the violet power spark in his fingertips.

"It's almost time, isn't it?" Riona asked.

Griffin nodded. "We must prepare."

Darkness still coated the sky, but if the magic had been returned, it could only mean they'd found a way to bring the sun back. For now, they had to take it on faith.

Hector rose and started issuing orders to his soldiers. Any who weren't going to fight made their way to the village. Gulliver pulled a crying Nessa away from Shauna and held her hand as he led her away.

"He'll take care of her." Griffin slipped a chain mail shirt over his head.

"I know." Shauna sighed as she strapped on her sword belt.

Grooms brought the few horses the Dark Fae had, and Griffin pulled himself into his saddle. Riona jumped into the air with a flap of her wings, now nearly half black against the darkened sky.

"Riona." He looked up at her hovering beside him.

"I know, Griff. Be careful."

He nodded. "That... and I love you."

Her mouth opened, but no words came out. He didn't need a response from her, not now. He'd just needed her to know.

The Dark Fae joined the lines of Iskaltians, Fargelsians, and Eldurians preparing to march. It was a united fae realm like Griffin had never thought possible.

At the front of the combined force, Lochlan rode with Finn and Myles. Alona led the archers, their fingers curled around bows as they sat atop their horses.

Brea should be there, but she'd done her part. She'd made this all possible. And Queen Neeve had one more task to perform. She had to bring back the sun.

Operating on faith, knowing Neeve would come through for them, the army marched across the sands separating them from the city.

And still, the sky remained dark.

Egan's forces scrambled to form lines at the edge of the western canyon, Dark Fae running and flying from the streets behind them.

And still, the sky remained dark.

Griffin drew his sword, the metal scraping against its sheathe. He was ready to fight.

And still... A cry wound through the Iskaltian, ranks and Griffin looked back over his shoulder to see a fire raging through the tents they'd left behind.

But the sky... Light appeared on the horizon, a dim ray of hope for an otherwise hopeless battle.

Looking toward the moon, Griffin caught sight of the blazing ring of light growing larger as the sun appeared from behind the moon until it was halfway visible.

"A partial eclipse," a soldier nearby cried out.

An event where both night and day existed together at the same time. Something the humans experienced, but no fae alive had ever seen. He looked to the Eldurian lines where they tested the magic returning to them after too long away.

The Iskaltian magic didn't fade from Griffin. Instead, it pulsed inside him, eager for an escape.

His eyes hardened as he readied to ride into battle.

Iskaltians. Eldurians. Fargelsians. Dark Fae.

Only when good bonded together could they wipe evil from their kingdoms.

Griffin

The noise of battle filled Griffin's mind and stirred his blood. Swords clanged, and warm blood spurted from fresh wounds. Iskaltian fought beside Eldurians, their magic working together against their enemy. It defied nature, and should never be, yet it was a thing of beauty to see them united together under the partial eclipse.

Gathering his magic close to his core, Griffin fought alongside Riona with Hector and Shauna, Dark Fae and Light Fae fighting for the good of them all. Casting his magic toward the desert sands beneath their enemy's feet, an explosion of ice and sand sent them scattering, blinded by the sand in their eyes.

They'd learned quickly that the Dark Fae's defensive magic could be penetrated with much effort. But the Light Fae could expend too much energy trying to get through their defenses. It was a far better use of their magic to use it on their surroundings, creating explosions and obstacles to block their enemy's path and cause confusion. After that, it came down to which side was better with a sword.

Beside him, Hector snorted like a bull, sinking into a crouch. As the dust cleared, he charged ahead, locking horns with a fae twice his size.

Riona and Griffin moved to flank him with Shauna at their backs, their swords making quick work of those moving in to surround Hector and his opponent.

"Griffin! Above you!" Riona called as she leapt into the air and sank her dagger into the thick neck of an enormous ogre. She held on as the ogre fell to his knees.

Griffin whirled around just in time to block a volley of arrows with his magic. The roughly hewn arrows fell to the ground, and Griffin sent out a blast of icy wind to blow the angry Slyph off course.

"What you said back there." Riona hacked away at the ogre's back to ensure he was dead. It was hard work, killing an ogre. Gore smeared her face and wings.

"I've said a lot of things, Riona." Griffin moved to block an Asrai from barreling over her. "Can you be more specific?" His sword glanced off the Asrai's scales. They were even harder to kill than ogres.

"You know I feel the same way, right?" She called as she climbed down off the ogre, just in time to help him take on the Asrai. She blocked the creature's massive sword, shoving her back.

"I know." Griffin shot her a grin as he threw a punch, sending the Asrai woman to the ground. Her scales were like stone against his fist.

"Well that was stupid." Riona moved in, hip checking him out of the way. Tossing her dagger from one hand to the other, she moved like quicksilver until her blade found purchase, and the Asrai went down like a dead fish on dry land. "Aim for the gills." She panted, wiping the gore from her dagger against her boots. "If you hit them like that, you'll be the one coming away with broken bones."

"I'm going to need to hear you say it." Griffin jumped in front of Riona, throwing up a shield to block a Light Fae's killing curse—a Fargelsian criminal from the prison realm. They would have to do something about all of them when this war was over. They couldn't leave the worst criminals of their world roaming free.

"Say what?" Riona leapt over him to clash with a Slyph with massive black wings. A ripping sound followed by screams and a shower of blood had Griffin looking up to the sky to make sure she was okay. The huge Slyph came crashing to the ground, his wings a bloody mess.

"I said the words, Riona, now it's your turn," Griffin shouted over the din of battle.

"Fine!" She turned toward him, her sword dripping blood. "I love you, Griffin O'Shea!"

"I love you too." Griffin grinned, making his way toward her. "Now was that so hard?" He threw a knife at an oncoming fae with tusks, the blade sinking into his forehead.

"Is this really the time for your nonsense?" Hector raged at them both. "We have a battle to win here, and we need you to focus."

"We're focused," Riona shot back.

"It's Griff." Shauna rolled her eyes. "He's never had the best timing."

"Quit your antics and come help me take this side of the canyon so we can get into the palace." Hector waved to his troops, and together they charged toward the western side of Raudur City. The palace sat perched among the city streets carved right into the sides of the eastern canyon below. Egan would be manning his forces from the safety of the palace.

"This isn't over until Egan is dead!" Griffin cried as they surged toward a line of Dark Fae protecting the Western road into the city.

Swords clashed, and Griffin's magic sent the Dark Fae scrambling for cover. They were almost through the ranks when a contingent of Slyph came surging up from the canyon, and Griffin barely managed to get his shields up in time to block the arrows raining down on them.

"Griffin!" Riona shrieked from the sky. Her brethren had swooped in to grab her, pulling her high above the battle.

"Riona!" Griffin called for her as he sent shards of magic toward the Slyph carrying her toward the palace, not stopping until the sharp bite of a blade tore into his leather armor, getting to the flesh beneath. Riona's panicked eyes met his once more before he stumbled back, losing sight of her.

Pain lanced through him, quickly chased away by the adrenaline surging in his veins. Hector's heavy axe ripped into the Asrai who'd wounded Griffin, dropping him to the ground.

Having no time to think of his injury or the warm blood seeping through the tear in his armor, Griffin charged toward the palace, Hector right behind him. His steps only faltered slightly before he regained his pace.

"Griffin, focus on what's in front of you," Hector reminded him. "You're no good to her if you get killed because your mind is elsewhere."

Griffin let out a scream of frustration as he hacked his way through the Dark Fae standing between him and Riona. His wound stretched and widened with each movement, but he did not stop. They would not take Riona away from him now that they'd found each other. Not now when they were finally on the same side. She'd risked her life to keep his son safe and again when she brought him home to his parents. He was not about to let her die for it, no matter how many times their swords struck him. He knew as sure as if they'd told him where they were going, the Slyph were taking her to Egan, and he would make her pay for her betrayal.

"She can take care of herself, brother," Hector called to him.

"I'm going to her. I have to find her."

Shauna's hand slipped into his. "We will help you." She turned her back to him as a swarm of horned fae came at them. Together they fought back to back, making their way closer to the canyon road that would lead them into the city.

Griffin's body ached with the effort of swinging his sword and wielding his magic, but the adrenaline of battle kept him focused on the fight ahead instead of his wound. The eclipse kept his night magic alive, but like everything, it came at a cost, sapping his energy faster than it should, faster than even his wound did. He absently wondered if the Eldurians were experiencing the same. They needed to win this battle quickly.

The last of Egan's defenses gave way, and Griffin ran with Shauna into Raudur City. The streets were empty, Eldurians hiding in their homes with windows and doors boarded up.

They met a troop of Egan's soldiers along the road up to the tiered gardens that overlooked the canyon from the eastern side. Griffin caught a glimpse of Egan pacing along the top tier of the garden. Beyond him, Enis—Griffin's traitor mother—worked to perform spells from that cursed book.

The only good thing was they didn't have Tia this time. Enis might know a lot about magic, but she wasn't as strong as Tia.

Griffin and Shauna darted up the road to the gardens. When Griffin's feet stumbled, Shauna shot him a worried look, her eyes flicking to where he hadn't realized his hand pressed to his side. She knew him better than anyone, so she let him keep going. Griffin had to dig deep, but he kept a shield over them, letting the arrows from Egan's crossbows bounce right off them.

Egan had strategically placed ogres and vicious Asrai at intervals along the pathway up through the gardens to the top where he directed his side of the battle. Griffin could make out Egan's angry shouts and the crack of a whip.

A woman's screams filtered down through the din of battle.

"Riona!" He cried, rushing in to help Hector and Shauna take down an enormous ogre. The ground shook beneath them as the Eldurians charged down into the canyon to take back their city.

With the Iskaltians coming in from the south, they would take this battle as a win. But they had to get to Egan now. Even with their numbers, they weren't able to fully surround Raudur City because the canyon and the Dalur river cut them off, leaving an escape route wide open for Egan.

"To the top!" Hector roared. He understood as well as Griffin that they couldn't let Egan escape down the back side of the pyramid-like structure of the gardens. They fought their way up each level, tearing through Dark Fae Egan had left to slow them down.

"Egan!" Griffin roared just below the top tier. He couldn't get through the swarm of bodies.

"This is not the end, young Griffin." Egan leaned over the side of the garden wall, his beard and arms covered in blood and gore as if he'd been fighting among his men this whole time. But men like Egan didn't fight their own battles. They hid behind others, forcing them to do the fighting for him. "Well, it may be for you." The Dark Fae king flashed an evil smile before he disappeared behind the wall.

"Egan." Griffin shoved his way through the swarm of battle, Shauna hot on his heels. When they reached the top, Egan was gone, Enis and his last remaining loyal soldiers with him.

Griffin stumbled to the other side of the garden only to see Egan fleeing on horseback through the fire orchard and to the road that would lead him into the unforgiving deserts of Eldur.

"We need to go after him!" Griffin shouted, knowing he'd be no good in any chase.

"We will." Hector panted beside him. "I'll go myself once we know this battle is done. He won't get away, Griffin. We will see him pay for his crimes. But that day is not today." Hector waved overhead to call down his Slyph from the skies. "I'll send a few sylph to track him and then follow once I can leave here." He turned to Griffin. "But you... Shauna needs to tend your wound." He walked away to talk to his fae.

"Who is she?" Shauna reached for Griffin's shoulder, having not heard Hector. She pulled him back to the aftermath of a battle just winding down and the force almost sent him falling to the stones.

"Who?" Griffin let his gaze wander across the gardens. And then he saw her. Strapped to a whipping post, the former Queen of Eldur lay slumped against it. "Faolan?" His voice shook as he ran to her side. He didn't want to have to tell his brother that the woman who raised him as her own might be dead.

Her back was a mass of shredded skin and welts. Some half healed and scabbed over as if she'd succumbed to this treatment on multiple occasions.

Shauna reached to check her for signs of life.

"She's Brea and Alona's mother." Griffin moved to cut her down from the post, using his last bits of strength as pain replaced the adrenaline inside him.

"She lives," Shauna whispered, making the swift adjustment from soldier to healer in an instant. "Bring her into the shade." She guided him toward a corner of the garden shaded under a canopy of trees with enormous waxy leaves. "Lay her on her stomach. I will tend her wounds." Shauna reached for the herb kit hanging over her shoulder. "You, Griff, stay. Don't think I forgot your wound. It needs tended to. Remove your armor while I help Faolan." She turned her attention from Griffin.

Faolan was in good hands, and Griffin needed to find Riona more than he needed Shauna to bandage his wound. He feared Egan might have taken her with him.

"We need to address the Dark Fae," Hector said, returning to Griffin's side. "Now that Egan is gone, most of them are laying their weapons down. You need to tell them it's time to choose which side they're on. The side of a king who has treated them like slaves all their lives or the side that will give them something they've never known. Free will."

"They need to hear that from one of their own, brother." Griffin clapped him on the back and winced. "And you are far more eloquent than I am."

"Me?" Hector stared blankly at him.

"Yes, you. Like it or not, you are a leader, and your soldiers respect you. The other Dark Fae will too if you give them a chance to come to your side."

"Mine?" Hector shook his head, his great bull horns nearly gored Griffin.

"It's time, Hector." Griffin led him to the garden wall overlooking the carnage below. Most of the fighting had stopped as news of Egan's escape spread like wildfire through the armies. "Stand still." Griffin placed his hands along Hector's throat, his magic pooling in his hands to enhance Hector's voice. "They will all hear you now." Griffin stepped back from the wall, each movement harder than the one before.

The Griffin of old would have jumped at a chance to take the reins after an epic battle, wound or no. The old Griffin would have seen it as an opportunity to seize power now that

Egan was on the run and no longer in a position to rule over the Dark Fae.

But Griffin learned the hard way that power corrupts, and he wasn't that man any more. The thirst for power had long since died out of him. All he wanted now was to make sure his family was safe.

"Dark Fae." Hector's voice boomed across the city. "What are you fighting for?" His steady gaze swept the crowds below. "Why do you fight for a king who does nothing for you? It is time to make a choice, my brothers and sisters. Myrkur is our home. It will always be our home, but we are no longer enslaved to a king who demands loyalty, but gives none. We are no longer held in bondage by a magical boundary erected hundreds of years ago to keep us contained. The people who did that to us are long dead and long forgotten.

"This is a new day." Hector gripped the edge of the wall, looking down over the people of all the realms. "We stand on the precipice of a new future. But we must decide what kind of future we want. I for one, stand for peace. Peace among the Dark Fae who wish to live openly in whatever land they choose to call home. I stand for peace between those of Myr and those of the three kingdoms. We are all fae. I ask my Dark Fae brethren to lay down their weapons in the name of peace."

A great roar of approval swept through the city, surprising Hector with its vehemence.

"Wrap it up, big guy, you've won them over." Griffin was eager to search for Riona and check on Gulliver. He needed to know all of his family had survived the battle before he could tend to himself.

"But to those who insist on resisting peace," Hector's voice grew harsh. "Light or Dark Fae, know this. We are coming for you. We stand united as the four kingdoms never have before.

Fargelsi, Iskalt, Eldur, *and* Myrkur are united as one, and we *will* have peace."

Just as Hector stepped back from the wall, the magic that created the partial eclipse subsided. The sun burst free from its place behind the moon, and light swept across the land, chasing the darkness away.

Griffin watched as those of the four kingdoms rejoiced. Dark Fae moved in droves to lay their weapons down, but he saw those who would resist as they crept away in small groups here and there. They were the ones who would find their way back to Egan.

The kingdoms won a huge battle today, but the war was not over. Not by a long shot.

CHAPTER ELEVEN

Riona

Riona slumped against the wall as the Eldurian troops surged into the palace. Blood trickled from a cut near her hairline, but other than that, she was unharmed—unlike the Slyph who'd carried her into the palace. Unlike Griffin who'd taken a sword to the side as her captors carried her away. She'd never forget the cold dread of that moment, the calm efficiency she'd used to dispatch the fae keeping her from protecting Griffin.

Loosening her fingers, Riona let her sword fall to the ground, its blade coated in the blood of her own kind. She leaned her head back, breathing heavily.

They did it.

She hadn't seen Hector give his speech, but his voice had carried throughout the halls as she dispatched the remaining attackers with a quiet efficiency. During the battle, she'd enjoyed fighting the army she'd pretended loyalty to, resisting a king who abandoned his troops while their enemy cut them down.

He lost. Egan had one chance to take control in the fae realm. Now, he had his life and the book but no army.

Her wings pushed against the wall, and she stumbled forward, needing to get outside, to escape the halls that were now stained with blood as well as the filth from Egan and his soldiers.

The grand palace of Eldur had been reduced to a hovel for Dark Fae who didn't know any different. It wasn't hard to see why the palace of Myrkur had been in such disrepair.

Riona crept up the winding stairs, finally bursting through the doors that let out into the gardens. A woman lay on her stomach on a stone bench with Shauna applying a paste to her back. As she neared, Riona recognized the Dowager Queen of Eldur, Faolan. A groan escaped her lips, and Riona released a breath. Leaving Faolan in the palace had been on Riona's mind, but she'd had no choice.

Across the garden, Hector also tended to his people with a surprising softness as he bandaged wounds. She turned as someone ran into the garden, expecting to see Griffin.

But it wasn't him.

Alona dropped her bow and sprinted down the path toward her mother, dropping to her knees at her side. Blood streaked through her blond hair, giving her more of a warrior queen look than the human she was. It suited her.

Everywhere Riona turned, injured fae tried to pick up the pieces of the battle. Walking to the wall looking down into the streets, she watched fae mourn over the dead as their blood still warmed the streets. In the distance, Eldurians tentatively came out of their homes.

Riona jumped into the air and flew the short distance into the city, landing among the people. They gave her a wide berth, and she looked down to find blood gleaming on her leather armor.

Above, the sun beat down on them, bringing with it the harsh Eldurian heat they'd avoided during Egan's endless night spell.

A fae she recognized ran toward her, a canvas sack over his shoulder. "My Lady!" He waved a hand over his head.

Riona paused, waiting for him to reach her. "I'm not a lady, sir." That title implied a status she didn't pretend to have, especially not after a battle where the enemy looked like her. She'd noticed the only Slyph who'd stayed were the ones already a part of Hector's army. The others were either dead or scattered.

The fae shoved his bag at her. "I tried to reach your army before the battle, but my wife forced me back into my home."

"Your wife is smart." She looked into the bag, finding the sunglasses not unlike what Gulliver wore in the human realm.

But the Dark Fae no longer cringed at the light during the day. She shook her head. If they were going to have peace, they had to adapt to this world. These glasses wouldn't help. "I'm sorry, sir. You can keep the payment, but we have no more need of a device to protect us from the sun. It is our sun too." She handed the bag back. There was no time for this when Griffin was out here somewhere injured.

He gave her a confused look but didn't try to follow her as she stepped onto the road heading outside Raudur.

The battle hadn't lasted long, but it drained every bit of energy she had. As she walked, she pulled on her wings, checking them for tears. The darkness that had crept into them since she first left Myrkur now covered more than half of the delicate surface. She didn't know what that meant. Nihal's wings were dark, but she'd questioned everything about him since Enis revealed herself to be in league with Egan.

Even now, she escaped with him.

She reached the edge of the city and kicked her toe against the ground, letting her wings stretch to their full span. Before her, Iskalt, Fargelsi, and Dark Fae soldiers trudged across the hot sands to return to their camps. Riona lifted into the air, hovering for a moment before letting her wings carry her to the camps.

As she neared, she caught sight of burned out tents and black marks scorching the sand. Soldier's belongings lay in charred messes. Spotting Lochlan directing the healers, she touched down. They'd done what they could to set up an area for the wounded, but it seemed they lacked supplies.

Lochlan didn't scowl as she approached—a welcome change in their relationship.

"You're hurt." He crossed his arms. "Take a seat, and I can have one of my healers help."

She shook her head. "I just need to find Griffin."

"Another who refused my help." Lochlan released a tired sigh.

"So, he's alive?"

He nodded. "He's a fool, but alive."

Riona's gaze searched the destroyed camp. "What happened here?"

"From what Myles says, the spell bringing about the eclipse went awry the first time they tried it. It sent streams of fire through the camps, lighting up the dark with flames instead of the sun."

Riona didn't know how magic worked, but she nodded, knowing the explanation was as good as she'd get. A familiar face looked up from a spot laying on the ground.

"Your Majesty?" Riona moved closer. "Do you need help?"

The King of Eldur stared at her like he was trying to figure her out. "You're the one who saved my children."

She wasn't sure how he knew that, but she opened her mouth to refute it. It had really been Gulliver who saved the Eldurian kids. Lochlan jumped in, cutting her off. "Finn, this is

Riona. I don't know her last name, but I'm sure I'll learn it. And yes, she saved Darra and Logan." His eyes met hers. "And our Toby too."

Finn offered a weak smile. "Then never again call me Majesty. I'm Finn... just Finn."

She wouldn't remind him they'd met before in the human realm, not now when his brow scrunched in confusion, and his eyes slid shut.

"No, Finn." Lochlan kneeled at his side. "Come on, brother, keep your eyes open."

"Alona," Finn whispered. "Where's my Alona?"

Lochlan cursed as his hand came away covered in blood seeping from the back of Finn's head.

Riona dropped to his other side, her wings helping her keep her balance. Lochlan called for one of the healers as Riona gripped his hand. "Alona is alive, Finn. She's well. I saw her at the palace with her mother."

Lochlan's eyes snapped to hers. "Faolan... she's..."

"In rough shape, but alive and being tended to."

He nodded, releasing a breath. "Good, that's good."

An Iskaltian healer ran toward them, and Riona got to her feet, backing away.

"Riona?" Lochlan turned from the healer to her, a worried frown on his lips as his eyes flicked to Finn.

"Yes?"

"I can't leave him." He gestured to the hordes of injured. "Any of them. We're going to prepare to move the badly injured to the village while tending to minor injuries here. More will pour in, and I'm determined to help all we can. But I don't know where my brother is. Will you find him and make sure he's not bleeding out in an Aghadoon alleyway?"

He didn't have to ask. She wanted nothing more than to

search for Griffin. But she sensed Lochlan needed to say the words, to know he'd tried to do something to help his brother.

Lifting into the sky, she flew over the destroyed camps to reach Aghadoon, dropping to the stones outside the library. The door stood partially open, and she pushed it wider, finding Brea collapsed in a chair next to her equally exhausted looking sister. Neeve leaned forward with her head on the table.

Myles bustled in behind Riona, a silver tray balancing on one hand. Blood caked under his fingernails, providing a contrast to the small moment of having tea sitting in a library that didn't belong near a battlefield.

The human looked unharmed, which surprised Riona. She'd struggled in the battle even with her fae advantages.

But there was someone missing.

Tia.

The young girl had been a part of their magic too.

Brea lifted her pale face, fixing her eyes on Riona. "I heard Griff was seen back in Aghadoon. You can find him if you go look." Riona hadn't needed to ask any questions.

Riona paused at the door. "Lochlan is with the healers tending the wounded."

Brea released an audible breath. "I've been so scared since he didn't come find me right away."

"Finn has been hurt."

Brea closed her eyes for a brief moment and nodded. "Only his family could keep him from me. Will Finn live?"

"I don't know." It was honest, at least.

A tear slipped down Brea's cheek. "Go find Griff. He's hurt too and wouldn't let me help him until he found that boy of his."

Just like Lochlan, family was the most important thing to Griffin. Riona rushed from the library. She stopped when she noticed drips of blood on the stone, all leading the same way.

A soldier bumped into her as he led a large group through the streets, cheering in celebration. A huge battle had been won this day, but Riona didn't feel like there was anything to celebrate.

Egan and Enis got away. They still had the book. This wasn't over. Not yet.

But no one knew what they'd do next.

Riona couldn't help feeling like this battle was only the beginning. This wouldn't end until Egan was dead.

The trail of blood led her to the door of a shop with an image of a loaf of bread hanging crooked over the door. A bakery.

She braced herself for what she'd find inside. It was only when a scream pierced the air she forced her way in.

Chapter Twelve

Griffin

Griffin managed to get back to Aghadoon atop his horse after giving Hector instructions to go after Egan with the journal that would let him report back. As soon as he's reached the village, he slid from the saddle and crashed into the stones below. He watched his blood fill the cracks between stones, remembering Shauna stitching up a similar wound from another lifetime.

But Shauna wasn't there this time. He'd managed to crawl toward the library, but his blasted horse left him. The door had been so close, but he hadn't made it before two sets of arms dragged him across the road into a nearby shop that smelled of yeast.

He hadn't had the energy to fight them, but he forced himself to look up at them as they leaned him against the counter.

Two familiar faces frowned down at him.

"Griff." Gulliver slapped his cheek. "Don't you dare pass out on us."

A crease formed between Tia's brows. "I can fix you."

He wanted to tell her no, that they'd seen what happened when she tried to fix Gulliver's tail with a spell she'd forged together herself. Fargelsians weren't supposed to be able to craft their own words of power, but Tia seemed to defy every rule.

Gulliver turned his cat eyes on her. "Are you sure?"

"Gullie, there is no one else here to help us. If we don't fix Griffin, he could die. It's up to you and me." Griffin tried to focus on the ten-year-old manipulating the older boy, but he couldn't get his mind off the pain throbbing through his side.

Gulliver studied Griffin for a long moment.

Tia bent to look into Griffin's eyes and took his hand. "I don't want you to die."

She knew. Griffin could see the truth of it in her eyes. "How long?" How long had she known Lochlan wasn't her biological father?

"Since I first saw you in my dream."

The dream. Tia had seen the prison realm and Griffin in her mind before ever seeing either in person. She'd known Griffin would save her before they'd ever met. And with that knowledge, knowledge she'd kept to herself for so long, there was a bit of trust.

Seeing no other option, Griffin nodded, preparing himself for whatever consequences of her uncontrollable magic he had to face.

"What do you need?" Gulliver asked her.

"Focus. To craft spells, I need to draw on Toby's strength."

Gulliver slid onto his butt at Griffin's side. His tail curled into his lap as he reached forward to wiggle the leather armor over Griffin's head. It took some doing, but Griffin breathed more easily without the weight on his shoulders.

"Take his shirt off," Tia said. "I want to see the wound."

Opting to tear it instead, Gulliver ripped the already fraying and faded shirt so nothing stood between Tia's magic and Griffin's bare chest. He breathed heavily, wondering how these two kids would ever look at him the same after seeing him coated in blood.

This wasn't his first battle, but it was the first where he wondered if it would be his last. The moment the Asrai sword bit into his flesh, he saw the last few months flash before his eyes.

Had he brought this upon the realms? If he'd never gone in search of the book for Egan, if he'd never left Myrkur in the first place, maybe none of this had to happen.

But then his eyes met Gulliver's, knowing the kid would get to live in the sun. He'd see himself as an equal to Tia and other Light Fae. And there was power in that. Some things were worth fighting for, worth giving up peace.

Because peace could not truly exist if it wasn't peace for all fae.

Tia closed her eyes, trying to call on Toby's strength.

Gulliver leaned down. "Where's Riona?"

A tear slipped from Griffin's eye. Riona. He'd tried not to think of her being carried away by her own kind. Did she now lay among the bodies in the palace? Or had Egan taken her with him? This time as a prisoner rather than a loyal subject.

Either fate was almost too much for him to bear.

"She loved me." She'd admitted as much. There was a time Griffin didn't think he'd ever have what Lochlan and Brea found in each other. Something to overcome even the sharpest pains of the marriage magic.

And he never once imagined Riona would say the words.

Gulliver's eyes glassed over. "Is she..."

Griffin nodded. "But she didn't die before making a difference, before doing something good. I think that's all she wanted." He knew because he'd wanted the same thing. After Regan, he'd arrived in Myrkur thinking there was no good in him.

He'd been wrong.

And Riona had been wrong about herself too.

Tears flowed down Gulliver's cheeks, and his eyes flashed in anger. "He took her from us."

"What?"

"Egan. He took Riona, and for that we'll make him pay." Seeing his own anger reflected in the kind-hearted Gulliver scared him.

Tia's eyes snapped open, breaking their moment. "Something is wrong."

"What do you mean?" Gulliver wiped his cheeks.

"Toby..."

"Is your magic broken?" Gulliver would probably never truly understand how magic worked.

She shook her head. "My brother isn't in the village."

Alarm shot through Griffin, and he tried to push himself up but Gulliver had a surprisingly strong grip and held him down.

Tia tried to hide the fear on her face, something Griffin had learned she did often. Toby was more open with his emotions like his mom, but Tia was more like him. She got to her feet. "I... I can feel him but not close. Where is he?"

Gulliver looked up to her, his voice pleading. "We can find Toby, but we still have to close Griffin's wound."

Griffin shook his head. "I changed my mind. Don't fix me with your magic. You need to find Toby."

Tia pursed her lips. "I'll be back." She disappeared, leaving Griffin alone with Gulliver.

Gulliver pressed the ripped shirt to the wound. "You're going to be okay. I won't lose you like we lost Riona. I refuse."

We.

Griffin tried to muster up some encouragement, to tell Gulliver it would be okay.

But he didn't want to lie to the kid.

"Everyone else?" Gulliver met his eyes, looking scared of whatever answer was coming.

Griffin forced out the words Gulliver needed. "Hector and Shauna are uninjured. Lochlan is fine as well."

He bit his lip. "But someone else isn't?"

"The King of Eldur—Finn—he's badly injured." Gulliver barely knew Finn, and Griffin had never been friends with the guy, but still, he couldn't help the ache at the thought of what his loss would do to Lochlan. "A lot of fae are dead, Gullie."

"But we won? Soldiers came through here celebrating and saying we won."

Griffin nodded, his breathing growing labored. "But Egan got away." It was Griffin's biggest regret, not capturing the Dark Fae king and his mother. They wouldn't know what to do next until Hector made contact.

But Griffin had never been good at waiting.

Tia burst through the door with Nessa on her heels. A steely look replaced the youth in Nessa's eyes. She was an eight-year-old on a mission.

Nessa clutched a bag in one hand.

"The village healers have left to go transport the injured. This girl says she's going to fix you, Griff, but she's just a kid!" Tia paced in agitation. "I can still do it with Toby far away, I can still draw strength from him over the distance like I've done before, but I'll have less control, and I could hurt you, and..."

On a normal day, Griffin would have laughed at the thought of Tia saying someone was "just a kid." He'd seen enough things now to realize youth did not mean a lack of necessary skills.

And Nessa...

"Go, Tia. You need to find Toby." If he was near the battle... "Please, go."

Nessa lowered herself next to Gulliver. "I can help you, Griff. I swear I can."

Nessa had spent her entire life helping her sister tend to the villagers, learning everything she possibly could about healing. He looked from Gulliver—the child thief who'd saved the Eldurian prince and princess—to Tia, the child who'd brought down the prison magic.

And finally Nessa. "Do it."

"I'm going to find my papa." Tia turned on her heel and ran from the room, her words trailing behind her. She might know who Griffin was to her, but Lochlan was Papa, the man she wanted when every fear came to the front of her mind.

Gulliver watched after her, torn. "Lochlan can protect her."

Pain seared through Griffin as Nessa probed his wound. "I don't have any of that gross brown liquid my sister gives patients or even the numbing herbs. This is going to hurt, Griff."

"Just do it."

Nessa looked so much like Shauna as she bent forward, a crease between her brows. This was better than using Tia's magic, more controllable, the outcome sure.

The moment she pierced his skin with the needle, he bit back a cry. Not everyone was as strong. Gulliver screamed as if it had been his skin Nessa stitched.

Griffin was so focused on Gulliver and on not passing out,

he didn't notice the door opening or the woman rushing in. Not until her gasp drew all his available energy.

Riona stood in bloody leathers, half dark wings curling into her back and light pouring in behind her.

Griffin grit his teeth as Nessa continued to stitch his wound, but he couldn't take his eyes from the woman he'd seen carried away. The one he thought dead or a prisoner.

But she was here.

"Riona?" Gulliver choked back a sob. "You're dead."

Riona rushed forward as she took in the scene before her. "What are you doing? Nessa, stop right now, and I'll find a healer."

"I am a healer," she squeaked in her little voice. Her tongue poked out between her lips as she concentrated.

"Let her finish, Riona." Griffin's voice was weak.

She lowered herself to the ground on the opposite side of Gulliver and Nessa, taking Griffin's limp hand in hers. "You're okay." It was like the whispered words were only for herself.

He looked up at her. "You're okay."

"I'm okay," Gulliver piped in.

Riona reached across and gripped Griffin and Gulliver's clasped hands. There'd be time for explanations and worrying about Egan later when Griffin didn't have to worry about losing too much blood if he stood.

"Shauna is going to be so mad." Gulliver shared a smile with Nessa as if this here was their contribution to the fight. They too got to be a part of it despite their ages.

Worry for Toby mixed with relief at being with these three warred within Griffin. Squeezing Gulliver's hand tighter, he bit back another scream.

Riona's brow furrowed. "That's got to be painful, Griff. You don't have to be silent just because I'm here. I heard you scream."

Red crept up Gulliver's cheeks. "That was me."

"I'm done." Nessa sat back on her heels and wiped her brow. "It's not perfect, Griff, maybe not even good. I had nothing to clean it with and don't have any salve now. But your guts won't fall out, and the bleeding will stop."

Griffin nodded, staring down at the jagged stitching holding his skin together. "Ness, thank you."

She shrugged. "You and I save each other. It's what we do."

She spoke with the words of a much older fae, but Myrkur stole any hope of a childhood from her. Nessa didn't grow up playing with toys. From the time she could walk, she accompanied Shauna to treat patients. The children of the village worked from a young age. They too had to fight to survive.

Gathering his remaining strength, Griffin pushed himself up, so he was sitting. "We need to find Toby."

"Griff." Riona sat back to stare at him. "Nessa just stitched you back together. You aren't going anywhere."

"No choice."

"His father is out there looking for him." She said the words pointedly, telling him Toby wasn't his responsibility. Not anymore. Both Griffin and Riona had done their job protecting the kids. Now it was up to their parents.

"I love them, Riona." Whether he was their father or just the uncle he was supposed to be, that wasn't something he could forget. He loved Toby and Tia from the moment he'd met them.

And he'd do anything to keep Brea's children safe.

"Let me bandage you." Nessa dug through her bag for a roll of bandages.

"There's no time."

"Griff." The kid gave him a stubborn look. "You love Toby. Well, we love you."

"Yeah, we sort of don't want you to die." Gulliver matched Nessa's stance.

Griffin sighed, inching forward so Riona and Nessa could wrap the bandage around him.

The door opened, and Myles peered in, his floppy hair soaked with sweat and who knew what else. Curses flew from his lips. "I wondered where the blood was leading. Yikes, Griff, you don't look so good. Was it an ogre?" He said it as if an ogre was the only creature who could defeat Griffin.

"Asrai." Griffin winced as Nessa tied the bandage. "Myles, can you get me a horse?"

His words faltered. "Uh, Griff, you really don't look like you should be riding a horse."

Griffin leaned forward, trying to push himself to his feet. "I'm guessing Brea hasn't recovered from the magic. If you don't help me, I'll have to tell her we don't know where her son is, and then you'll have a weak Brea demanding to join the search. So, that horse?"

Myles stared at Griffin in stunned fascination. "Who knew Griff could be such a manipulator? Oh wait, everyone." He laughed. "If you want to kill yourself for Toby, who am I to stop you?" He turned on his heel and marched back out of the bakery.

"Help me up." Griffin reached a hand out to Riona. When she didn't move, he looked to Gulliver. "I am going to find the boy."

Reluctantly, Riona and Gulliver helped him to his feet. He tried to step away from them, but his body tilted forward, and Riona slid one of his arms over her shoulders and gripped his waist before he could fall. Pain shot through his side. Yet, he couldn't sit here and recover while Toby could be out somewhere on that battlefield injured.

Riona helped Griffin outside to where Myles lead a horse

toward them. It was already saddled, and Griffin knew all he had to do was get to the city. He had to find Lochlan and Tia and make sure they didn't lose one of the people they loved most.

Injured soldiers streamed into the village, directed to one of the many homes and businesses that had been set up for them, filling the village streets with hobbling fae. The people would recover, but Griffin was more worried about his family.

Before they reached the horse, Riona pulled Griffin to a stop and turned to face him. Some emotion he didn't recognize sparked in her eyes. She reached up, trailing her fingertips over his cheek. "You'll find him, Griffin."

"No one has ever had such faith in me before." He didn't understand how she could stand with him, holding him up because his strength had failed him, and still look at him like he was a battle-ready warrior.

Rising up on her toes, Riona pressed her mouth to his. He wished their moment didn't have to end, that it wasn't just another in a steady stream of dangers.

"I meant what I said before the battle." He ran a finger over the cut on her head, making sure she was okay.

"Well, I thought the ogre was going to kill me. And in that moment, all I could think, all I wanted, was for you to know this isn't like your battles ten years ago. Now, you're fighting for people who love you, people who will fight for you too."

"Come on, lovebirds." Myles waved to them, lifting the reins in the air. When a curse slipped past his lips, Griffin turned his head to see Brea stumbling from the library, her face pale.

"What's going on?" She looked from Myles standing next to the horse to Griffin leaning on Riona just to stand at all. "You're injured. We should get you to a bed."

He shook his head, not wanting to utter the words he had to say. "It's Toby. We don't know where he is."

Only hours ago, Griffin ran through the streets of Raudur City fighting the fae who now stood on their side. Dark Fae and Light Fae together cleared the dead from the streets. Eldurian families watched in horror. The stain of battle would never be scrubbed free.

And now, Griffin held on to a saddle, doing everything he could not to fall off. It was a slow ride from the village to the city, especially because he was not the only person on this horse who could hardly sit up on their own.

Brea clung to him, refusing to be left behind as they went in search of her son. They left without Myles, but he caught up with them after going in search of a second horse. Riona had flown ahead to lend her assistance to Lochlan.

Now, as Griffin surveyed the carnage, he wondered if they would ever find Toby alive. There were too many dead in a war that hadn't had to happen. The Dark Fae that had turned to their side once Egan fled, outnumbered the Light Fae.

They could've prevented this by realizing sooner the way to gain freedom from the prison realm was not by controlling the other kingdoms, but by seeking peace with them.

This battle would fade to the back of their minds, but there were many Dark Fae out there who ran rather than surrender, and they would have to be dealt with. As would Egan and Enis. It wasn't even close to being finished.

But this wasn't about that. They had to deal with the consequences of this battle before moving onto the next. And one such consequence was a missing prince.

Griffin found Lochlan in front of the wall where Hector had given his speech. Lochlan and Tia called for Toby, using Tia's magic to make their voices carry through the streets.

Sliding down from the horse, Griffin stumbled when his feet touched down. Brea managed to be slightly more graceful than him.

When Tia caught sight of Griffin, she hiccupped back a sob. Running toward him, she jumped over the body of a hooved fae. Riona caught up to her before she could reach Griffin. "Careful."

She skidded to a halt in front of him, careful not to touch him for fear of his injury.

"Hello to you too, daughter." Brea held out her arms.

Tia fell into them. "I'm sorry, I've just been so worried Griffin died because I left."

"Still here, kid." He gave Lochlan a nod. To his brother's credit, he made no comment about his wife being here when she hadn't regained her strength. "Now, let's find your brother."

Riona helped Griffin walk through the streets calling for Toby. He could hear Lochlan, Brea, and Tia ahead of them.

"Do you feel him?" Griffin yelled up to Tia.

She looked back over her shoulder. "Sort of. He's struggling."

"So, that means he's alive?" Griffin's heart ached at the hope in Brea's voice. He hoped she didn't have to lose it.

Tia nodded. "I think so. But it doesn't mean he'll stay that way. We have to hurry, Mama."

"What was he doing joining the battle?" Brea's shoulders dropped. "And how could I not have kept him safe?"

It was Tia who answered. "Because he wanted to do something. Toby's life has always been about me. But he was held hostage for much longer than me, he has more reason to fight. Just because we're kids, doesn't mean this isn't our war too."

Griffin wanted to say that he was just ten years old, but that didn't matter anymore. He continued to call the boy's name. He didn't know how long they'd been searching or how he remained upright when his side radiated pain, but when he heard a faint reply, it was worth it.

Lochlan took off running with Tia at his side. Brea tried to keep up, but she wasn't in much better shape than Griffin. By the time they reached the others, they found the body of an ogre and something moving underneath.

"I'm here." The cry that reached them was weak.

"Under the ogre?" Brea's eyes widened. Only months ago, she hadn't known such creatures existed.

"Help," Toby cried. "Please. I can't breathe."

Lochlan clenched his fists, probably realizing what Griffin already had. Griffin and Brea would be no help, and Lochlan and Riona couldn't lift it alone.

But it seemed they didn't have to. Tia crouched down next to the ogre, not showing an ounce of intimidation as she pried the giant green arm away to peer down into the small space created underneath its twisted body. "Toby, are you hurt?"

"Tia," he cried. "You're here."

"Of course I am."

"It's on my legs. I can't move them."

"Tia." Lochlan put a hand on his daughter's shoulder. "Back away. We're going to try to move the ogre."

She didn't move except to look up at him. "No."

"What?" Lochlan crossed his arms. "This is no time to—"

"Save the day? Again? Yeah, I think it kind of is. Please stand back, Papa. I don't want to have to make you."

Riona snorted and shared a smile with Brea.

Lochlan, obeying his daughter with amusement in his eyes, joined them in backing up. Griffin shook his head, pride blossoming inside him. "She's her mother. Every bit of her."

"I know." Lochlan groaned. "It's going to be the death of me."

And yet, he remained back, trusting his young daughter. Griffin was proud of him too. The Lochlan he'd known was prideful, arrogant. He'd had trouble trusting anyone.

"Okay, Toby," Tia started. "I don't want to move the ogre off you in case it hurts you further. You're going to have to do it."

"I can't."

"Yes, you can. You survived a battle all by yourself." She patted the slimy shoulder of the ogre. "I'm guessing you killed this ogre here. My brother, the ogre killer. You didn't need magic to be great, Tobes, because great is who you are."

Griffin sent himself a mental reminder to go to Tia when he needed a pep talk. Every moment with the twins amazed him just like the time he spent with Gulliver and Nessa. When he was their age, he played with other kids at the Fargelsi palace and spent time at his studies. He didn't go to war, stitch wounds, or travel across four kingdoms and the human realm.

Tia kept going. "It's just like taking down the prison magic. I couldn't have done that without you, and I can't do this alone either. I'm going to funnel magic into you, Toby, and this time, you're going to save yourself. Are you ready?"

A moment passed before he said, "I'm ready." Griffin couldn't help noting the added strength in his voice.

Tia concentrated on the ogre as she muttered Fargelsian words under her breath. The ogre shifted, its other arm dropping to the ground, cracking the stones underneath.

It shifted again, its giant body rolling to reveal the boy they'd all been searching for.

Lochlan, Brea, and Tia rushed forward as Toby scrambled out, covered in the ogre's blood. Together, they collapsed into a family hug.

Griffin watched their reunion, reaching a hand out for Riona, this time for a different kind of strength, the kind that let him turn away. He stumbled over his own feet.

"That's it." Riona kept him steady. "We're going to the palace."

"What's at the palace?"

"Not what, who. Shauna is there caring for Faolan and other wounded. Come on."

By the time they reached the palace gates that stood open, Griffin wasn't sure how much longer he could keep going. Servants bustled by, returning the palace to its pre-Egan grandness.

Soon, there'd be no sign of the battle. But they'd always remember.

Dark Fae wandered listlessly, no one giving them orders.

Griffin's shoulder slammed into the corridor wall, and pain lanced through him. He started sliding down the wall, but Riona wouldn't let him.

"You," she called to someone Griffin didn't see. "I need help."

Strong arms scooped him up, and he looked into the hairy face of a horned fae with a giant red beard.

Riona directed them through the palace to the infirmary where not a single bed was open. "Set him near the wall."

The fae put him down and walked off.

Riona crouched next to him. "We'll get you some help, Griff. You should have stayed in Aghadoon to rest."

Even if Tia hadn't needed him, he'd needed to be there. "I-I… know." It was all he'd had the energy to say.

"Griffin?" Shauna rushed toward them, wiping a bloody hand on her apron. "What are you doing here? And where's your shirt?"

He looked down at his chest and the bandage where dots of

red soaked through. Shauna followed his gaze. "I told you to stay and let me treat this, you big oaf."

"Had to get to Gulliver." He couldn't admit he'd thought Riona had died and needed to be with the one person who'd feel that as deeply as him.

Shauna lowered herself to her knees, ignoring the bustling infirmary around her. "All right, let me see the wound." Riona helped her remove the bandage, and Shauna pursed her lips as she began muttering. "You idiot man. This wasn't cleaned before it was stitched, was it? Whoever did it has some skill, I'll admit, but it should have been me."

She reached into the bag slung over her shoulder, producing a tiny ceramic pot he recognized as the salve she put on to help wounds heal. "I'm going to have to open it up again to clean it out and make sure it's just a flesh wound." She shook her head. "You need to start caring what happens to you."

"It was Nessa." He leaned his head back.

Shauna froze for a moment before slapping him upside the head. "She's better than most of Egan's healers, but Griffin! My sister is eight. Eight!"

"It was either that or die, Shauna. What would you have me do?"

"And how many healers did you pass on your way to almost dying, you idiot man?" He couldn't tell what else she muttered as she searched the room. "I need a bed for you."

Riona shrugged. "This palace is full of beds."

Shauna's eyes lit up. "Riona you're a genius. Will you return to Aghadoon and let Gulliver and Nessa know what's happened?"

Riona stood, and Griffin appreciated that she trusted Shauna to take care of him. She met his gaze. "Do *not* die." With that, she hurried away.

Shauna rubbed a hand over her face. "This is going to hurt,

Griffin. A lot." She stood. "And it's all your fault, so I don't want to hear any complaining."

He closed his eyes. "I can handle it, Shauna."

He could. The battle was over, and the people he loved lived through it. It was a miracle, one he hadn't expected but had been afraid to hope for.

Now, they had to survive what came next.

Griffin

Griffin's hand drifted down his side. The bandages wrapped tightly around his torso made it difficult to get a deep breath.

But he was healing. They all were.

"We're going to be late." Riona tugged his hand as they made their way through the battle-torn streets just days after Egan fled Raudur City with his few remaining loyal followers.

"Hurry, Griff." Gulliver ran ahead of them. "I'm starving."

The Eldurians had spent the last two days cleaning their city. They still had a long way to go, but they were in high spirits. Now that their king—though he wasn't conscious—and queen had returned with the young prince and princess, they could see the light at the end of the tunnel. For them it was a matter of celebrating their victory and picking up the pieces to continue on, hoping King Finn would wake to join them soon. And celebrate they did. Even now, Eldurians danced in the streets, singing ballads of the epic battle for Raudur City.

But for Griffin and his family, there was no light at the end of the tunnel. At least not yet. Egan would be back. He was not the type to disappear after failing to get what he wanted. He would rise again. This would never be over until he was dead and the book of power was somewhere safe.

Griffin leaned on Riona for support as they made their way up the winding path to the tiered gardens that sat above the canyon city.

Egan and his brutish followers had destroyed the once beautiful garden—mostly through neglect—but Alona would have it put to rights again soon. For now, the pathway danced with light from the torches perched at intervals to light their way.

Though none of them felt like celebrating, the banquet was just that. A celebration for their victory over the Dark Fae king.

Griffin was sweating by the time they reached the top. Alona's court was in full attendance. Tables lined the open terrace, and Eldurians mingled with Iskaltians and Fargelsians as well as Dark Fae. Griffin even spotted a few ogres among them.

"Over here, Griff!" Gulliver called them over to his table. For a moment, he was torn between the two sides of his family. Part of him wanted to seek out Tia and Toby and their parents, and another part of him was desperate to hear how things were going for Shauna and the others.

"Look, Griffin." Riona nodded across the room, giving his hand a gentle squeeze.

Gulliver sat between Tia and Nessa. Hector's mother and Lochlan were in deep discussion over something serious. And Brea and Shauna were discussing Faolan's condition. For once, all his family were together, except for Hector who'd gone to track Egan, and for a moment, he couldn't catch his breath.

Griffin O'Shea didn't get this. He didn't get to keep both his old and new families.

"Let's find a seat. You're dead on your feet." Riona guided him toward the long table.

"There he is." Lochlan's smile caught him off guard. "It's about time you showed up."

"Griffin." Brea beamed a smile at him. "We saved you two seats."

"Right here between Toby the Ogre Killer and Shauna the Mighty Healer of Myrkur." Lochlan clapped a hand on his son's shoulder, and Toby's ears turned red just like Griff's did when he was that age.

"I have yet to hear the full tale." Griffin groaned like an old man as he took his seat.

"There's not much to tell." Toby shrugged. "I wanted to fight. I've trained with Papa for years, and I thought I was ready." Toby cast his eyes down at his lap. "I'm thinking there's not much that can prepare you for what battle is truly like."

"Wise words, young prince." Riona raised her glass, and the others followed suit.

"I was mostly staying out of the way, looking for ways to help our soldiers who might need an extra hand. I helped a few fight off their opponents, and then the ogre caught me. He picked me up by my collar and waved me around like a feather. I thought he would kill me."

"Ogre's like to play with their enemies first."

"That they do." Toby nodded. "And that's what got this one killed. He dropped me to the ground and was going to kick me, but I rolled out of the way and tried to gut him with my sword. Their skin is awfully thick."

"You have to get them from the back," Griffin said. "Right at the waist where their skin is fleshier."

"That's where I stuck him. Several times." Toby's eyes glassed over at the memory. "He started to fall back. I knew I wouldn't get out of the way fast enough so I lunged for a gouge in the ground, left over from some explosion, but I couldn't get my legs out of the way. The great stinking ogre landed right on top of me, but the hole in the ground kept me from getting smothered. Did you know ogre blood is black like sludge? And it stinks. Like, really stinks."

"He was covered in it when we pulled him out of that hole," Lochlan said proudly. Griffin was certain the Iskalt king had partaken of copious amounts of wine.

"How are your legs?" Griffin leaned in to ask his son. When they pulled the ogre off him, the boy's legs were badly bruised and swollen. Brea feared there might be permanent damage.

"All healed," Toby said, rubbing his leg under the table. "Shauna took care of me."

"It still twinges a bit, doesn't it?" Griffin nudged him.

Toby nodded. "That numbing salve she uses makes me feel funny."

"It'll feel that way for a while, but you'll be good as new soon enough." Judging by the somber look in his eyes, Griffin was certain the battle with the ogre would haunt Toby for years to come.

"Have some wine, brother." Lochlan filled a glass for Griffin. "It will help with the pain of Shauna's stitches."

"My stitches are what's keeping his guts inside him." Shauna shoved him playfully.

"How is Queen Faolan?" Riona asked.

Shauna's smile wavered. "She is going to pull through. I've never seen anyone take such a beating and still hold on. That woman is a force of nature."

"It would take more than a whip to break Mother's will," Brea said softly. "But if you hadn't been there to care for her when you did, I shudder to think what would have happened to her." Brea reached for Shauna's hand. "I can never repay you."

"I'm just glad we were able to keep her pain under control with the Eldurian medicines. I've learned much from your healers."

"And I've heard they've learned much from you too." Brea squeezed her hand.

"How is Finn?" Griffin asked, not sure he wanted to know.

"He still isn't awake." Shauna sighed. "The healers from all the kingdoms have been working together to treat him. We believe he will wake soon as the swelling from his injuries continues to improve."

The crowd murmured behind them as Alona entered the gardens with Prince Logan and Princess Darra holding her hands. Of all the things Griffin might have expected to see tonight, he never would have imagined Alona, the human Queen of Eldur to be accompanied by Egan's highest ranking general, Padraig—an ogre.

Alona looked weary but every inch the queen she was. With both her mother and her husband gravely injured and a hurting kingdom to run, she hadn't slept in days.

Alona stood at the front of the gardens with all of Eldur spreading out behind her to the east. "My friends." Her voice rose above the silence that had fallen at her arrival. "Eldur thanks you for everything you've done to aid us in this terrible war." Her fierce gaze fell across the terrace. "Tonight we celebrate our victory and our unity, but we are not done. We have a common enemy."

Cries of agreement rang out across the crowd.

"Egan must be defeated, and the book of power must be contained," Alona continued.

"Burn it!" several shouts rang out.

"Burn the library!" others agreed.

"I invite the leaders of Eldur, Iskalt, Fargelsi and Myrkur to join me this evening for a council meeting in the throne room where we will discuss what must be done in that regard." She turned toward the tables where the nobles sat. "General Padraig and I will meet you there in an hour."

With that, she took her children and made her way back to the palace.

"I am looking fer one called Tobias the Ogre Killer." The gravelly voice made Griffin flinch. Both Lochlan and Griffin reached a protective arm over Toby at the sight of the massive General Padraig towering over the little boy.

Griffin and Lochlan stood together, but Lochlan spoke for his son. "You seek my son, Prince Tobias of Iskalt." Lochlan's voice grew icy.

Padraig cleared his throat, a sound like an avalanche of boulders crashing down a mountainside. "I wish ter shake yer son's hand, Majesty. It's na small feat ta kill an ogre in the heat o' battle. Tobias is already a great warrior. You should be proud."

Lochlan looked stunned.

"The ogres have great respect for those who manage to best them in battle." Gulliver leaned forward to explain. "It happens so rarely, they recognize the great skill of their enemies."

"Tobias the Ogre Killer isna our enemy, nor tis his father, the mighty King o' Iskalt." Padraig gave a courtly bow.

"Go on, son. Shake the general's hand." Lochlan stepped aside.

Toby stood on shaky legs and approached the ogre with more confidence than Griffin would have in his shoes.

"I am sorry I had to kill one of your soldiers, sir." Toby stuck out his hand.

His little hand disappeared in the ogre's massive gray hand. Padraig leaned down to Toby's level and winked. "Now tha' we're on the same side, see that it doesna happen again." He chuckled, patting Toby's shoulder as he turned to shake Lochlan's hand. "I ha' never agreed with Egan's way o' ruling, and I'm grateful for a chance fer my people ta do better."

"Well, that is something I've never seen before in all my life." Riona shook her head. "An ogre playing at diplomacy."

"We should head to the throne room, Loch." Brea took her husband's hand. "I've asked Rowena to take Tia and Toby to spend the night with Logan and Darra. Gulliver too." She turned to Griffin.

"We'll take Gullie back to the village with us." Griffin draped an arm around Riona's waist.

"If you think you two are getting out of this council meeting, you'd better guess again," Lochlan said.

"We aren't leaders." Griffin looked to Riona in confusion.

"You forget you're a Prince of Iskalt, and though Riona might not have a title, you've each played integral roles in this war. You're coming with us." Brea tilted her chin in the stubborn way Griffin remembered.

"I wish Hector was here to represent the Dark Fae," Lochlan said.

"He has a more important mission." Griffin stood. "We can't lose Egan. Shauna and I can represent the people of Myrkur. Nessa can go with the other kids."

"What? How did I get dragged into this?" Shauna frowned.

"You're going to give us a report on the injured." Brea linked her arm through Shauna's, and they all made their way down the winding path to the palace.

Griffin and Riona walked with Lochlan down to the throne room. It was going to be a very long night.

"Thank you all for coming." Alona sat at the head of the long table in the throne room.

Myles and Neeve were already there, pouring over maps of the three kingdoms. Finn was still under the care of the palace healers, but it seemed that General Padraig and Alona had become fast friends.

Lochlan and Brea sat to Alona's right, and that left Griffin, Riona, and Shauna feeling uncertain about where they fit into this war room.

"My brother is here as a Prince of Iskalt and a representative of the Light Fae who have lived in Myrkur all these years."

"And we've asked Shauna to stand as a representative of the Dark Fae of Myrkur," Brea added. "She's also our resident Dark Fae healer." Alona gave her a grateful nod.

"And why am I here?" Riona cast an uncertain glance at Griffin.

Brea patted the seat beside her. "You, my friend, are here because of all the fae in all the lands, you know Egan's mind. You have insight we desperately need."

"We have much to discuss." Alona sat forward. "And everyone in this room is vital to the future of all the kingdoms."

"The people cry out for us to burn the library," Brea said. "We do not have the book, but burning the library would destroy the book and the source of vital magic. My sisters and I do not believe this is a solution."

Neeve nodded in agreement. "We believe to destroy the library or the book would destroy far too much magic. The Fargelsian's in particular would suffer greatly for the loss of the ancient language of power contained in the library."

"Forgive me, your Majesties," Shauna interjected. "We do not know the ways of magic. Could you explain how burning a building would affect your knowledge of magic?"

"Of course," Brea continued. "We discovered a way to

destroy any bit of magic so long as we can find the corresponding spell in the library. Destroy the record, and the magic will never work again. It will fade from the minds of those who once knew it. We believe the library contains the origin records of all magic. It cannot be destroyed, at least not all of it."

"We must study everything within the library and destroy the records of the most dangerous magic there." Brea turned toward Alona. "We would like to leave the rest as a public record for everyone to study and benefit from."

"Do we all agree this is the best measure to take?" Alona asked the room.

"Perhaps a committee should be selected to study the contents of the library," Shauna said uncertainly. "With representatives from each kingdom?"

"That's an excellent idea," Lochlan said. "And a task to tackle after we win this war."

"Of course," Alona said. "We're in agreement not to burn the library."

"We should move it," Griffin spoke up for the first time. "It's not safe here. Most still can't see it, but they know where it is and they see it as the source of all our problems."

"I have a suggestion." Brea stood up to address the room. "I want my kids with me. All of them. And I know Neeve and Myles want their kids with them too. The village could be the safest place for the realm's princes and princesses. We must protect them."

"We could portal to the three kingdoms," Griffin suggested. "Get the kids and bring them to the village and then move the village somewhere safe."

"We can't let Toby use his portal magic any time soon." Brea shook her head. "He's able to do more with his portals than you two can, but I can't risk his health. He needs time to recover from his ordeal."

"I can do it," Griffin offered. "At least, I think I can."

"I'm lost again," Shauna whispered to Riona. "What's a portal?"

"The O'Shea's have portal magic that allows us to travel from the fae realm to the human realm," Griffin explained. "But we can only travel to a place in the human realm where we've visited before, and once there, we can only return to the place where we portaled from here."

"You think you can portal from here to the human world and then to Iskalt and back to bring our children here?" Brea asked.

"I did it once before. I portaled from Myrkur to the human realm and then from the human realm to Gelsi."

"Wasn't that because the prison magic wouldn't let you return to Myrkur?" Riona asked.

"Yes, but since then, we also managed to get to the Eldur forces. Toby was with us and directing the magic then, but I can do it without him. I can at least try."

Lochlan nodded. "So maybe it's possible. But you need to rest, brother. I should travel to get the children."

"I'll go with you through your portal to the farm. Once we're there, I'll open the portal to Iskalt for you. So, even if we must return to the place we've left, your portals have only been opened between Aghadoon and the human realm. Mine will have been opened between the human realm and Iskalt."

"I think I followed that... it might work," Lochlan said. "We will try it after you've rested tonight."

"Who is watching over your throne, brother?" Griffin asked. It hadn't occurred to him how long Lochlan and Brea had been away from Iskalt.

"My advisor, Lord Brennan Cormac of Isvasi serves as my regent when I am not there."

"I know that name." Griffin frowned.

"He served as father's general. We used to call him Uncle Bren when we were children."

"Very well, once we have the children here, we will move with Aghadoon to somewhere safe in Fargelsi, then our children can join us there." Neeve scribbled notes in a journal. "Aghadoon should rest somewhere remote in the country where Egan won't find it."

"Brandon should be an invaluable help with researching the contents of the library," Lochlan said.

"I believe we might be able to study the darkest magic in the library and discover what Egan might do next." Neeve lifted her nose from the book in front of her where she made notes. "If we can find and destroy the magic he seeks before he can have Enis perform it, then we might be able to cut him off at the knees."

"Brandon has been busy since we left," Myles said. "Droves of confused Dark and Light Fae who did not join Egan's army have been making their way across into Fargelsi, refugees fleeing the harsh conditions of Myr with nowhere else to go. We will have to move them from the current camp Brandon has set up to more permanent lodgings."

"You can count on Iskalt's help to create a place for our Dark Fae friends who do not want to return to Myrkur," Lochlan offered.

"Eldur as well," Alona added.

"They will need a province, perhaps in northern Fargelsi near the shores of Loch Villandi," Neeve offered. "The country is wild, and few villages call that part of the kingdom home. Perhaps we can appoint a Dark Fae governor of the region, though they would need to abide by Gelsi law."

"It is decided." Alona leaned back against her chair. "We will gather our children and send them to Aghadoon, which we will then move to Gelsi. The library and our children will be safe there. I must remain here in Eldur to see to my people while Mother and Finn are recovering. I would ask that General Padraig go with you in my stead until I can join you."

"I would be honored ter serve ye, my Queen." Padraig gave a bow as if he'd spent his life in the court of the highest queen in the lands.

"Then the only thing that remains is Egan. What will he do now that he has lost Toby, Riona, Aghadoon, and Eldur?"

All eyes turned to Riona, and Griffin could sense her distress. She didn't like to be in a position of leadership. He reached for her hand under the table, giving her as much reassurance as he could in that gesture. Her fingers wrapped around his, and she held on tight.

"He will seek power wherever he can find it." Riona spoke softly. "If that is no longer possible here in the three kingdoms, he will probably return to Myrkur and those who have remained. He will gather his followers, creating an army once again. If given the time to gain his footing ..." Riona paused, casting a look at Lochlan. "I believe he will set his sights on Iskalt, and if he cannot reach for your throne in your absence, he will grasp power by any means necessary. Whenever he makes his next move—whatever that might be—we will know immediately."

Riona

Making changes to the way the O'Shea magic worked wasn't as hard as they'd imagined it would be.

Making changes to the way the O'Shea brothers *viewed* their portal magic was a different matter entirely.

They couldn't break the rules that had existed for hundreds of years, not like Toby could. Instead, they had to learn to work together.

And they figured it out.

Three weeks ago, Griffin and Lochlan left Aghadoon together through Lochlan's portal. It took many attempts, but they soon learned if they then used Griffin's magic to come back to the fae realm, they didn't have to return to the exact spot Lochlan had left.

Riona expected the brothers to celebrate when they managed it the first time, but they'd come back arguing instead, and they hadn't stopped since.

"I found another one." Lochlan dropped a heavy book onto

the table, and a cloud of dust erupted from the pages. He opened it to the page he'd marked, and Griffin sidled up next to him, his eyes scanning the words.

"Absolutely not." Griffin scowled down at the book. "Loch, you can't be serious. That spell isn't even dangerous. Veto."

Lochlan sighed. "You can't veto everything." They'd been having the same argument for weeks. Lochlan wanted to destroy Fargelsian spells Griffin thought needed to be preserved. "It lets the spell weaver create a barrier. Haven't we all had enough of those?"

Now, he'd done it. Riona hid a smile as she stared into the book in her lap. They searched the library in shifts to avoid getting in each other's way, shifts Brea scheduled. Riona got the feeling the Iskalt queen had some ulterior motives throwing the brothers together so often.

Griffin grit his teeth and ran a hand through his already messy auburn hair. He'd made Riona chop the length off last week as the Fargelsian humidity made anything touching his neck unbearable–his words.

"Loch." Griffin dropped into a chair beside his brother. "I feel like I've said the same thing over and over. Not all spells are the same even when they appear to be. I know because I—"

"Grew up in Fargelsi." Lochlan rolled his eyes toward the ceiling. "Yes, Griffin, I remember."

"Plus he's said it a million times," Riona muttered.

Both brothers looked to her as if they'd forgotten they weren't alone. They looked as exhausted as she felt with dark circles under their eyes and rumpled clothing.

No one had gotten much sleep over the last few weeks. The royal children were now in Aghadoon, even Darra and Logan whose parents weren't here, and it gave the village some much needed life after all the death Riona had seen here. But it had become the unofficial center of the fae realm, with four of the six rulers spending the majority of their time here.

And that meant no one had a moment to breathe.

They'd destroyed hundreds of dark spells. Even if they didn't find Egan, they were making this world a safer place. Yet, they hadn't found anything that looked like something he'd attempt.

He'd been quiet since the battle, returning to the palace of Myrkur according to the messages in the journal they'd started receiving from Hector. It wouldn't last long. Riona knew he was up to something.

The majority of the army stayed in Eldur to bolster their own decimated forces and help Alona rebuild. They'd come if needed.

And Riona knew eventually they would have to fight again.

Lochlan and Griffin continued to argue, their voices filtering through her mind.

"Loch," Griffin groaned. "Do you see these words here?" He pointed to a Fargelsian phrase. "Those are safeties, preventing the spell from growing in power over time. This is the kind of boundary spell Fargelsians use to keep their chickens from escaping, to keep intruders from entering their homes uninvited. It is impossible for it to grow large enough to cause the kind of problems you're suggesting."

Lochlan's shoulders dropped, and he slumped into a chair. "I feel like we're still in the dark here." He rubbed his eyes and pushed the book away. "You're right."

"I'm what?"

"Don't make me say it again, Griff. These aren't the type of spells we're searching for. But my Fargelsian is rusty at best and staring at these words is making my head hurt."

"Then take a break." Brandon entered the library, looking way too wide awake. Brea and Neeve's father knew more about this place and the book than any of them because he was part of the Fargelsian royal line. But it didn't mean he knew a lot.

Brandon stopped behind Lochlan's chair and put a hand on his shoulder. "I passed Brea on my way here. She's feeding the children, and then she'll come. You all should go get some rest and come back with fresh eyes."

Neither Lochlan nor Griffin argued with that as they pushed to their feet. It was only when they stood side by side one could see the similarity between them. It wasn't in their looks, but their mannerisms, the way they held themselves.

Riona couldn't look away.

Griffin paused at the door and met her gaze. "Are you coming?"

She shook her head, not wanting to stop when she'd just found what she was looking for. "Not yet."

"Don't stay too long."

"I won't."

He attempted a tired smile, but it fell quickly and he ducked out, leaving Riona alone with the intimidating Fargelsian. She'd heard the stories about Brandon O'Rourke. Kept in the dungeons for eighteen years by his own sister, Regan, he hadn't known Faolan gave birth to a baby girl—Brea—or that she'd exchanged her with the human Alona as an infant for her own safety.

"Which book are you reading?" He had a kind voice, one that held none of the pain she imagined he hid.

Lifting the book from her lap, she showed it to him. "I don't know Fargelsian, so I'm not much help with finding the spells. But there's a section of books on the histories of the fae realm, and these, I can read."

"Ah." He smiled. "Yes. After my sister studied in this library when she was young, she told me about such books. The books themselves are spelled to appear in whatever language the reader wishes to see. It was once a way to make sure no one was able to forget. If everyone could read our earliest beginnings, they could not be denied. And then the books were hidden in Aghadoon, and much of the histories were forgotten behind the prison magic."

He walked to the back of the room and retrieved a black leather-bound book. "I found this yesterday. It may be of more interest to you than—" he looked over her shoulder at the book in front of her. "—Iskaltian histories."

Taking the book from him, she set it on top of the other. It had no title, but the moment she opened it, she knew what it was.

This was an accounting of Myrkur.

A kingdom only those in this village in the human realm knew existed, and they'd kept it secret for generations.

It was a handwritten book, the calligraphy hard to read. But something kept her eyes pinned to the words, straining to know their meaning.

Brandon gave her a knowing smile and went to another shelf to dive back into searching the spells.

Others came and went while Riona read. Brea and Neeve both had children on their laps as they focused on their research. Myles came, leaving when Neeve kicked him out for being annoying.

Riona read first of the depiction of Dark Fae, creatures with horns and tails and wings. She flipped through hand drawn images showing them as vicious animals with sharp teeth. "This book was obviously written by a Light Fae." She shook her head and kept going, ignoring the rumbling of her stomach, her dry mouth.

A heading started a section on origins of the Dark Fae, and the image drawn made her breath stutter. It was a Slyph with the gills and scales of an Asrai. Rubbing a hand up her arm,

Riona needed to feel her scale-less skin. There was no denying what the drawing was supposed to be. Someone like her, like Nihal.

Half Slyph.

Half Asrai.

The story of Riona had always been that she was the product of a Slyph and an Asrai coupling, that her village had been full of such fae until it was destroyed. That was what Egan told her.

But this book said something different. "They come from us."

"What?" Brea lifted her eyes.

Brandon and Neeve stopped reading to focus on Riona.

"This book... is it possible it can be wrong?"

Brandon studied her for a long moment. "There's always that possibility, but I wouldn't think so. Not here. You found something, didn't you?"

She held out the book to him, needing him to confirm what she was really seeing.

"The Slyph and the Asrai come from the same ancestors," he read. "Creatures of both the sea and the sky, they are the earliest known Dark Fae. Their fates intertwine with that of Myrkur."

Fates. She'd tried not to think of what the book said about the tattoos on her skin, but there was no hiding from it. Her fate was to find the rightful ruler of Myrkur.

Shoving that from her mind, she shook her head. "I... I've always been treated with such scorn as if my very existence was wrong. An abomination." A tear slipped down her cheek as she remembered how those in Myrkur looked at her.

Brea handed her daughter to her grandfather and stood, crossing the room to Riona. "Riona...," she paused as if trying to figure out the rest of Riona's name.

"Nieland." Riona wiped her cheek.

"Well, Riona Nieland, no matter your birth, whether your people were the first Dark Fae or a mix of others, it doesn't matter. Not here. We accept everything you are."

Embarrassment flooded Riona when she couldn't hold back the tears. She'd never had a friend, not until Griffin. And now, this perfect queen didn't look at her as something different from her.

"Warning." Brea smiled. "I'm going to hug you now. I know we aren't the hugging type of friends yet, Riona, but I think that's friend goals for us." She wrapped strong arms around Riona. "I mean, a part of me wants to squeeze the life right out of you for being in love with my first husband, but lucky for you, I won't let the marriage magic win. And oh, holy cow, your wings are so soft. Neeve, get over here and hug Riona."

Neeve crossed her arms. "No. Can we go back to saving our kingdoms now?"

Myles walked in, one hand held up in surrender. "Don't make me leave again, wifey. I know I can't read the spells, but we have a problem." He dropped the journal they used to communicate with Hector. They'd tasked Myles with handling these communications.

Riona reached for it, flipping through the pages that had told them Egan was back in Myrkur struggling to gain many new followers. They hadn't erased any of the intel in case they needed it. She reached the last page with writing and stopped, reading the words. "We've been found."

No one spoke for a long moment until Brea stood. "Gather everyone in the center of the village. Lochlan won't like this, but I'm going to have Toby take him to Eldur." She walked from the room with the air of a queen. For someone who claimed she didn't want to rule, she was good at it, going from sentimental human to fae queen in minutes.

A million scenarios filtered through Riona's mind as she thought of Egan and what he'd do next. Would he return to Eldur now that they'd left? Try to make a move on the weaker Fargelsi, not knowing Aghadoon was within its boundaries?

There had to be something more, something none of them had thought of.

Night had fallen on Fargelsi by the time Riona reached the crowded square. Once, this village was home to many families who'd lived here for generations.

Until the slaughter.

Riona still saw their faces in her mind, and she wondered if Toby did as well. She met the watchful black gaze of Padraig, a general she'd worked with many times before when they both served Egan. The Light Fae had been so desperate to trust those who'd put aside their weapons in the battle she worried they didn't really know who they were dealing with.

She'd never met an ogre she could trust, one with the intelligence for true leadership—until Padraig.

The other fae in the village gave him a wide berth, and she didn't blame them.

Tearing her eyes away, she searched for Griffin. Only he'd understand this foreboding feeling inside her. He too would have guessed Egan wouldn't be content just sitting in an empty palace with Enis and the book.

Not when there was still so much dark magic left in it.

It would take years to finish combing the Aghadoon library for dangerous spells to destroy. They didn't have years.

Brea clapped her hands together, and the sound reverberated against the stone, amplified by her magic. All chatter died down.

Neeve and Myles joined her, the only other royals currently in the village. "A moment ago, King Lochlan and Prince Tobias left for the human realm. They will portal from there into Eldur to make sure our brothers and sisters in the desert kingdom are secure." She kept emotion out of her voice, and Riona didn't know how she did it. Brea O'Shea was the most emotional fae she'd ever met—other than Gulliver, of course.

"What's going on?" Gulliver hissed, joining her.

Riona slipped her arm around his shoulders but didn't answer him as Brea continued. She couldn't voice the words she knew would hurt him. Hector, he...

"When Egan Byrne fled the battle like the coward he is, a group of the noble Slyph went to follow his movements led by the Dark Fae leader, Hector. I'm sad to say we no longer believe them to be alive." She lifted her chin. "But their deaths will not be in vain. We know where our enemy is, and we will prepare to meet him once more. Our troops who have been resting and recovering in Eldur while helping to protect Raudur City will be recalled to join the fight. This time, we take the fight to—"

Her words cut off as icy blue magic ripped through the air, a portal opening right in the middle of the crowd. Fae scattered out of the way as Lochlan and Toby practically fell through. Lochlan snapped the portal shut and turned to the expectant faces. "It's dark."

Riona never would have imagined seeing fear on the face of the seemingly fearless king. But it was there, and she wasn't the only one who noticed.

Griffin appeared at his side, his face stony with a lack of emotion over Hector's fate. She knew it was a lie. "What's dark?"

Lochlan shook his head, unable to get the words out.

Toby's next words carried over the crowd, settling an ominous weight around them. "The human realm. It's daytime there, but their light... it's gone."

Riona wouldn't believe the blinding sun of the human realm was gone until she saw it for herself. She shook off any lingering sadness and weariness from the last few weeks as she clothed herself in the least fae looking thing she could find. Brown trousers that gave her ample room to move, a white linen shirt, and black boots she'd scrubbed the blood off only days before.

She left her sword behind to join the traveling party.

This was it, she could feel it. The darkness in the human realm had something to do with Egan's next step. It had to.

Which was the worst thing of all. The fae realm wasn't supposed to have an impact on the humans—unless an O'Shea was involved of course.

In this moment, nothing else mattered. Not the histories she'd uncovered or even the spells Neeve and Brandon would continue searching with their team. Even Hector's unknown fate, his possible death after being found and the journal destroyed, had to fade into the background.

Lochlan and Toby had only spent a few minutes in the human realm before portaling back, so no one knew what they'd find at the familiar farmhouse in Grafton.

Which was why their party wasn't small.

Brea insisted on leading them herself, and no one argued. It was her home, after all. She and Myles had more stake in this than anyone.

"Are we ready?" Lochlan asked, his power winding through the air.

Griffin nodded. "Let's do this." His violet portal opened, and he held out a hand for Riona. There'd been so little time to spend together over the weeks that just a simple touch had her heart speeding up.

She'd been prepared for the darkness after suffering through so much of it, but there was something wrong about it in the human realm. A familiar feel of magic buzzed through the air. Did the humans feel it too?

It took her a moment to get her bearings as she stood in the field across from Brea's house. The last time they were here, Aghadoon stood where she now did. Well, according to Griffin. Riona hadn't been able to see it then.

Memories of that time came at full force. Nihal sitting under the drooping tree by the front porch playing his music.

The sun blazing down on them.

"This isn't right," Brea whispered. "Do you feel it?"

Griffin tugged Riona close to his side, whether for his comfort or hers, she didn't know. Her wings stretched out behind her, ready for a fight should that become necessary.

"Myles." Brea gripped his hand, and Riona wondered how much worse this was for them.

Riona was used to her home being shrouded in darkness, and that's when it hit her. The thickness in the air, the way something felt so off. It wasn't a feeling she'd have noticed if she'd never left Myrkur, but then she'd experienced the fresher air of the other kingdoms.

This felt exactly as Myrkur had.

The hairs on her arms stood on end.

None of them spoke as they walked toward the house. It was as if they were afraid of voicing what they were all thinking.

Egan was coming after the human realm, and the humans would stand no chance.

But how? How did he get here to use the book? That was the question no one could answer.

"I thought we destroyed the darkness spell when we created the eclipse." Myles' voice was low.

It was Griffin who answered. "We did."

That was the problem. They'd destroyed it, and still, the human realm was dark.

Brea pulled a key from her pocket and ran up the steps to unlock the house. "Okay, first thing's first. Myles, you know the box in my room under my bed?"

"The one you used to hide things from your parents in when we were kids?"

She nodded. "I'm still paying for internet here, so it should be up and running. I want the laptop and the phone from that box."

He ran off to retrieve the items, though Riona wasn't sure what a laptop or internet was.

Brea turned to Lochlan and Griffin. "Don't just stand there. Be useful. We don't have to stay the night here since we don't want your magic lingering too long like last time, but I don't want to sit in the dark. Turn on lights, open up the house."

"What can I do?" Riona rubbed her suddenly cold arms.

Brea ticked her head toward the sitting room. "You and I are going to do some searches."

Riona nodded. "Tell me where to look and what I'm looking for. I can fly further into town if you'd like."

"Any other time you'd be cute, Riona, but right now I really just wish you spoke human. Okay, short lesson." Myles returned and handed her a slim silver metal thing. "This is a computer. It will tell us any information we need to know." She sat on the couch and opened the computer to reveal a bright light and rows of letters.

Riona perched on the arm of the couch.

"We don't have time for your stand-offishness." Brea patted the seat next to her.

Riona reluctantly joined her.

Myles threw himself into a chair and started hitting letters on the phone.

Lochlan and Griffin watched from the doorway.

Brea's fingers flew over the letters, and before long, a list appeared. She used her finger to choose an item.

Riona read over her shoulder. "A week?" She sat back. "The human world has been dark for a week."

Brea nodded. "It looks like it's only Grafton right now, but it's spread from where it began. The reporters are calling it a weather phenomenon and linking it to global warming."

"Global what now?" Lochlan asked.

"Warming. The humans are killing the planet, but that's not our issue right now. This isn't a global warming issue. How could they even consider that? It's not weather! The sun is just gone." She huffed out an angry breath.

Griffin pushed away from the doorframe. "When something unexplainable happens, humans will find logical explanations—they just won't be right. Humans do not know magic exists, so what else can help them understand an entire town going dark?"

Lochlan nodded. "The bigger issue is you said it's spreading. The computer told you that?"

Myles held up his phone. "Look, there's a map showing how it's grown. These articles... the humans are freaking out. I mean, I would have too before I knew another world existed."

Riona met Griffin's gaze, wondering if he felt the same similarities to the prison realm. "This... thickness, that lack of fresh air... it feels very much like the prison realm, like whatever magic caused the endless night in Myrkur."

But that wasn't supposed to be possible. The humans would be helpless against magic.

Leaning forward, she rested her elbows on her knees, not

looking away from Griffin. "Is it time to consider if there's a breach between the fae and human realms?"

Everyone spoke at once, denying that could happen.

Except Griffin.

Because, like Riona, he knew Egan. He'd seen the book. Anything was possible.

Myles stood. "I need to call my folks."

Brea nodded. "Then we must get back to Aghadoon." She rubbed a hand across her face. "If we're to entertain the notion that Egan has caused some kind of rift between the worlds—since he has no O'Shea to bring him here—we at least know what to look for in the library."

The moment they returned, those who'd stayed behind had a million questions. Riona wanted to seek her bed, to curl up and forget this day for a few hours. But she didn't get that luxury.

Not now that she knew Egan's next steps.

The others might be skeptical, but she'd never been more certain of anything.

Brea led them to the library for a meeting before they decided what to do next.

She spoke much more calmly than any of them felt. Griffin sat next to Riona and reached for her hand.

Her entire body relaxed at his strong grip as she listened to Brea tell the others what they'd discovered.

Neeve had many questions, but Riona watched Brandon, noting how quiet he'd become.

She cut off whatever Neeve had been saying. "What is it, Brandon?"

The man who knew more about this world than any of

them sighed. "I never wanted to speak Regan's final truths. I figured she's dead so her true mission didn't matter."

"She wanted to control the fae," Griffin said. "What does that have to do with this?"

He shook his head. "No, son. She wanted to control all life. My sister... she was much darker than even you realize. I may know how Egan managed this. But... we're going to need Regan's grimoire."

Griffin's breath quickened as they spoke of Regan, and Riona leaned closer to him, letting him know she was there. "That book was destroyed when she died."

Brandon shook his head. "I saved it."

Griffin

"It's happening." Brandon's hands shook as he paced the span of the library. He'd left to retrieve Regan's Grimoire. A book Griffin had grown up seeing. It was never far from Regan's reach, but she never let him touch it.

It was spelled so that no one could open it without her permission. It seemed her death was her final permission because Brandon O'Rourke set the book on the table, letting it fall open.

Griffin gasped at the sight of Regan's handwriting. It shouldn't hurt to see it after all this time, but it did. Like a knife right through his heart.

"I am so sorry, Griffin." Brandon turned his sad gaze on him. "I hoped the truth of her darkness had died with her." He thumbed through the grimoire, searching for whatever he believed was relevant now. "She was your mother." He slid the book toward Griffin.

"The legacy of her darkness is my burden to bear." Griffin's voice came out strangled, and he couldn't seem to meet his brother's gaze.

"It is not, brother." Lochlan placed his hand across the book, forcing Griffin to meet his eyes. "She was your mother, and you loved her. You remained loyal to the woman who raised you. We ... I should never have blamed you for that."

Griffin nodded, not trusting his voice as he pulled the book toward him and began to read. It took his breath, reading his mother's words. He could hear her voice as clearly as if she stood behind him reading over his shoulder.

Shock and revulsion rolled through him as he realized how truly unhinged Regan was. He'd always known she craved power. Absolute power.

Griffin stood to pace as he read through pages and pages of research and dark spells. Dangerous spells. Some she'd constructed herself—a perilous pursuit that rarely ended well for the fae involved in such things.

"Well?" Lochlan finally spoke as Griffin flipped through the pages.

"Give him a moment, Lochlan," Brandon said. "It's likely a shock."

Griffin sat back in his chair, dropping the book on the table in front of him as if it burned him.

"She was ... insane." Griffin reached for Riona's hand, needing her strength. "We all know she craved power. She wanted to unite the three kingdoms as one under her rule. In her twisted mind, she found her pursuit to be a noble one.

"She used to tell me about a world where there was no more war or conflict. She painted a picture of a beautiful life for all fae, one I wanted to help her create. But I was wrong. So very wrong." Griffin leaned forward, pressing his forehead against the table.

"She writes of her time studying here in the Aghadoon

library. She was an O'Rourke descendant, so they could not deny her access, but they wouldn't let her copy the spells she studied. She writes of one spell in particular." Griffin pulled the book closer. "A complex weave of magic she describes as wickedly beautiful in its construction. It came from an ancient scroll filled with dark magic. She tried to tear the spell from the scroll, but the paper wouldn't rip. The main subject of this scroll was on the fragile veil that exists between our world and the human world. She wished to destroy it. To bring magic to the human world where she would rule as mistress over all." Tears welled in his eyes and splashed on the page in front of him.

"How did I let her become this? This monster? How did I not see that she wasn't in her right mind?"

"That fault lies with me, son. Not you." Brandon laid a weary hand on his shoulder. "You were just a boy who loved his mother. You believed her to be right and true. Whereas I was her elder brother. I knew what she was when we were young, and because I loved her, I looked the other way when I should have done something about it. I should have gotten her the help she needed."

"The fault is Regan's." Brea stood up, coming to Griffin's side. She leaned down until he couldn't help but meet her gaze. "She went down a dark path that lead to her end. This is not your fault, Griffin O'Shea. It was never your fault, and I can't believe we let you enter the prison realm to pay for the crime of believing in the wrong person."

"I did terrible things, Brea. Don't kid yourself. I deserved what I got. But right now we need to find this scroll."

"Griffin is right." Neeve placed a careful hand on Regan's grimoire, as if asking his permission to see it. He nodded, letting her take it from him. He never wanted to see it again. "There are thousands of scrolls here. But knowing we are looking for a scroll and not a book narrows our search considerably. We will find this bit of magic, and we will destroy it."

"If Enis has somehow found this magic within the book," Lochlan began. "And created a tear in the veil between our worlds, allowing the darkness of Myrkur to ... leak into the human realm, will destroying the magic repair the tear?"

"It should." Brea came back from a far corner of the library with a stack of dusty scrolls. "At the very least it's the first step to making sure that fool who calls himself a king doesn't destroy the veil completely."

"Enis is likely not powerful enough to do that," Neeve said, helping Brea shift through the scrolls. "It will only be a matter of time before Egan realizes he needs a stronger spell caster. And comes for one."

"Griffin!" Brea stormed into the room he shared with Riona and Gulliver. Aghadoon was bursting at the seams with people, and the royals were sharing one small house.

"Oh, I'm so sorry." Brea's face flushed at the sight of Griffin and Riona in the same bed together. Not that there was anything remotely interesting happening between them with no privacy to be had these days.

"Whas happening?" Gulliver sat up from his pallet at the foot of the bed. His tail flicked nervously over his head. "We being invaded?" His tail knocked over a stack of scrolls Griffin and Riona had spent most of the evening poring over.

"Go back to sleep, Gullie." Griffin slipped out of bed, feeling nervous and ashamed to have Brea find him here in a completely innocent embrace with the woman he happened to be head over heels in love with. They had to do something about this marriage bond holding them together. He'd always seen the marriage bond as a romantic thing one shared with the love of their life. But what happened to free will? He didn't want to be connected with Brea like this. Not anymore.

"What have you found, Brea?" Riona asked, rising from the bed in the clothes she'd slept in. They'd fallen asleep reading late into the night.

"We found it. Early this morning, Lochlan found the spell we've been looking for. We need to destroy it, but we want everyone in agreement before we destroy the whole scroll."

Griffin and Riona gathered the scrolls they borrowed the night before and followed Brea across the narrow cobblestone road to the library.

"It's truly awful magic," Brea called over her shoulder as they rushed through the library doors. "Neeve has read each spell carefully to make sure we don't destroy anything important."

"Whoever created this magic hated humans." Neeve set the scroll down when they all gathered around the table. "I mean, really despised humans. This is written on some kind of leather I'm truly afraid might be human skin."

"It's just like I've always said." Myles sat back in his chair looking like he hadn't slept in days. None of them really had. "Human legends are always rooted in truth somewhere. Listen to this." He gestured to Neeve, and she began to read.

"This is a spell designed to fool humans into believing the fae are beautiful souls who only want the best for them. And this one creates spelled music that will force a human to dance for the fae's entertainment. It says here they will dance until their feet are bloodied and they finally die from exhaustion."

"That's horrifying," Riona said.

"It's also the kind of magic that shows up in every human fantasy book with fae characters." Myles looked ill at the thought that such magic existed. He held the evidence of it in his hands.

"This magic cannot be allowed to exist." Neeve sat back with a sigh. "It's always bothered me that we are sitting here destroying magic. No one should get to decide what magic should exist and what shouldn't. It's a dangerous precedence that cannot be helped. We are dealing with such an extreme situation. It calls for extreme measures."

"Are you saying we should preserve these spells? And others like it?" Brea asked.

"No, but I worry what the future kings and queens of the realms will have to say about us. What happens generations from now when we are all long dead and others look back at what we've done here and either judge us for it, or use it as a precedence to ... censor all magic, or worse, destroy it completely. Who are we to decide these things?"

"We do what we must," Lochlan said. "We cannot look back, and we cannot look forward. We must do whatever we can to ensure our survival and that of the human world. Let history mark us as traitors or heroes. None of it will matter if Egan wins."

"You are right." Neeve nodded.

Griffin cleared his throat, wondering if what he was about to suggest would force them all to remember he was the criminal in the room. "No one needs to know what happens here. Neeve is right to worry about how history will judge us for how we deal with this threat. But who says history needs to know any of this? If we all take this to our graves, we aren't setting a precedence at all."

Silence fell across the table, and Griffin immediately regretted the suggestion.

"I'm good with that," Lochlan said as he stood, taking the scroll from Neeve.

"Yeah, I can live with it," Neeve agreed as her husband nodded his consent.

Lochlan dropped the scroll into a charred bucket at the center of the room. They had burned dozens of spells they deemed dangerous, but none so complex as this. Unlike the books, most of the scrolls they destroyed refused to burn by magical means. Lochlan struck a match—a human match—and dropped it on top of the aged leather.

Fire blazed as the scroll burned followed by an unnatural green flame that destroyed the words of magic written with such hate and vengeance it couldn't be allowed to exist.

They stood around in silence, watching the scroll burn to ash.

"By destroying such a dark part of our history, may we not be doomed to repeat it," Neeve whispered.

"This history will die right here, sister." Brea took her hand. "Because we will teach our children not to harbor such hate in their hearts."

It didn't work.

After burning the scroll, Lochlan and Griffin traveled to the farmhouse to find the darkness still spreading from the breach in the veil. A breach they could not find because it was invisible. But with the destruction of the dark magic that created the breach, they had ensured that Egan would not be able to destroy the veil or create a larger tear.

"This is the sort of darkness you lived in for ten years?" Brea asked as they stood in the field near her childhood home the following morning. The sun was still absent from the skies over this part of Ohio. But they were here to rectify that situation.

"It is." Griffin nodded. "But you get used to it. Myrkur has its own beauty if you know where to look. The darkness wasn't so bad. I still enjoyed this time of day."

"How do you know what time it is when it's always the same?" Brea asked.

"It's in the subtleties. The early mornings are quiet. Fresh and cool with the morning dew. The darkness is still there, but it's not as heavy when the day is young."

"You always could find the beauty in everything." Brea smiled as she moved into the clearing with her daughter and her sister. The three women held hands. As they performed the magic that would chase the darkness back into Myrkur, they leaned on each other so the strength the spell demanded of them would not drain them.

Griffin only had eyes for Tia as she spoke the words of power with confidence. She was incredible, his daughter. He would never cease to be proud of her. Together with her mother and her aunt for support, Tia guided the darkness back through the invisible veil, sealing the rift behind it.

Sunlight burst through the clouds, and they all cheered in triumph. They thwarted Egan again. And this time, they wouldn't let him recover. This time, they were going to bring him to justice.

Riona

Riona sat on the edge of her bed as her thick black hair hung in wet braids around her face. She tried to dry her hair with a bath sheet, relishing the feeling of being clean. Time away from the library was hard to come by, and she closed her eyes, letting the rare quiet wrap around her.

Reaching behind her, she pulled the tips of her wings to the front to study the inky darkness that seemed to expand almost daily now. Would she end up with entirely dark wings like Nihal had?

Thoughts of Nihal always left her confused and a little angry. He'd pretended to be on their side, to give them answers, but it was Enis who held his loyalty in the end.

And none of them quite knew what that woman's goal was yet.

Nihal died for his trouble, to save Enis, taking the rest of the answers Riona needed with him.

"You took a bath?" Gulliver walked into the room and

stripped off his shirt. "Griffin told me I couldn't bathe for another few days."

She hid a smile. He'd surprised her this morning with the bath, lugging the water himself. "Carry the water yourself, and you don't have to listen to him."

He shrugged. Riona had never spent much time around kids, but now she was surrounded by them. She'd learned quickly that they didn't prioritize privacy, nor cleanliness, especially if it meant extra work. "No time today. I have a game to play." He flashed her a smile and slipped a new shirt on before running out the door.

From what she'd learned of Fela, the village in Myrkur where he grew up, there'd been so little time for playing. But now, with all of the royal children in the village, they spent hours playing a game Myles called soccer, running through the town square without the heavy burdens on their parents' shoulders.

That was one thing the adults had all agreed on. Other than occasionally using Tia's magic or Toby's portals, they wouldn't put this weight on their children. Not after all they'd been through.

After all everyone had been through.

Had they done it? Had they thwarted Egan's grand plan? Kept him from the human realm?

It felt like a win.

But she had no delusions about it. This wouldn't be over until he was dead.

Standing from the bed, Riona twisted her braids to wring out the water. She laid the bath sheet over the back of a chair and walked from the house into the sun she'd come to appreciate. The brightness still bothered her at times, but its warmth on an otherwise chilly Fargelsian morning was welcome.

Signs of life entered the village with shops opening to keep the royals and soldiers supplied. They'd managed to change the village magic once again, allowing all those with honest intentions to see it, which meant trading with the Fargelsians was possible.

Yet, the people who'd lived here before were never far from her mind. They too had lived lives with purpose.

She crossed her arms as she reached the square near the library at the center of the village. Gulliver kicked a ball in front of him with Tia and Logan chasing. Little Darra trailed along after them. It was good the Eldurian prince and princess were occupied. It kept them from asking too many questions about their father who still had yet to wake.

Riona barely knew Finn, but she could see the worry in Lochlan's eyes.

As if the thought of him called him forth, cold blue light flashed in front of her moments before Lochlan stepped through a portal with a familiar little girl at his side.

"Nessa?" Riona walked toward them.

Lochlan met her gaze, and it still surprised her whenever he did so without scorn. The battle changed him, learning the truth about his world changed him. "Where are the others?"

"In the library, I'm guessing. I was just headed there."

He nodded and took off toward the most important building in the entire realm.

Inside, the realms' rulers looked fresher than they had in a long time. They were still searching for dangerous spells, but there was a sense of hope that what they were doing had worked.

Griffin stood from his seat at the table and walked toward them, bypassing Lochlan and Riona to get to Nessa. "Hey, Ness. I thought you were staying in Eldur with Shauna."

"Eldur." Lochlan sighed. "Just one of our problems. I spent the last few days with Alona and Faolan—who is mostly recovered thanks to Shauna's attentive care. Bands of fae who'd chosen to leave rather than join us after the fight have been attacking the city, forcing Eldur and Iskalt soldiers to work day and night to keep them out. We need to call our men back, but I won't leave Eldur unprotected. For now, they will have to stay."

He looked down at Nessa. "Shauna thought the village would be safer for her."

Nessa crossed her arms. "I was helping. That's more important than safety."

Griffin smiled and put a hand on her shoulder. "Shauna just worries, but you can still help here."

"Help you figure out why the human realm is dark again?"

Riona sucked in a breath as every eye in the room focused on Nessa.

Lochlan rubbed a hand across his face. "I was getting to that. We just portaled through Grafton on our way back. Our bigger problem right now... whatever we did to save the human realm... it didn't work."

Weeks of darkness did something to a fae... or a person. Riona and Griffin were well versed in living without light in the sky, but most were not.

Which was why it didn't surprise her when the news out of the human realm was of societal breakdowns. Their governments had no answers, nor any solutions to the increasing crime and dissolution of order.

This time, the darkness didn't linger over Grafton. It spread rapidly and without slowing to the neighboring towns and beyond. Nearly all of Ohio was dark now.

Weeks had gone by, and they still hadn't found the tear or how Myrkur's darkness leeched through it.

Griffin, Riona, Brea, and Lochlan had started a rotation at the farmhouse. There was never a time when two of them weren't in the human realm searching for answers while the other two searched in the library.

Riona flopped onto the bed, too exhausted to keep her eyes open. They'd spent the entire day scouring Grafton for any sign of the breach. Just like they'd done every other day. At least they could return to the village soon for a break.

Griffin crawled into bed beside her and released a long sigh as he rested his face on one of her soft wings. The hope that bolstered them after they thought they'd sealed the breach and chased the darkness away had long since evaporated, leaving them drained.

"Riona," Griffin whispered.

She didn't open her eyes. "Hmm?"

"Do you think we'll be able to stop this?"

Turning onto her side, she slid her eyes open to study him, this beautiful fae she'd once tried to kill. "Do you remember what you said to me in the arena?"

He hummed in the back of his throat. "Not really. What I remember was how fierce you looked as you tried to gut me. I like to picture warrior Riona."

She pinched him. "I was being serious."

"So was I."

"Griff, I will never forget your words that day. I think they were the start of everything changing for me. You told me you weren't scared of me. When I asked why, you said it was because you had something to fight for." She put a finger under his chin and turned his face up. "I didn't understand it then, but I do now. I don't fear Egan or the book of power, because we will never stop fighting until he's gone. Do you know why?"

"We have something to fight for."

She nodded. "We do. That day in Myrkur, you did not let fear control you, and you bested me because of it. The only way we will beat Egan is if we do not fear him."

Griffin wrapped an arm around her waist and pulled her closer. Riona had never before considered love as something she sought. But this fae... he changed that too.

Riona wrapped a blanket around her shoulders as she stared out on the back deck where Griffin watched the moon overhead, his shoulders hunched forward. Beside him lay a book he'd taken from Aghadoon to study while they were here. He'd been using his magic to light the pages, but now he looked deep in thought.

Tomorrow they'd return to Aghadoon for another neverending round of reading in the library until no one could make out another word and waiting to come back to the human realm.

It was all they had.

And it wasn't enough.

Riona walked into the bedroom and lifted Griffin's bag onto the bed. She knew he still held out a small hope that Hector was alive somewhere and would contact them. He blamed himself for his death, claiming he should have been the one to go after Egan. It was his mother helping him after all.

That had led to one of the more epic arguments between Griffin and Lochlan—who held more blame for their mother's actions, a mother neither of them knew. Both of them were way too self-sacrificing for their own good.

She dug through Griffin's bag until she found the book only

he cared about now, needing to see what it was he wrote in it every day.

Flipping the cover open, she thumbed through the pages, watching his desperation play out. He wrote to Hector, begging him to answer, to let him know if any were alive. There was no information regarding troop movements or plans, nothing about burning spells in the library.

Griffin was too smart for that. An idea struck her, one that probably wouldn't matter. If Egan found the Slyph, he probably had the book now. Was he too smart for them to deceive him? Wanting to test her theory, Riona reached into the bag for the quill.

Her hand bumped against a worn leather scroll, tied with a fraying silk cord. Glancing toward the door to make sure Griffin wasn't there, she untied it and rolled it flat. It looked old, older than anything they'd seen thus far. Instead of parchment, leather held the words she realized belonged to a spell. A complicated one. She couldn't read much Fargelsian, but she recognized the language. Why did Griffin have an ancient spell from the library hidden away with him in the human realm?

So many questions rolled through her mind, questions she wasn't sure she wanted answers to. If he'd kept it with him, it had to be important, something he wanted to protect.

The back door slammed, and Riona jumped, shoving the journal back into the bag and putting it on the floor. The scroll, however... if it was something that could help them, she had to know.

Gathering her strength, she sucked in a breath and marched from the room, ready to confront whatever this was.

"Hey." Griffin had his head in the strange ice box when she approached. "So, there are what Brea calls frozen burritos. They're not awful if we want them for dinner. I can heat them again with my magic." Brea refused to let him touch the new microwave after the old one blew up when he'd tried to reheat leftovers in a metal pan two weeks ago and almost set the house on fire.

When Riona didn't respond, he shut the ice box and turned to her, his eyes going to the scroll in her hand. His mouth opened, but he didn't say anything.

Riona stepped forward, letting only the kitchen island separate them. "Why do you have a scroll from the library with you here? The books, I can understand for studying purposes, but a single spell? Why this one?"

It seemed like such a simple question.

He placed a hand on the countertop, his fingers curling in. "That's none—"

"If you finish with 'of my business,' I know what that human phrase means. It means you're hiding something. Griffin, we are in the human realm that has been dark for weeks, and it's still spreading. We can't find the breach or why it didn't close when we tried. Nothing we do works. This is not the time to keep spells hidden. What could possibly be so personal from that library that the rest of us don't need to see it?"

Griffin leaned against the counter. "I don't owe you an explanation."

"You know what? You're a coward. The only reason you'd keep that spell from us is if it scared you."

"It's the marriage magic," he burst out, stealing the breath from Riona's lungs. "The scroll... it's the origin magic that every marriage bond in the three kingdoms stems from."

Riona stepped back, taking a moment to let this information filter through her mind. The marriage magic... if it really came from a Fargelsian scroll, it could be destroyed just like all the others. "And you couldn't let her go?" It was the only explanation.

For months, Riona told herself Griffin didn't love Brea, but they were connected, and that meant something.

Something more than she'd ever mean to him.

Neither of them spoke for a long moment. "Have you told her what you found?"

He shook his head. It was the answer she'd expected.

"You don't understand, Riona," he pleaded. "The bond... do you think I like being connected to my brother's wife? That I like flashes of long past memories invading every thought when she's near? And yet, most of the time it's awful, but it's also a connection like something you could never imagine. The minute it returned to me, I knew I wasn't alone in this world. There's power in that. As long as I have the marriage bond, I'll never again have nothing."

"Have nothing?" Her voice was low. "Nothing? Gulliver isn't anything? Shauna, Nessa, Hector? Griffin, you were never alone in Myrkur. Their love for you wasn't tied to some piece of magic. That isn't how love should work. It shouldn't be a compulsion. There has to be choice, it has to be allowed to grow out of nothing instead of just appearing. Or else, what value does it have?"

Griffin stared at her with glassy eyes. "How would you know? You and I both grew up with false love, false belonging. Neither of us knows how to love, let alone be in love."

"That's what you think? Griffin, I hated you. But even when I hated you, there was something more. I saw the way you protected Gullie, the way you risk everything time and again for kids who will never call you father. And your brother... even Brea. I don't think all your affection for her is the magic. I envied them all, because even when I hated you, Griff, I still fell in love with you."

She stepped around the corner, wanting him to see what she'd learned in her time around him and his two families. "You don't have to learn to love, just like you don't need magic tying you to someone to keep you from being lonely. Regan and Egan never loved us like parents should." Her steps stopped in front of him. "But we are different than them. Because we choose to be. You taught me that."

"I… Riona." There was so much desperation in his voice.

Riona set the scroll on the counter because it didn't matter anymore. There would be more discussions to come once they showed it to Brea. But right now, Riona just wanted to prove to Griffin, to herself, that they could have this. Despite all their trials, everything they'd done and said to each other, they could hold on to some kind of hope in the darkness. Hold on to each other.

The thought was so unlike her, but she was tired of never taking what she truly wanted.

"I love you." They seemed such simple words, and it wasn't the first time she'd told him. But there was a difference between declarations in a battle and standing in front of each other laying themselves bare.

Reaching up, Riona trailed a hand over the curve of his neck and repeated herself. "I love you. I'm not saying it because we might die, not this time." She pulled him down, and when their lips met, his sigh gave her life.

"I love you," she whispered against his lips.

There was a time he was the wise one, giving pep talks and making her question her loyalties. Now, she had to be the strong one for him. Give and take, that was what love meant.

Griffin's kiss turned more forceful, and he picked her up, setting her on the counter. Her wings stretched out behind her, the pleasure tingling all the way to the tips as Griffin's lips trailed to her ear. "You're right." His breath warmed her skin. "I don't need the magic."

His hands dipped under the loose t-shirt she'd borrowed

from Brea's room, his fingers sliding along her rib cage. It had been so long since they had any privacy, and Riona needed more. She needed Griffin to prove to her his hesitation about destroying the marriage magic had nothing to do with her.

She slipped her shirt over her head as he pulled his off, revealing strong muscles shining in the moonlight. Only a tiny bulb illuminated the kitchen, casting them mostly in the darkness they knew so well.

Needing to touch him, she leaned forward, kissing a line across his shoulders, wishing they could stay this way forever.

Griffin lifted her up to slide her pants down her legs, and it was just the two of them with nothing separating their bodies, their souls.

Riona's wings splayed out, the white and black plumes stretching as far as the tendons could go as she cried out.

"I love you too," Griffin whispered as they collapsed against each other.

Riona trailed a finger down Griffin's chest. The air felt like early morning, meaning they'd slept through the night after eating dinner sans clothes in the kitchen. He was beautiful when he slept, when the lines of worry eased from his face.

One day, she hoped their days could be filled with as much peace as their nights.

But today would be another day of fruitless searching before returning to Aghadoon.

"Mmm." Griffin's lips curved into a smile. "I like waking up to you."

Riona couldn't believe moments like these existed in either

world right now. Moments of being content, despite everything happening around them.

"I had an idea yesterday before you distracted me." She didn't want to think of the marriage magic that had been the cause of her distraction.

Griffin's eyes slid open. "It involves getting out of this bed, doesn't it?" He sighed as his hand gripped the curve of her waist, the other massaging the joint where her wings met her back.

Riona tried not to give into the pleasure, but she couldn't help moaning.

"So, this idea?" Griffin smirked.

"Right." She pushed his hand away. "I noticed you still have the journal that can communicate with the other."

He nodded. "But it's useless. I've tried. Our spies are truly dead."

"Which means Egan probably has the book."

Griffin sat up, the sheet pooling at his waist. "He wouldn't get rid of something like that."

Riona pushed herself up and rested her chin on his shoulder. "Maybe we can use that to our advantage."

"I'm such an idiot."

"Well, I won't argue with that."

"I've been trying to communicate with Hector as if it's truly him. But if Egan has the journal—"

"—we can feed him information," she finished for him.

He turned to her, taking her face in his hands and planted a kiss on her lips. "Riona, you're a genius. We need to get back to the village." He jumped from the bed in all his naked glory and marched from the room.

"Might want to put on clothes, first," Riona yelled after him. "Don't want to scare the children!"

Chapter Seventeen

Griffin

Griffin's bloodshot eyes ran across the page in front of him, the ancient Fargelsian words and letters a jumble of nonsense.

"Drink this, it'll help." Brea poured him a steaming cup of Eldur brew. The stuff she claimed was the fae equivalent of human coffee. It was the one human vice she refused to give up. "This is the good stuff too. Straight from the human realm."

"Not Eldur brew?" He peered into the mug with slightly less contempt.

"Of course not, I wouldn't dare serve a royal fae such a common drink." Her sarcasm dripped like venom from her smart mouth.

"And here I thought you liked me better than you did when we were married." His tone was teasing, but his words reminded them of the bond they still shared. The bond that made everything awkward between them. He glanced at his bag where the scroll sat hidden from her. It was time they had that discussion. "Brea, I—"

"You drink it with cream and sugar, and it'll perk you right up." Brea mixed the dark brew until it was the color of sweet toffee. He had to admit it smelled much more appealing this way. Taking a tentative sip, he refused to admit how it warmed him from the inside out and revitalized him with its potent jolt of caffeine. Not that he knew what that was, only that Brea had constantly whined about needing caffeine in the mornings.

With a sigh, Griffin kicked his bag under the table, vowing to find the right moment later. And soon.

The words on the page began to make more sense as he read through the complex spells for growing buildings and structures from the ground using nature as the source for the power to fuel the spell. It was really fascinating to learn just how complex Fargelsi magic was. His Iskalt magic came to him intuitively. He'd had to study growing up, and practiced for years and years before he mastered his natural abilities, but he'd never had to work as hard as those with Gelsi magic did.

He mustered up his courage again. "I need to tell you—"

"We have a problem." Neeve came to sit with them. Blowing her dark hair from her face, she gave a big sigh. Griffin hated how relieved he felt at the interruption. "At least I think it's a problem. That or I truly need to rest and possibly see a healer."

"Care to tell us what you're rambling about, sister?" Brea sipped her coffee looking more refreshed than either Griffin or Neeve.

"Come with me." Neeve stood, guiding them through the stacks to the desk she and Myles were using toward the back of the library.

"What's going on?" Griffin asked, watching the way Myles stared at a stack of books like he thought they might disappear.

"We cleared out a whole shelf of books on primary Eldurian magic this morning. We were going to ask Brea to give it a quick look before we moved on. Myles has been shifting the books and scrolls around, creating a system to set aside those books we've reviewed and deemed safe."

Brea nodded. "So, what's the problem?"

"This." Myles stood and turned her around to face a bookshelf bursting with leather-bound tomes.

"Use more words, Myles. I'm too tired to guess what you're trying to tell me." Brea frowned.

"That's the shelf we cleaned off this morning," Neeve said.

"The one with all the kid's books on Eldur magic," Myles added. "It's full again."

"So just move these books back to wherever you found them."

"We didn't move them here." Neeve sighed. "The library did."

"What now?" Griffin turned to her, confused.

"Come again?" Brea echoed his confusion.

"I think our little pea brains have made some rather dumb assumptions." Myles scratched his head.

"Like?"

"Like this rather smallish library houses everything in a pretty substantial collection of knowledge... at first glance. But I think what we've got here is your basic Room of Requirement situation."

"Oh." Brea's eyes widened. "Oh my." She looked around the room, seeing more than Griffin saw.

"Explain using more fae words." Griffin rolled his eyes.

"If we took all the books off the shelves and moved them outside, the shelves would just fill up again. Not everything housed here is altogether ... visible."

Neeve sank back down to her chair. "Which means we've barely put a dent in this search for dark magic."

"So you're saying this is going to take longer to accomplish."

Neeve nodded. "Once we figure out how to get the library to show us everything on record here."

"Guys, we can't keep this up." Brea rubbed a tired hand over her eyes. "What we are doing here is important work, but we have to move on. We're in the middle of a war, and Egan is getting stronger every day we let him live."

"I think you're right. Father can spearhead this project," Neeve said. "He's the most knowledgeable fae we could ask for in terms of researching what magic is catalogued here."

"It's time we make a big move." Griffin set down the book he'd spent the morning reviewing. "Let's get everyone here."

"It's clear we need to move against Egan." Lochlan stood at the head of the rough plank table in the library. "But we need our army to do that, and most of them are still in Eldur helping Alona deal with the remaining Dark Fae roaming around Raudur City."

"We can't wait the weeks it will take for them to arrive." Brea twisted her hands in her lap. "By then it could be too late."

"We will have to ask Toby to create a portal large enough to bring at least a small force of soldiers ready for battle."

"I don't like it, Loch. He's just a baby, and he's just getting back to his normal self after being sick for so long from the way Egan abused his portal magic. We're his parents, we should do better by him."

"He is not a baby, Brea. No matter how much you might like him to stay one, our boy is growing up. He killed an ogre all by himself. I don't like it either, but what choice do we have?"

"Um, we could use this rather fancy party bus we're sitting

in and go pick up an army and bring them back." Myles looked at them both like they were rather dim.

"You mean the village?" Brea smiled.

"That's a rather smart idea." Griffin shot Myles a patronizing smile.

"I've been known to have them from time to time," Myles muttered.

"But the village is so full," Neeve said. "We'll have to move the children into the Gelsi palace as well as the injured and anyone not needed for battle. Myles and I could watch over them with Father's help. We'll keep the young royals safe. That is, if you can do without me in the coming battles with Egan? We aren't the most useful leaders in a fight, and my soldiers will follow Lochlan."

"You have done enough, sister." Brea reached for her hand. "We all need to face the fact that Eldur and Fargelsi need to stay strong while the rest of us deal with this threat. Lochlan's regent is strong enough to hold Iskalt should we fail. Should that happen, it's more important than ever for the realms to stay united."

"You will not fail," Myles said. "You two don't have it in you."

"Then it's decided," Lochlan said. "We will empty out the village and then move Aghadoon to Raudur City. It will be a good time for us to check on Alona and Faolan. And Finn," he added uncertainly. His best friend still had not recovered from his battle wounds. Griffin feared he might never recover and wondered what that would do to Lochlan. Finn was the brother Griffin never had a chance to be. Like Hector was to Griffin. The pang of loss struck him, but there'd be time to mourn fallen friends. Right now, he had to focus on the task ahead.

"From there we will fill Aghadoon to bursting with strong soldiers ready for battle and we'll move to Myrkur near Egan's palace. None who are our enemies will be able to see the village."

"And once we are there, we will seek out Egan and make our move against him," Griffin said. "His days are numbered." He'd pay for Hector's death and every other dark deed.

"Don't argue with me, Gullie. You're not going. Not this time." Griffin crossed his arms over his chest and stood his ground against the persuasive Gulliver.

"But Griff, you know I can be useful." Gulliver's tail thumped irritably against the wooden floorboards of their room. Getting Gulliver packed and to the palace had proven to be an undertaking. The kid did not want to go, and Griffin couldn't blame him.

"Know and should are two different things. I know you're more than capable of helping us fight this war, but you are only twelve years old—"

"Thirteen." Gulliver's tail wilted to a lifeless coil behind him. "My name day was weeks ago."

Griffin felt like the worst father in the world. He'd forgotten his name day. He'd given Gulliver his gift months ago, right before their world turned upside down. He'd seen Gulliver using the carving kit whenever he had free time. But he should have recognized his name day.

"I should have remembered." His shoulders drooped as lifeless as Gulliver's tail.

"We were kind of busy, Griff. Truth be told, I forgot it too until it was over."

"We were kind of busy." Griffin smiled, draping his arm over his son's shoulders. He would be a man before Griffin could blink. "You've been right by my side through all of this Gulliver." He leaned down to look him in the eye. "But I need to know you and the others are safe. Go with Tia and Toby to the palace and help Myles and Neeve."

"I'm a lot more useful in battle, and you know it."

"You're not going anywhere near Egan and his men." Riona marched into the room, giving them both a glare. "And that is final."

Gulliver opened his mouth like he was about to argue.

"Final." Riona glowered. "Egan is a desperate man, and desperate men do desperate things. He's used you against Griffin in the past, and I will not let that happen again. Do you hear me?"

Gulliver's tail coiled around his leg, and he dropped his head. "Yes ma'am." Grabbing his bag, he tossed it over his shoulder and shuffled toward the door.

"Hey, where's my goodbye?" Griffin pulled him back by the scruff of his shirt.

Gulliver grinned and threw his arms around Griffin's waist. The kid couldn't stay mad at him for long.

"Do try to behave yourself while we're gone."

"Don't I always?" Gulliver blinked up at him.

"You do not want me to answer that. Just don't steal the crown jewels while you're a guest in Neeve's palace."

"I swear, I will only steal food."

"You know." Griffin pulled Gulliver against his side. "They'd probably just give you whatever you want if you'd go to the kitchens and ask for food."

"It's more fun to steal it. It tastes better."

"Take care of yourself." Riona pulled him into a hug.

"Love you guys." Gulliver squirmed out of her arms. He leaned back in to whisper in Riona's ear. "Take care of Griff for me."

"You got it." Riona winked.

"I heard that." Griffin scowled at them both.

"Later gators." Gulliver tipped his hat onto his head and made his way to the center of the village to meet the other kids traveling to the palace this afternoon.

"You're the mean one, you know." Griffin moved to put his arm around Riona. "I'm the nice one."

"That's why the kid never listens to you."

"We have a system."

"Whatever, he likes me better." Riona elbowed him playfully.

"Does not. I'm his favorite. He just thinks you're pretty."

Riona smiled and took his hand, leading him to the small table in the corner of their room. "I have an idea."

Griffin pulled up a chair to sit beside her as she shuffled through her bag for the spelled journal. "We talked about using the journal to manipulate Egan. Feed him some false information. Now that we have a plan in place, I think we should test it."

"What did you have in mind?" Griffin folded his arms against the table and leaned closer.

"The message needs to be subtle at first. Similar to the messages you've written to Hector previously. But we make it look like a careless slip of too much information. A tip we didn't realize we'd given."

"Enough to get Egan to respond, hoping for more." Griffin nodded.

"Exactly." Riona handed him the quill.

Griffin stared at the blank page, letting his eyes drift over his previous messages before he began to write.

Hector,

It has been some time since we've received word from you and your team. Should you be in need of assistance, please respond. We are nearly in position to aid you if you can let us know where in Myrkur you're being held.

Griff.

Griffin leaned back, hoping the hint that they would soon be within striking distance of Myrkur would spurn Egan to respond. They waited not so patiently until it was clear he would not be responding so soon.

"It's nearly time." Griffin sighed.

"I think I prefer portaling." Riona winced. She didn't like the disturbing sensation of an entire village moving of its own accord.

"It's definitely not my favorite way to travel." Griffin took her hand and left for the town center. After weeks of living on top of each other in the confines of Aghadoon, the village was eerily quiet without the children and their families.

"Feels huge now with just the four of us here, doesn't it?" Brea asked as they joined her and Lochlan on the green lawn surrounded by the ancient numbered stones.

Brea spoke the words of power that set the stones in motion. The village turned in a slow circle, gaining speed as Brea finished the traveling spell that would transport Aghadoon to Eldur. A thick fog crept across the village as they disappeared from the rolling green hills of Fargelsi.

"Yeah, I'd definitely rather portal." Riona clenched Griffin's hand, her wings spreading to wind around them. As the spinning village came to an abrupt stop, Griffin smiled down at her from the cocoon of her silken wings.

"You freaked out," he teased.

"That was a freaky thing we just did." She let her wings slip from his shoulders with a shrug.

"We are so not in Kansas anymore," Brea said.

As long as he lived, he would never understand that woman.

As the fog cleared from Aghadoon, the vast night sky stretched across the Eldur deserts. They would leave for the palace in the morning to meet with Alona and catch her up to speed with their plans. But for the evening, they would do what they had done every night since leaving Eldur. Study.

"If I never see another book on Fargelsi magic, it will be too soon." Lochlan slammed his book closed and leaned back in his chair. "The spells are a nightmare, I don't know how any of you actually learn to perform your magic."

"It's tedious work." Brea nodded. "But it's fascinating." She hummed as she kept her nose stuck in a book on the complexities of spell work involving herbology. "I never knew there were so many poisonous plants in Fargelsi. Everything there really is trying to kill you." She turned the page.

Lochlan shared a bored look with Griffin. If he knew his brother at all—and he was getting to know him quite well—Lochlan was ready for a chance to fight. Anything to bring them out of the mind numbing task they'd been at for months now. Griffin was of the same mind.

"This is interesting." Riona paced back to the table with a weathered scroll trailing behind her. "It's about the book of power."

"So you're saying you've found a book about a book?" Lochlan leaned his head against the table.

"It seems to explain the nature of the book and how it works as a key to the library. Neeve was right, the contents of the library are vast." Her eyes scanned the faded script, and her breath hitched.

"What is it?" Griffin pressed a hand against her back as she sank into the seat beside him.

"For the book to function properly, it must have a keeper. A fae tasked with tracking the movement of the book. This keeper is responsible for what the book chooses to show those who come in contact with it." Riona lowered the scroll to the table looking to Brea for confirmation. "Like some sort of ... filter."

"Grainne must have been the last keeper," Brea mused. "I wonder ... do you think she and her descendants created this village to ... take over the role of keeper? So a single fae keeper couldn't become corrupted by the power of the book?"

"If she was the last, then Mother has surely taken on that role now." Griffin ran his thumb across the spine of the book he'd been studying.

"Which would make her responsible for the tear in the veil." Lochlan's jaw grew rigid with tension. "She's responsible for Tia and Toby's suffering. All of it." He pushed back from the table. "I need some air." He stormed out of the room, his footsteps thudded across the cobblestones leading away from the library.

"I'll go check on him." Brea rose from her seat.

"Let me." Griffin moved to follow his brother.

Griffin found Lochlan sitting on one of the ancient stones in the town center, his elbows resting on his knees as the moonlight illuminated his blond hair that was so like their mother's. In many ways his older brother was a lot like their mother. Stoic and firm. But he had a nobility that came from their father. A strength of character Griffin completely lacked.

Griffin sat on the ground beside the stone.

"Do you remember her?" Lochlan asked.

"Not really." Griffin pulled his knees up toward his chest. "I have vague ... feelings of her. But no clear memories."

"I don't have a single memory of her." Lochlan's gaze drifted toward his. "Not one."

"We were both terribly young when they died."

"I remember Father." Lochlan shook his head. "I remember so much of him. Yet, I can't recall anything about the woman who gave us life." He leaned back, lifting his face to the moon. "This whole time I've been trying so hard to see the good in her. Father was a great man. A respected king. He would not marry a woman without honor. At least that's what I told myself."

"I have struggled with similar thoughts. Unable to decide which side she's on or if she can be trusted at all." Griffin turned toward his brother, hoping to find the right words to comfort him.

"I am afraid Enis is on Enis' side," Lochlan scoffed.

"The book has been her life for so long—"

"Don't make excuses for her, brother. She could have come home when we were young. She and Father took Brea to the human world when she was a baby. After Father died, she was trapped in the human realm. But Enis knew where Brea lived. She knew one of us would be watching over her. She knew one or both of us would come for her when the time was right. She could have found us."

"She didn't want to, Loch. It's as simple as that. She gave us up for the power of the book. I know that hurts. It cuts deep. But the fact is, we were both raised by loving mothers that were nothing like Enis. As unhinged as Regan proved to be, she was still there when Enis was not. She loved me as much as if she'd given birth to me. As much as Faolan and Tierney loved you and Alona."

"Aye, they loved me well." Lochlan looked down at his hands.

"Perhaps the O'Shea brothers are destined to choose their own family?" Griffin said softly. "Blood has never mattered to us."

Lochlan nodded, laying a hand on Griffin's shoulder. "Maybe it's never mattered before, but you and I are brothers through blood and by choice."

"It took us long enough to get here." Griffin snorted a laugh.

"Thirty years too late is better than never, I suppose." Lochlan grinned.

"It's getting late, maybe we should call it a night. I do have a rather pretty Dark Fae waiting for me. And I'm sure Brea is twisting herself up into knots wondering if you're okay."

"Riona is good for you, brother."

"I don't think you approved of her much in the beginning." Griffin and Lochlan trudged through the dark streets back to the temporary home they shared with Riona and Brea.

"I did not trust her."

"What changed your mind?"

"She took care of my son when I could not. For that, she will always have my loyalty and respect. And she has very good taste in fae. She had the good sense to choose my slightly less handsome brother." Lochlan clapped him on the back.

"You underestimate the red hair. The ladies–and the males–quite like it."

"I said slightly less." Lochlan shrugged. "That's the most you'll get out of me."

Griffin let them into the dark house with a laugh. "You are every inch the ice king they call you."

"Who calls me that?" Lochlan blanched.

"Everyone. Night, Loch." Griffin chuckled at the blank look on his brother's face.

Without the kids running amok, the house was quiet.

"Riona?" Griffin stepped into the room they normally shared with Gulliver.

"Everything okay?" She turned to him from her seat at the table.

"We're good." Griffin nodded, not wanting to let himself think overmuch about what just passed between him and his brother, not when he was keeping the key to breaking the marriage magic a secret.

"Good, because we got a response." The spelled journal sat on the table in front of her. "But it's not who we thought it would be."

"Who's the response from?"

"Your mother."

CHAPTER EIGHTEEN

Griffin

Raudur city looked as if a battle had never taken place among the streets. The windows that were boarded up after Egan's arrival now stood open, letting the Eldurian people resume their lives once more. Shopkeepers sold their wares in the marketplaces across the city where the people congregated.

As Griffin followed Lochlan and Brea through the busy streets, he took everything in. It all seemed so... normal. Even the Dark Fae mingling with the Eldurians didn't look out of place.

It was mid-morning when they rode past an ogre standing guard at the palace gates. He stared down at them, his dark eyes finding Riona, recognition lighting in their depths. With a simple nod, he let them pass.

Eldurian, Iskaltian, and Dark Fae soldiers stood at intervals, guarding the royal family and all others inside the palace from dangers Griffin hated that they faced. The human queen had been left to fend off waves of stragglers from Myrkur, Light Fae prisoners—now released—and Dark Fae who didn't know how to live in peace.

And yet, the city thrived. Griffin didn't know what he'd expected. Egan had all but destroyed parts of the palace, but now it looked as it always had.

They reached the inner courtyard doors, and a familiar figure sprinted out, her pale pink dress bunched up in her hand to keep her from tripping. Griffin jumped from his horse to wrap his best friend in a hug. "Shauna." He squeezed her tighter. "You have no idea how good it is to see you."

Lochlan slid down and handed his reins to a groom who'd come running when they entered the courtyard. "I'm going to find Finn." He marched inside without another word.

Shauna slid her arm through Griffin's. "He's friendly, that one, isn't he?"

"Takes some warming up to." He laughed.

Brea joined them, turning a hopeful smile on Shauna. "My mother... is she—"

"She's well, Majesty." Shauna grinned. "And she awaits your arrival with your sister in the gardens."

Brea gripped her arm. "Shauna, thank you. For taking care of them." Griffin knew who she meant. It was the reason Shauna stayed in Eldur. To care for Faolan and Finn.

"Oh, it was a simple thing, your Majesty."

"Stop calling her that," Griffin hissed, jabbing her with his elbow playfully.

"Don't embarrass me in front of the queen," she hissed back before turning her attention back to Brea and dipping into a curtsy. "Your mother has been telling me stories about you, your Majesty."

Brea laughed at that. "You mean she's been filling your head about the great Brea Robinson." She held out a hand, urging

Shauna to take it. "Come. We aren't strangers just because you now know my story, Shauna. On the way to the gardens you can tell me what lies my mother has filled your head with. And my name is Brea. I'm not really a queen, you know. I just married a king."

Shauna's eyes widened as she stepped away from Griffin and took Brea's hand before walking into the palace.

Griffin shook his head, wondering if it was wrong to smile when everything else was so dour. Maybe it was the only thing that was right. "And Brea steals another heart." She and Shauna had met briefly a few times, but Griffin hadn't seen them speak to each other directly before. Brea was a warm figure, one who was easy to love. And Shauna took to people easily, wanting, needing to trust them.

Riona lifted one brow and followed the other women. Griffin brought up the rear. He'd never spent much time in Eldur, always begging Regan to send others on missions to the kingdom his brother had grown up in.

Now, he saw it with new eyes. It was beautiful in its own way. Too hot and too crowded. But there was a kindness in the way servants met their eyes as they passed, offering smiles and nods, a warmth in the way the palace was designed to feel like one was almost outdoors. Archways lined the halls leading into various courtyards where fountains sat to be admired and gardens to be enjoyed.

But there was no time to enjoy Eldur. They had to be gone by nightfall. There was a purpose in their arrival here, a dark purpose.

Shauna led them to the tiered gardens where hanging vines wound up the archways leading to beauty that could only be found among the oasis cities of Eldur.

Alona saw them first, jumping from her seat. "Brea." She rushed forward to give her sister a hug. "We didn't know you were coming until we saw the village arrive last night. I will never get used to that." She pulled back.

Brea gave her a sad smile. "I'm afraid we can't stay long." She crossed the garden to hug her mother.

Griffin watched as Shauna took a seat next to Faolan and the two shared a smile. No. That couldn't be right. He hid his gasp behind a cough and thumped his chest. Ten years ago, he'd seen Faolan's wife die in the battle against Regan. Since then, she'd lived in the palace she once ruled, though she abdicated the throne for Alona.

"Ignore Griffin." Brea shot him a look. "He seems to have forgotten how to breathe."

"Would you like tea?" Alona waved to a tea cart at the edge of the garden with a queenly flick of her hand. Of all the fae queens, the human was the only one who'd been bred as royalty, and it showed. There was a stiffness to her the others didn't possess.

Only her husband softened that in her.

"Brea." Faolan smiled. "There's also Eldur brew."

Brea pumped her fist and ran toward the cart while Riona stepped to the edge of the gardens, peering out over the city.

Griffin sat on a stone bench across from the two Eldurian queens. "We have a lot to tell you. And none of it is good."

It took longer than Griffin wished to explain everything that had happened with Alona's frequent questions interrupting him, and even longer to tell of their plan.

She leaned forward. "So, your plan is really that you have no plan?"

He bristled at that. "That is not a fair assessment. We are going to Myrkur."

"With soldiers. And once you get there, you will find this rift... somehow. Then you will seek out King Egan by doing... something."

"My mother." Lochlan's voice shocked them all as he stepped out into the gardens. "Enis will tell us what to do."

"And you trust her?" Alona gave him a skeptical look.

"We have no other choice." His face softened. "Finn is asking for you."

Alona shot to her feet. "He's awake?"

Griffin leaned against the door to Finn's room, wondering if he should be here. They'd moved Finn from the healer's ward so he could rest in his own bed. Alona and Lochlan wouldn't leave his side. His father, a member of Alona's guard, came by, speaking in low tones with Faolan.

As Lochlan sat on the edge of the bed laughing with his friend, Griffin waited for the jealousy to come. He'd spent his life watching them at dual state functions act as brothers in a way Griffin never got to. Envy was a normal feeling for him.

But now, it didn't come. Instead, he only felt an immense relief his brother didn't lose someone who meant so much to him.

Riona and Brea had left to gather a unit of soldiers to bring them into the village. Griffin tried to go with them, but Alona had more to speak with him about.

She crossed the room to stand at his side and folded her arms across her chest. "You told me my children are in Fargelsi with Neeve, and I trust her with their lives, but I need you to tell me they're okay. That I will get them back when Eldur is safe."

Despite her skepticism of him, Alona was not only a queen, but a worried mother, and he had to remember that. "They're smart kids. It's hard on all of us, you know. I left my son in Fargelsi. Brea's four children are there as well. It is the safest place for them with Neeve and all of Fargelsi protecting them. I know you think we are trusting the wrong person in Enis, and I'm as skeptical of her as anyone, but we can no longer just sort through a library we'll never get through to prevent Egan from doing evil. We have to stop him."

"I know. We will not be safe until he is gone."

"I don't make promises about children anymore." He pushed away from the doorframe. "But I can say we won't stop fighting Egan until every last one of us is dead. Because we are fighting for your children, and for mine and Lochlan's, and every other fae child."

A small smile curved her lips. "You're not such a bad fae, Griffin."

"We are who we choose to be." It was a lesson he'd had to learn the hard way—by making the wrong choices.

Alona returned to Finn as Lochlan walked toward the door. Faolan stepped in front of him, and Griffin couldn't help watching them, imagining if things had been different, if a better version of Regan could stand in front of him now.

Faolan reached down to take both his hands. "I just need to say this, Loch. Enis O'Shea was once my best friend. She gave birth to you and saved Brea. I never imagined she was still alive or that she'd get mixed up in such a mess. But Lochlan, whatever that woman does to you, she is not your mother. She cannot break your heart because she does not belong in there. Do you hear me? *I* am your mother."

Griffin didn't like to see his brother so vulnerable. As Lochlan let Faolan wrap him in a hug, he turned away, needing to escape the palace before everything became too much. There was too much emotion that sounded like goodbye.

And he refused to say any goodbyes.

Marching through the halls, he burst out into the courtyard, not bothering to call for a groom as he started up the road to the stables. It was time for him to be a soldier, to prepare for the next step in this war.

He led his horse from one of the stalls and saddled him quickly before pulling himself up and thundering down the road and across the bridge into the desert sands and the village that would take them to the final battle.

Faolan's words to Lochlan ran through Griffin's mind. *I am your mother.*

She was right. Enis didn't deserve to be trusted just because she gave birth to two Iskalt princes.

Griffin held the quill hovering over the journal. It was strange knowing his mother was on the other side of these messages now, talking to him more than she ever had.

But he needed to know he could believe her when she said it was time to get the book away from Egan. If she truly was this keeper of the book, she only wanted it safe.

And she'd have to prove it.

Enis, I need to know everything you tell me is the truth. How will I know you won't betray us to Egan again?

He waited a long moment, staring at his own words before closing the book and setting it aside. She'd respond when she saw the message.

A crash sounded from the room next to his, but he was supposed to be the only one in the house. Taking silent steps, he retrieved a knife from the table near the door and walked from his room. Rounding the corner, he prepared to fight an intruder. It was probably a Dark Fae who'd found their way into the village by tricking it with their intentions. When they'd altered that magic, they all knew it was a risk.

The door stood ajar, and Griffin pushed it open slowly before bursting into the room, his knife raised. He froze when three familiar and terrified faces looked back at him.

"Oh, it's just Griff." Gulliver relaxed and flashed his ornery smile at Tia and Toby. "It's okay."

Griffin lowered the knife slowly, anger burning in him at his son. "What are you doing here?" he grit out.

Gulliver backed up. "Okay, I know you're mad, but Griff, there's a good reason. I promise."

Setting the knife down, Griffin crossed his arms. "Speak, boy."

"Well." Griffin shot Tia a helpless look. "We... uh... we wanted to stay."

That was his good reason?

Tia jumped in. "He means you need us."

"Oh, we do, do we?"

She nodded, her hair bouncing around her shoulders. "You're going into Myrkur, and after everything, you can't tell us we're too young for this."

"Don't tell me Nessa is hiding somewhere here too." He searched the room.

"Oh, no." Gulliver rolled his eyes. "She's *such* a rule follower."

"Well, at least one of you has sense." He rubbed a hand over his face. "Brea and Lochlan are going to—"

"Freak?" Gulliver smiled proudly at his human phrase. "We know. Sooo..."

"You could just not tell them," Toby finished.

"You too?" Griffin sent him a look of betrayal. "I figured these two dragged you into this."

"No way." Gulliver gave Griffin a stern look. "I'm a good boy. This was all Toby's idea."

Toby snorted-laughed, but Tia ignored them both, stepping in front of Griffin.

"What if we're right?" She looked up at him with pleading eyes. "Hasn't everyone kept saying we'll do what it takes? What if it takes me and Toby?"

"And me," Gulliver piped in.

Tia continued. "We brought the prison magic down. Please, Uncle Griff, let us finish the job. This is our world too, and we don't want to keep having to fight. Maybe if we're there, it can be the last time. For all of us."

Griffin sighed, unable to tell Tia she was wrong. When Lochlan told him he was making the twins stay in Fargelsi, something hadn't felt right about that. Maybe their magic would be needed, and he didn't want to fight anymore—just like her. "I have to tell your parents."

She shook her head, her eyes glassing over. "They'll take us to Fargelsi. Please, just keep this a secret a little while longer."

Brea would hate him for this. He thought about the marriage magic sitting in his room. She'd hate him for keeping a lot of things from her. But if it meant defeating Egan... he'd do whatever it took.

Gulliver gave him a triumphant smile the moment he recognized they'd won.

A knock at the door had the kids scrambling for cover. Except it wasn't their parents. Shauna pushed open the door, her brow arching as she caught sight of Gulliver's tail poking out from under the blanket he'd covered himself in.

Griffin joined her in the hall. "Shh, we aren't supposed to tell anyone they're there."

Shauna shrugged. "You'll have to give the kid a hug for me then. I just wanted to see you before you left."

His shoulders dropped as they stepped from the house to survey the activity of soldiers entering the village. "I was hoping you'd come with us." He eyed her, wondering if she'd admit what he suspected.

Her lips curved down. "I want to. For Hector. But I can't leave this place, Griff. I'm needed here. They lost a lot of their healers in the battle, and..." She pushed out a breath. "I can't leave her."

He wrapped an arm around her. "I know." His eyes found Riona directing a handful of soldiers. They planned to leave most of the Iskaltians who hadn't already returned to Iskalt in Eldur to continue keeping the roving bands of fae at bay and take most of the Dark Fae with them to Myrkur. "I would go where she is too."

Shauna leaned into him. "Be safe, yeah?"

"Always."

"This isn't goodbye."

"Definitely not." He kissed the side of her head, wondering how long it would be before he saw her again.

As Shauna turned to leave, Gulliver burst from the house. "Shauna!"

She turned to catch him in a hug. "Take care of our guy, Gullie."

"I will. I won't let anything happen to him in Myr."

She smiled and pressed her lips to the top of his head. "I know you won't."

They hugged for a moment longer before Shauna walked from the village. Griffin turned to Gulliver and swatted him toward the house. "Get inside before Brea sees you." He couldn't believe the words leaving his mouth, but he'd made his choice to keep their secret.

Gulliver skipped back to the room where the twins hid, and

Griffin returned to his own, flipping open the journal to find his mother's message.

You want good faith information?

Your fae inside Myrkur are alive. They gave this journal to me freely.

Hector. Could it be true? Griffin always figured Hector would have destroyed the journal before letting Egan get it again. But now... he was alive?

Griffin had to believe her. He scrawled his response across the page.

Okay, I'm listening.

She took little time to respond.

You cannot wait any longer if we are to save the human realm.

It is time.

Chapter Nineteen

Griffin

Rain soaked the village, welcoming the Dark Fae home to Myrkur. Griffin stood on the edge of the village, staring out at the sparse forest where trees struggled to keep their leaves. They weren't far from the rocky mountain passes leading to Kvek's stronghold he'd once broken into when he was injured.

When he'd thought he was going to die.

There were very few memories he had of Myrkur that were good, but a few hours ride from here was Fela where he'd become the person he was.

Somewhere in this harsh terrain was Hector, once again trying to survive under Egan's rule.

"This darkness feels familiar." Brea stepped up beside him. "There's a coldness to it, isn't there?" She had a hood pulled up over her dark hair, shielding her face from the drizzling rain.

"For a long time, it was all I knew." Brea and Lochlan experienced the darkness twice before, but they never had to live with it for a prolonged period. "But we cannot stay here long. A few days at most."

She nodded. They'd had this discussion many times. With Griffin and Lochlan having night magic, being in a fae realm where darkness was all they saw would exhaust them, maybe even kill them if they stayed too long. They'd seen it before.

"Is it day or night?" she asked, looking to the sky.

"It's early morning." Even with the rain, the air held a freshness in the mornings.

She nodded. "I've pictured the kind of place you lived, Griff, but I don't think I even imagined this." She gestured to the dark, barren land.

He had no energy for explaining the harshness of a life in Myrkur, so he turned away, eyeing the soldiers who went about their morning routines preparing for whatever was to come. The Dark Fae were used to the inky mornings.

"Have we heard from Enis today?" Brea asked.

Griffin sighed. His mother was supposed to send them the location of the rift. It seemed so simple, but she'd been silent for days. "No. But I'll keep checking."

She nodded. "So, there's a reason I came to find you before Lochlan woke."

He didn't like the sound of that. "And?"

She sucked in a breath. "So, this marriage bond. I've been thinking about it. It's something we haven't completely discussed between the three of us, well four with Riona. But I think we can live with it. I think we both know how much it'll hurt after this battle is over and we go our separate ways, so I have a proposal."

"Brea—"

"No, listen to me. The worst part last time was when we were too far apart. But we don't have to be. You and Riona can come to live in Iskalt. She can help any Dark Fae settle there who so choose, and you can join Lochlan's counsel where you belong."

"Brea—"

"Think about it, Griff. Both Iskalt royals back in the palace? The people would rejoice."

"I know how to break the magic."

Brea froze, her lips no longer moving.

A sigh rattled through Griffin. This was the moment she lost faith in him. Again. "Come with me."

Brea silently followed him back to the house. Lochlan slept still, and the kids didn't make any sounds. Riona had left in the middle of the night, telling Griffin she wanted to explore the village being rebuilt near the palace. She'd covered her tattoos, and her head, making her look like any other Slyph.

She knew what she was doing.

Unlike Griffin.

He led Brea into his room and retrieved the leather scroll from its hiding place. Handing it to Brea, he waited as she unrolled it, her eyes scanning the words. "Griff." She sounded more surprised than angry. "When did you find this?"

"A few weeks ago. I know I should have told you, but this magic... if we burned it and saved ourselves this pain, it doesn't only affect us. Every married couple in the kingdoms would lose their marriage bonds."

Tears gathered in the corners of her eyes. "We shouldn't have to make that choice."

He sat on the corner of the bed. "I've studied the scroll. Marriage magic once had a great purpose. It says it was created hundreds of years ago when fae couldn't perform magic on their own. They borrowed strength from others, and the bond made that easier. But the world has changed, fae and magic have evolved. Our powers have grown to immense levels, and we no longer need one another to use it."

Brea slumped onto the bed next to him. "It's like O'Rourke twin magic. Tia borrows power from Toby. Every fae used to do that?"

He nodded. "Twins were once the only fae who didn't need the marriage magic to... boost their natural abilities. Now, only O'Rourke royal twins do, and marriage magic has become an obsolete power, meant to hold people together for long fae lives. In the end... it strips us of our free will." He took her shaking hand in his. "You and I weren't meant to be together, yet the magic forced it on us. Loving someone should be a choice. Not once, but every single day. Magic can't take its place."

He knew that now, the difference between love and magic, his feelings for Brea and what he felt for Riona.

Brea swallowed a sob and leaned her head on his shoulder. "Every single day."

"Are you mad at me?"

She shook her head. "I can't say I know what I'd have done if I found it either. We all do the best we can, Griff. But I don't think it is only for us to decide what to do with it."

She was right. Of course she was. He looked down at her. "When this is over, once Egan can't torment us anymore, then we will make a decision."

"Griffin O'Shea!" Lochlan's voice echoed through the house.

Brea bolted up, and Griffin walked out into the hall to find Lochlan staring into the spare room where the three kids gave him sheepish smiles.

Now, this... this angered Brea. She rounded on him. "Why is Lochlan yelling at you?" There was an accusation in her voice. "Toby, did Uncle Griff know you were here?"

Gulliver groaned. "He already told Lochlan he had." He shot Toby a betrayed look.

Griffin wished he could disappear right then.

Lochlan and Brea both advanced on Griffin, their eyes holding a kind of anger he hadn't seen in them. He backed up until he hit the wall.

"Hey," Gulliver yelled. "It wasn't his fault."

"It's okay, Gullie." Griffin met his brother's eyes. "I made my choice."

"You let them come." Lochlan's eyes narrowed. "To Myrkur!"

"Actually, he didn't know we were here."

"Quiet, Tia," both her parents yelled.

"No." She stepped between them and Lochlan. "It's our fault. You leave Uncle Griff alone. We just want to help."

"You don't know what you're getting in to." Lochlan looked over her, not taking his eyes from his brother.

"I do. We all do. I've done more in this fight than you, Papa!" Her words echoed down the hall.

Some of Brea's anger dropped as she looked to her daughter and sighed. She wrapped an arm around Tia. "Let's let them talk."

"Mama, I deserve to be here."

"I know, honey." Brea sounded more tired than anything as she led the kids back into the room. "Now, tell me how you managed to keep yourselves hidden? That's impressive." She closed the door, leaving Lochlan and Griffin staring at each other.

Lochlan's jaw clenched. "You are not their father, Griffin."

"I know. Loch—"

"No, I need you to hear this. I don't care whose biological children they are. I have raised them since birth. I named them and held them when they hurt. I have feared for them every day of their lives because I love them so much it physically hurts. If anything happens to them—"

"I know. Loch, I know." He always had. It didn't matter who'd fathered them over ten years ago, only who'd been a father to them for ten years. "You have to believe me. I would *never* take that away from you. You, Brea, and the kids... that's *your* family. I'm their uncle and will never be anything more. But you also have to see how amazing they are. Tia and Toby could be the difference in this fight. They have been before. I've seen it."

"I don't want them to be the difference, I just want them to be my kids." He hung his head and moved to lean against the wall next to Griffin. "This wasn't your decision to make."

"I know."

"Then why did you make it?"

Griffin was quiet for a long moment. "Because I want them to grow up in the kind of world we never had."

"And what world is that?"

"One at peace. If they stay here, Loch, maybe they can get to be kids when this is over."

Lochlan leaned his head back. "Why do I always love the special ones?"

A laugh burst out of Griffin. Lochlan had fallen in love with Brea when she was destined to defeat Regan. "I am sorry, Loch. I should have told you they were here."

"I understand why you did it. I don't agree, but I understand." He pushed away from the wall. "I'm going to go be with my family." He gave Griffin one final look, nodded, and entered the room.

Griffin left the house behind, stepping out into the rain that had grown steadier as the day wore on. He walked toward the center of the village where their coordinates were burned into the stones. The human numbers transformed to ancient runes in the fae realm, but it still led them to their specific location.

Shaking wet hair out of his face, Griffin looked to the sky, ready for whatever came. He found a stone bench and sat down.

Movement caught his eye moments before someone sat beside him.

"You sure like to create trouble, Griffin." Gulliver nudged him. "You should try not to do that."

Griffin laughed. "Says the thief." He bumped Gulliver's shoulder.

"I'm sorry you can't be their father."

"You heard all that, did you?"

Gulliver nodded.

Griffin wiped rain out of his face. "Well, I'm not sorry. I still get to be your father."

He bit back a smile, water dripping from his lips. "True. Just stop fighting with Lochlan, please. It's kind of embarrassing for all of us."

Griffin wrapped an arm around Gulliver and pulled him close. "I'm embarrassing, huh?"

"Very much."

"Good." He smiled.

"You're very strange."

He only shook his head with a laugh. Through the rain, he caught sight of mostly dark wings and the fae they belonged to. Riona had returned, and it warmed him despite the rain to have her near.

She approached the bench and both of them stood to greet her. Griffin pulled her into a hug with him and Gulliver.

"What has gotten into you?" Riona groaned. "And how is Gullie here?"

"Old news, Riona. You know what's also old news? Griffin is acting odd." Gulliver agreed. "If you two are going to kiss now, I'm definitely leaving." He practically ran from them.

Griffin laughed, knowing this feeling of contentment

should wait until after they defeated Egan. But maybe it didn't have to. "I'm definitely going to kiss you."

The rain dampened the kiss, sliding his lips against hers. He'd wanted to prepare for whatever came here in Myrkur, and this was the best preparation there was.

Chapter Twenty

Riona

Riona and Griffin led the way along the rocky trail through the mountains far above Chieftain Kvek's fortress. Part of her worried they were walking into a trap. The other part of her genuinely hoped Enis would come through for her sons. They needed to know there was some spark of goodness within her.

She'd cared enough to help the children escape Eldur, perhaps she cared enough for her sons to help them defeat Egan.

"It's just up ahead." Griffin studied the map Enis had sketched in the journal for them.

The Iskaltians and other Light Fae trailing along behind them complained about the darkness, but to Riona, this was her natural habitat. She could make her way through these mountains in her sleep. As they crept along the narrow trail, they came to a ridge. A barren valley stretched out below them.

Wide and grassy, it would have seemed beautiful to her had she never witnessed the rolling green hills of Fargelsi.

"The rift lies at the north side of the valley." Griffin moved to pick their pathway down the steep ridge into the valley. Riona followed, moving between boulders and dry patches of dirt where nothing grew. Their friends trailed them, with the small force of soldiers they brought with them from Aghadoon.

"I think I can see it," Riona said, peering ahead of Griffin.

"Can you?" He gave her a skeptical look.

"No she's right. I can see it too." Gulliver squinted in the moonlight.

"I don't see anything."

"Well, we are Dark Fae, we can see better than you." She could just make out the faint edges of the tear. She couldn't see into the human world beyond, but she could almost feel the darkness seeping out of Myrkur through the narrow gap. "It's just there." She pointed with a shaky hand. "Can't you feel it? Evil magic has happened here." Riona and Gulliver grasped hands as if they could feel the taint of it. Riona had the sudden urge to leave the valley at once. "Do not leave my side." She pulled Gulliver closer.

"I don't feel or see anything." Lochlan pushed past her. "But if you do, that's good enough for us."

"I wonder if it's their defensive magic at work?" Brea moved forward, clutching Toby and Tia's hands. Riona knew their parents didn't want them here any more than she and Griffin wanted Gulliver here, but they had each played important roles in this war. It was fitting they get to witness the end of it.

"Let's get this done." Lochlan turned to direct the small army to surround them for protection should Enis betray them and show up with Egan and his dwindling forces.

"Can you handle this alone?" Griffin looked to Brea as she

approached the rift clutching a book from the library. It contained the spells she and Neeve had used in the human realm to try to seal the rift once before. They were hoping it would be more successful from this side of the rift, and now they were staring right at it.

"I can handle it." Brea nodded. "It was easier with Neeve's help, but I can manage it alone just as well."

"And I'll be here if you need me, Mama," Tia called from the sidelines where Lochlan stood guard over her and her brother.

"Good luck." Riona patted Brea on the shoulder and went with Gulliver to stand with the others.

Riona watched as Brea opened the book of spells and began muttering the ancient words that meant little to Riona. Griffin came to stand beside her, clutching Gulliver between them.

"I should fly up to the ridge and circle overhead to make sure we aren't taken by surprise."

Griffin grabbed her hand tight in his. "Please stay. We have sentries posted all across the valley."

Riona nodded, comforted by the thought he wanted her near.

Brea's Gelsi magic was different from her Eldur magic that glowed yellow whenever she embraced her power. When she used her Gelsi magic, it wasn't as flashy, but the massive effort and focus it took was so much more impressive.

"That's not gonna work, Mama," Tia yelled, causing Lochlan to shush her. "Well, it's not going to fix it," she muttered to herself. Having witnessed what Tia and Toby could do with their magic, Riona was inclined to agree with the kid.

"The darkness is shifting," Griffin said. "She's pulling it back through the rift." They watched in silence as Brea moved through page after page of complicated spell work. She reminded Riona of an adult version of Tia when she'd brought down the barrier surrounding Myrkur. If Brea was any indication of what her daughter would be like when she was grown, Tia would be a force of nature when she came into her full magic.

"It is done." Brea stumbled forward as she closed the book.

"It's gone." Gulliver looked up at Griffin. "I can't see it anymore, can you?" He turned to Riona.

"I don't see the tear either. It's sealed."

A cheer went up behind them as the news spread through the ranks of soldiers surrounding them.

"Lochlan, can you go check it?" Brea scowled up at the place where the rift was only a few moments ago. "Something doesn't feel right."

"Should we give it some time first?" Lochlan turned to his brother.

"We can portal to the farm once we get back to Aghadoon. I don't like being out in the open here."

"Agreed. Especially with the children and the eventuality of me and Griff growing weak without the sun to relieve us of magic for a time." Lochlan took Tia and Toby's hands, and they returned to the path they took to get here.

Riona looked over her shoulder, but she wasn't sure if what she saw was part of the rift or an afterimage of it. She agreed with Brea, something didn't feel right.

"The darkness is returning. Again." Griffin emerged from Lochlan's portal and dropped down beside Riona on the grassy lawn of the village center where she and Brea waited.

"So, it didn't work?" Brea's shoulders fell.

"No." Lochlan said as he followed his brother back from the human realm just moments after they'd left. "We will have to find another solution." He joined his family on the blanket Brea had set out for their evening picnic.

Griffin and Lochlan should have been gone for hours, waiting in the daylight of the human realm to return to the darkness of Myrkur once the moon rose. They arrived to discover it was already night in the middle of the afternoon, meaning the rift was still open.

"You didn't fix it right, Mama." Tia sat in the middle of the grassy lawn, making flowers grow up around her for the daisy chains she was making. She braided the long-stemmed flowers into crowns for Gulliver and Toby.

"I know, baby," Brea muttered absently. "Loch, I just don't think I can take another minute of searching in that library for a spell that might or might not work. It's exhausting."

"I second that." Griffin lay back in the cool grass, tugging at Tia's flower chains, trying not to laugh when she shot him a death glare just like her mother's.

"So where does that leave us?" Riona asked. She would be all too happy to never set foot in that library again, but they had to find a solution. Who knew what atrocities might happen to the humans if the rift was left open much longer.

"Why can't we just make a new one?" Tia said with a shrug.

"A new what?" Brea turned toward her daughter with a frown.

"A new spell. If the old one didn't work to close the tear in the veil, I should just make a new one instead of wasting so much time looking for some old spell that might not even work." Tia tied her chain of violets in a loop and placed it on Griffin's head. Then she went to work growing blue flowers for a new chain.

"No." Lochlan and Brea said in unison. "Absolutely not."

"Crafting new spells is dangerous, honey," Brea said. "Even the simplest spell can go wrong if you don't construct the words of power just so. For something as complex as this situation, it's impossible."

"No it's not, Mama." Tia glanced at Toby, sporting a crown of red poppies on his brow. "I know I could make a spell that would work."

"I don't know, maybe we should move the village back to Gelsi and brainstorm with Neeve and Dad. Between all of us, we have to find a solution that will work." Brea ignored her daughter, but Riona was beginning to think the girl might have the fresh perspective they needed. She was a child, but she was an inherently gifted one.

"We do need to move on soon. We can't take too much more of this endless night before it starts to affect our Iskalt magic." Lochlan scowled at his daughter when she stood to place a crown of blue irises on his head.

"That seems like an awful lot of moving around just to come right back here, Papa," Tia said, patting her father's long blond hair.

"Griff." Gulliver rolled his cat eyes at him. The orange marigolds on his head bobbed in the breeze.

"What?" Griffin stared blankly at him. But Gulliver just glared at him.

Finally Griffin sighed. "I think Gullie might have a point. We should listen to Tia's ideas."

"Griff, I don't want my daughter involved in this kind of dangerous magic. She's just a child." Brea was quick to put an end to such a discussion.

"And that decision falls to you and Lochlan." Griffin cast a worried look at Riona. She knew he was afraid of overstepping.

Well, Riona had no such hesitations. She'd never worried

about overstepping in her life, and she wasn't about to start now. "If I may, neither of you were there when Tia and Toby worked together to dismantle the prison magic keeping thousands in bondage."

"How dare you." Brea bristled like an angry cat. "Our children were taken from us."

Griffin sat up to move beside Riona. "I think Riona just means that we actually got to witness your children performing complex magic better than most adults could on their best day. Tia was in control the whole time. It was astounding."

"I meant no disrespect," Riona rushed to say. "Your children were nothing short of incredible. If I hadn't seen it with my own eyes, I wouldn't have thought it possible of any child. They are young and innocent, but they are gifted with strong intuition. Tia's knowledge of Fargelsian magic seems unparalleled. I just wonder if we should hear her out."

"Thank you, Auntie Riona." Tia placed a chain of silver rosebuds around her neck.

Riona looked down at the flowers Tia had grown for her and something swelled inside her. It was an unfamiliar feeling, this ... emotion for a child that wasn't hers to love.

"You don't like it? I didn't want to give you dark flowers, so I thought silver would match your pretty wings." Tia stroked the silvery gray part of Riona's wings where the black and white met.

"They're beautiful." Riona smiled, patting the blanket beside her. "Why don't you sit and tell me why you think you can just make a new spell."

"I make new spells all the time." Tia shrugged and sat down on Riona's lap, still braiding a chain of yellow daisies. "It's easy for me. Even the hard stuff. Mama and Papa think I'm being reckless, but I know what I'm doing. The language of power comes to me easily."

"Sweetheart, I know you are talented," Brea said. "I don't want you to ever think I don't believe in you. I do. I just don't want you to *have* to do this kind of magic before you're ready."

"But I am ready, Mama."

"Before we go so far as to make an entirely new spell, let's think about other options," Lochlan interjected. "What can we do that isn't so drastic, but also doesn't send us back into that library to chase phantom spells from now to the end of time?"

They all fell silent trying to think of a solution. Riona didn't have a clue when it came to all things magic, but she watched Tia's hands move through the motions of braiding. The little girl's mind was clearly somewhere else.

"What if we reversed it?" Tia finally said, picking up her chain of daisies.

"Reversed what?" Brea moved to sit in front of her daughter.

"The spell you did, Mama. The one that didn't work the other two times."

"Reverse it how?" Brea frowned.

"If you won't let me make a new spell, we could reconstruct that one. Reverse the magic so it doesn't pull the darkness from the human realm back into Myrkur, but instead pushes the daylight from the human world back here."

"This land has always been dark," Riona said. She couldn't imagine a version of Myrkur that existed in daylight.

Tia leaned her head back against Riona's shoulder and looked up at her. "Yeah, but what if it wasn't?"

"Can you do that?" Riona asked Brea, though she had no doubt in her mind the child sitting in her lap playing with flower chains could do it with one little hand tied behind her back.

"That is ..." Brea trailed off, staring at her daughter in awe.

"Brilliant," Lochlan finished for her. "Our daughter is a magical genius."

"I told you, Papa." Tia rolled her eyes, draping the chain of yellow daisies around her mother's neck.

Riona stared at the colorful flowers Tia had used for each of them. In her own way, she'd given them each a flower that represented the color of their magic.

Griffin

It turned out that Lochlan made Tia nervous with his loud pacing and grumbling, so Brea threw him out of the library. But then Tia asked if Uncle Griff could stay since he knew more of the ancient Fargelsian language.

That did not go over well with Lochlan.

"Loch." Griffin stood on the front porch of the building. "She's just afraid of disappointing you. It's messing with her work."

Lochlan gave a curt nod before he left them to their work.

Brea had turned the reconstructive magic project into an art project. The library table was covered in brown paper and an assortment of crayons and markers.

"Darling, is this part right?" Brea pointed to the childish blue scribble Tia had just handed her.

Tia rolled her eyes and read the phrase.

"Snúou töfrunum við til ao koma ljósi til lands þar sem aeins er nótt."

"That's right, Mama. It basically means, 'turn the magic around to bring light to a land where there is only night.'"

"Are you sure? Do you think the intent should reverse with the subject?"

"No," Toby said from his end of the table where he and Gulliver were drawing crayon doodles. "Tia said it right. The subject of the spell *always* comes first, even in a reversal. Intent comes last because it's the most important part of each phrase that makes up a complex spell. Unless it's just one word. Then the intent is in the body movement and state of mind."

Brea and Griffin exchanged looks of confusion.

"I knew that." Brea erased what she'd just written on the brown paper.

"Toby can't perform the spells himself, Mama, but he knows the language and construction as well as I do. This is right." Tia slid the scrap of scribble back to her mother. "Can you trust us?"

"You know what, kiddo? This is your rodeo." Brea copied the partial spell into the notebook so they had a clear record of their work that wasn't in crayon. "I came into my magic when I was a lot older than you, but my magic was unique, like yours and Toby's. I need to remember how irritating it was when people used to tell me what I could and couldn't do with it."

"It is irritating." Tia's eyes scanned the spell they were trying to reverse engineer. She started to scribble more words and phrases, the tip of her pink tongue poking out between her lips. Some words she copied straight from the book—just in a different order that made little sense to Griffin—and some words he was almost certain she'd made up on the spot.

"What does this mean, honey?" Brea pointed to a word Tia had written in black marker surrounded by other phrases in pink crayon.

"*Sköpurn.*" Tia wrinkled her nose. "That's a bad word, Mama. But it's necessary for the intent."

"I have a whole new appreciation for what my mothers went through when I was learning my magic." Brea bent to copy the new phrases into the book.

Pretty soon, Brea stopped asking questions and let Tia work her translations. Occasionally, Tia would call Toby over and the two would have what amounted to a philosophical discussion on the construction of sentences.

Brea looked up at Griffin as the two kids worked together on a particularly difficult part of the spell. "Am I a bad mother because my kids' power scares me?" she whispered, leaning in close to Griffin. "They're freaking me out."

"No, you're the best mother in the whole world, Brea. But I'm glad it's not just me." Griffin ran a hand through his hair. "How did they get to be so much smarter than us?"

"And they're only ten." Brea shook her head, stifling a laugh. "What happens when they're twenty?"

"They'll have solved all the world's problems by then." Griffin shared a look of pride with Brea and for the first time, he didn't feel uncomfortable about their unique family situation.

This time when they traveled to the valley where the rift in the veil was, they took as many soldiers with them as they could. They were lucky the first time, and neither Griffin nor Lochlan felt like their luck would hold out much longer. Egan was bound to make his next move soon.

"According to Enis' communications, Egan has been busy trying to browbeat her into widening the tear between the worlds, but she has told him that's beyond her abilities. It probably is." Griffin and Lochlan made their way into the valley with the others following close behind. The rear guard would protect them until they were in position.

Lochlan nodded. "He will figure out soon enough that Brea and Tia are more powerful than Enis, and he'll come for them."

"I have every confidence in our daughter's spell work." Brea and Riona came to stand with them. "We will fix this matter today, and then you two can go kill that awful man who calls himself a king." Brea patted Lochlan's arm and took Tia by the hand to approach the rift with Riona and her sharp eyes guiding them.

"You do realize we're just the brute force here?" Griffin stood watching with his arms folded across his chest.

"They don't even need us," Lochlan agreed with a grin.

"Speak for yourselves." Gulliver cupped his hands around his mouth. "A little to the left, Riona."

Riona guided Tia and Brea where Gulliver directed until they were right in front of the tear in the veil.

"I still don't see anything," Lochlan muttered.

"It's okay, your Majesty. I've got this." Gulliver patted the king's arm, and Griffin coughed to cover his laughter.

"It's cold in front of the tear." Riona rubbed her arms as she came to watch with them, their soldiers fanning out around them for protection.

Tia's clear voice joined Brea's as they worked together to perform the complex magic.

"This makes me insane." Lochlan paced. "I want to run up there and take my baby girl home to play in her nursery until she's forty. She shouldn't have to do this."

"No, but I'm grateful she *can* do this." Griffin clapped a hand on his brother's back. "She's so much like you, Loch."

Lochlan snorted irritably.

"I'm not just saying that. That kid adores you, and she's as stubborn and loyal and smart as her papa."

Lochlan shook his head. "She's smart like her mama. But I did always wonder where she got that red-blond hair from."

"Majesty!" A Slyph swooped down from the sky, her eyes wide with fright. "King Egan's guard is marching this way."

Lochlan immediately started issuing orders. "What are his numbers? Captain Macleod?"

"Slightly more than ours, your Majesty."

"Take your Slyph and prepare your archers."

"Yes, sire."

"And Macleod, please be careful. There are precious few of you, and we don't want to lose any of you."

Captain Macleod looked startled at Lochlan's kind words. "Thank you, your Majesty. We will be careful."

Lochlan shouted orders to his guard, sending them marching around the valley to protect Tia and Brea.

"I'll take the east side, you take the west?" Griffin gripped his sword.

Lochlan pointed to the line of soldiers across the grassy glade in front of them. "Nothing that passes through our soldiers goes anywhere near Brea and our kids."

"Nothing." Griffin grasped his brother's hand.

"*We'll* take the east side." Riona came up beside him with Gulliver gripping a pair of daggers Riona must have given him.

"And I'll go with you, Papa." Toby stepped beside his father, lifting his chin in defiance. "I killed an ogre all by myself. I can handle this."

Lochlan nodded, handing his son a bow and quiver of arrows from his shoulder. "You're as good a shot as me. But stay behind me, son. Be prepared to help your sister if she calls for you."

"Yes, Papa." Toby gripped the bow, reaching for an arrow as

the first rumble of Egan's guard rushed down from the ridge to the south of the valley. A swarm of Slyph beat their wings as they soared above them.

Griffin and Lochlan threw up shields just in time to keep the archer's arrows away from Brea and Tia.

"Back up." Lochlan called pointing to the sky and the line of Slyph coming in to land behind their guard. Even with Gulliver and Toby, they were outnumbered by half.

"Gulliver, stay behind us," Griffin called as he and Riona moved to block the approaching Slyph.

Toby fired off shots as fast as a grown fae, hitting his target every time.

Griffin's sword clashed with the Slyph in front of him, and he cut through wings and flesh without hesitation.

Riona and Gulliver fought together. Gulliver moving so quickly, their opponents didn't even see him until it was too late.

Lochlan and Griffin crashed through the Slyph, armed with bows and little more than their incredible strength. The brothers hacked through them, but Egan's guard pushed their forces farther and farther back. Soon, Lochlan and Griffin fought back-to-back, protecting Brea as she worked through the magic with Tia.

The ground trembled beneath their feet, and Griffin looked to the mountain paths behind them. "Ogres." More than a dozen of them ran down into the valley to clash with Egan's army.

A contingent of Slyph flew in from the mountains behind the rift. Six of them circled above Brea, flying low to protect them from the enemy's archers.

"It's Hector!" Gulliver shouted, pointing to the foot soldiers flooding the valley.

At their helm was Hector, his bull horns catching in the light.

Light? Griffin looked over his shoulder to see faint daylight streaming in through the rift. "She's doing it, Loch! The reversal is working."

"Griffin!" Hector shouted over the din of battle. "Enis said you would be here soon. We've been waiting up in the mountains for days."

"I am glad to see you, Brother." Griffin gripped his arm.

"My soldiers will take care of Egan. You take care of your spell casters and then get them out of here." Hector charged into the fray. Little by little, the battle moved to the north end of the valley, leaving Griffin, Riona, Lochlan, and the boys to stand guard over Brea and Tia.

"I need you, Toby!" Tia cried out, sounding weary from the stress of the last hour.

"I'm here, Tia." Toby ran to his twin's side, taking her hand, even though she didn't need to touch him to draw from his strength. His touch and his calming presence were what she needed now. "I'll always be here when you need me."

Griffin listened to the spell, trying to determine how far into it they were. By the time Tia had finished deconstructing and reversing the spell, nearly half of Brea's notebook was full of neatly penned phrases that made up the complex magic.

He watched as Brea turned the page, her voice rising in sync with her daughter's. They were nearing the end of the spell. Daylight flooded the valley, causing confusion and pain among the Dark Fae on Egan's side.

Tia's voice rose like a clear bell drowning out the chaos of battle.

"Risastór ljúka er lokio og allt er rétt mei heimana!" Tia and Brea's voices filled with the power they wielded together.

"Hafou pao opi en láttu engan fara í gegnum pessa opnun!" Tia said these final words alone.

Griffin held his breath. The last time his daughter finished performing such a spell, she passed out from the demand of more magic than she could handle.

This time, she stepped back, looking weary but elated as she high fived her mom.

"Toby, portal." Lochlan shouted as he charged toward Brea, grabbing Riona and Gulliver as he went.

Toby's O'Shea magic gathered in a crimson swirl in his palm, and as he spread his hands wide, a huge portal opened, and all seven of them charged through it. Toby leaped through his portal, letting it close behind him. Unlike his father and uncle's magic, Toby's allowed him to take them straight to the stone pillars marking the entrance into Aghadoon instead of going through the human realm.

"Did it work?" Lochlan panted, picking Tia up to keep her from falling over. She was dead on her feet but in high spirits.

"Did you see all the light, Papa?" Tia smiled through a yawn.

"I did, baby girl. I'm proud of you and Toby."

"What am I, chopped liver?" Brea stood with her hands on her hips.

"You know I don't know what that means." Lochlan carried Tia into Aghadoon, holding Toby's hand.

"Of course it worked." Brea scrambled along behind them. "My daughter is a genius."

"Oh, so she's *your* daughter when she's smart, but *mine* when she's done something horrid?"

"I don't do horrid things, Papa." Tia's head drooped to his shoulder, and she gave Griffin a wink before she fell asleep in her father's arms.

Riona

Hector walked into Aghadoon like a hero returned from battle. Blood streaked his hair, and he could barely hold his sword up, but a smile curved his normally stoic face.

Riona caught sight of him from the doorway of the library and walked out to meet him.

Gulliver raced past her. "Hector," he cheered. "You were amazing."

Hector dropped his sword to the stones and wrapped an arm around Gulliver's shoulders. "That battle was a long time in coming."

Riona crossed her arms. "And we're not done yet."

His smile fell. "No. We're not."

Riona had wanted to head to the palace as soon as they finished with the rift. Sunlight from the human realm streamed in through the rift and spread slowly across the surrounding areas. It would take some time, but Brea believed the daylight would reach across the land, eventually fading in the distance to leave parts of Myr in its natural darkness.

What they didn't have time for… sitting around.

But Griffin insisted they needed to recover, that going to the palace could wait a couple of days.

"Where are the others?" Hector searched the streams of soldiers who'd taken up residence in Aghadoon.

"The library. Doing more talking. Now isn't the time for talking. We need to act."

His shoulders fell, and he leaned on Gulliver support. "Can you take me there?"

She turned on her heel and marched back to the library.

"I've got you," Gulliver told Hector. "You're barely standing upright."

Riona led them into the library where all talk ceased until Griffin shot from his chair. "Hector." He grabbed his arm and led him to a seat. "You have no idea how good it is to see you."

Hector slumped into a chair. "Egan's force is destroyed."

"I brought all those who wanted to come marching through the night to get here. They're setting up camp outside the village. We're maybe two hundred strong. Many chose to return to their families and prepare for whatever comes after Egan."

"After Egan?" Griffin leaned against a set of shelves.

Hector nodded. "You plan to kill him, right? I have fae blocking all exits from the palace so he cannot leave."

That was good to know.

Lochlan rubbed the back of his neck. "We're trying to come up with a plan to enter the palace."

That was the problem. Riona sighed. "And I keep saying that you Light Fae and your need to plan everything is going to allow him time to get away. Is that what you want?"

"Yes," Griffin said to Hector. "Egan must die."

It was as if Riona hadn't said anything.

Hector nodded at that. "Well, I have been living among the remaining Dark Fae in Myrkur since I followed Egan from Eldur. Most of them expect Griffin to assume the throne once the king is gone, and they will support that."

Griffin pushed away from the shelf. "Me?"

He said it like it was an incredulous notion, but Riona would be lying if she said she hadn't had the thought as well. He made sense. This war wouldn't be won without him. Despite his lack of Dark Fae heritage, the fae loved him, and he had experience leading. After the very first time she'd faced him in the arena, his name was all she heard in the villages.

It was one of the reason's she'd spared his life in Kvek's stronghold. Who wanted to kill the hero? It would have made him a martyr. Now, he was perfect for the job. Even his magic could keep them safe. But the dark expression on his face told her a storm brewed inside him.

Hector went on telling Lochlan and Brea of how Enis found him and how they'd started working together, but Riona's only focus was on Griffin.

Without a word to anyone, he walked from the library into the dim light. This far from the breach, the daylight was a subtle glow on the horizon throughout the afternoon. Riona followed him without a word.

"Go back to the library, Riona," Griffin said.

"Not a chance." She caught up with him in the middle of the street and grabbed his arm, forcing him to turn.

Pain swirled in the depth of his gaze. This was not a man who had just been told the crown could be his if he chose. "None of what Hector said matters, Riona. You will recognize the rightful ruler when the time is right. That is your destiny."

"Forget about destiny, Griffin. This isn't about that. You

and I understand each other. I know you." She stepped closer, her voice dropping. "You're scared."

"Scared?" he scoffed.

"Yes." She advanced on him, her wings reaching out behind her in dark intimidation. "You, Griffin O'Shea, are afraid to want power."

She could see the truth flash across his face as the stubbornness faded away. "I spent so many years being told I was going to be king of Fargelsi, and I did horrible things to make that come about. I can't be trusted, Riona. What if that yearning for power is what separates who I was from who I am?"

It was a similar question Riona had once. What if her yearning to be loved—once by her father figure in Egan—was what made her who she was? But she knew now it wasn't. "Griffin, your choices are what separates your past from your present. I don't think you could go back if you tried. I don't know if you have any right to be king of Myrkur, but even without the crown, you have power. Look at what you've done, what you've set in motion? It's because of you this war has happened, because of you we will finally be free."

He didn't speak for a long moment before reaching for her, folding her in a strong embrace. "Thank you."

"For what?" she murmured against his neck.

"Believing in me."

He kept an arm around her as they walked to the center of the village, neither ready to return to the library where those who didn't know Egan talked of what needed to be done.

"I get to kill him." She didn't need to explain her words.

A sigh rattled from Griffin. "Yes, you do."

"Come on." Riona tugged Griffin away, leading him to the edge of the village where they could see Hector's Dark Fae setting up camp.

Riona leaned her head on Griffin's shoulder. "This is why

we need to leave as soon as we can. These fae... they deserve to be free. So do we."

She knew what Griffin would say.

"We have to get back to the library." He turned and hurried away. Griffin's movement was so sudden, she turned to stare after him, but he was already heading back the way they'd come.

Riona ran after him, following him in.

"Brea... Lochlan... Hector," he started. "We've been trying to find a way to repair the breach now that the magic has been reversed. But what if we don't?"

They stared at him, not saying a word.

"Think about it. The humans know something isn't right after weeks of darkness. If there was ever a time to leave the worlds open to each other, it's now. We could spend our entire lives trying to find whatever spell in this endless library would close it. I don't want to do that."

It wasn't a horrible idea. Riona couldn't stand the thought of more time within these walls with books she couldn't understand.

Lochlan stood. "Absolutely not." He walked from the library, unwilling to even discuss the possibility.

Brea rubbed her eyes. "It's... Give me tonight to talk to him. I lived in the human realm for the first eighteen years of my life. Humans are stronger, more resilient, and more open-minded than most fae think they are. But, Griff, this is a big thing. It is not a decision for only the four of us." She stood and put a hand on Hector's shoulder. "Most of us have been up all night. Let's discuss this more tomorrow with fresh minds. If we do this, the decision won't be made until after we face Egan."

Brea followed her husband's path, leaving only Hector at the table. "We have to worry about the Light Fae accepting us, and you'd like us to appeal to the humans as well?" Hector shook his head.

Riona thought of Nihal and how he'd lived his life in the human realm. "Hector, I think you'd be surprised how many Dark Fae live as humans." It made so much sense. To the human eye, they appeared no different. How many lived among the unsuspecting humans?

"Get some rest, Hector," Griffin said. "You've earned it."

Now, there were no more questions in Riona's mind, no more battles to fight save one.

And she had to do it alone.

Slipping out from under the mound of furs Griffin slept with, she rummaged in his bag for the book that would let her talk to Enis O'Shea. They'd conspired once before, but this time was different.

This time, they were on the same side.

Finding the quill, she wasted no time writing to her, her Dark Fae eyes seeing the words even in the dark.

I am coming to the palace. She didn't mention it was her and not Griffin. *Can I expect your aid to get in unseen?*

Enis didn't respond at first, but then her words appeared.

I will meet you at the fighting pits.

The fighting pits. It was perfect. The tunnels would take her straight into the dungeons.

Closing the book, she set it on the table next to the bed, placing the quill on top of it. Griffin would see the messages she hadn't erased and know where she'd gone, but by then it would be too late.

Pulling on leather armor, she prepared herself for the battle she knew was waiting for her. She tied her black braids back away from her face and slipped into her boots.

With one final glance at Griffin, she picked up her sword and left the room behind.

Once outside, she walked toward the edge of the village, flexing her wings as she looked up into the clear night sky. A sliver of a moon provided little light, and not a single star hung overhead.

Kicking off the ground, she leaped into the air and circled the village, looking down on it once more.

Violet eyes stared up at her from a doorway, his magic sparking along his skin.

"I'm sorry," she whispered, knowing he wouldn't be able to hear her.

Turning away from Griffin, she headed toward the palace where the fight she'd dreamed of awaited her arrival.

Griffin

Griffin couldn't seem to shift his eyes away from the starless night sky, hoping for a glimpse of Riona's wings. There was still enough of their original white, he should be able to spot her.

"She's long gone, Griff." Lochlan urged his mount to keep up with Griffin's.

"That blasted woman is going to get herself killed." Griffin drove their horses to a breakneck pace over the barren plains. "Her and her blasted wings," he muttered, wishing he could travel by horse as quickly as she could fly.

"She's a capable warrior," Brea reminded him as she and Gulliver struggled to keep up with Griffin, Hector, and Lochlan. "But are you certain she's gone after Egan?"

"Positive." Griffin gripped the reins, urging his horse to go faster. "I know she can take care of herself, but this is not a fight she should face on her own. She shouldn't have to."

"Maybe she needs to face her demons, Griff." Brea reached

out to ease his grip on the reins. "A chance to slay them once and for all."

"I would slay them all for her if I could." Griffin reluctantly slowed their pace to give the horses a break.

"You know, that's where you and I went wrong," Brea said, and Lochlan gave a derisive snort.

Brea returned in kind. "Long before Loch was in the picture, when we first arrived in Fargelsi, I was just a scared kid, and I needed time to get my feet under me. You were there to take care of me when I really needed you, but then once I had my head wrapped around the fae world, you still wanted to take care of me. Sometimes, Griff, you have to let the people you love deal with their demons on their own."

"Easier said than done." Griffin slowed his horse to a walk as they approached the edges of the King's Forest along the road to the Castle of Myrkur.

"We should go in through the front and then sneak around back through the fighting pits." Gulliver steered his mount between Griffin and Hector.

"Surely you don't mean to let Gullie go into Egan's palace with you?" Brea sounded just like the concerned mother she was.

"Yes, but only because he's the best man for the job," Griffin replied.

"Gulliver has a way of sneaking into places he's not supposed to be." Hector clapped the boy on the back as if to congratulate him on his skill.

"People don't notice me till it's too late." Gulliver took a bite of an ochie fruit he'd pilfered from somewhere, wrinkling his nose when the bitter fruit no longer appealed to his more experienced pallet. "We'll ditch the horses in the forest and then head toward the castle gates." Gulliver tossed the fruit over his shoulder–something no inhabitant of Myrkur would ever do no matter how odious the fruit could be.

They found a spot for the horses to graze among the underbrush near a ridge overlooking the crumbling castle below.

"That's it?" Lochlan looked confused. "That... ruin is Egan's pride and joy?"

"It used to look a lot nicer." Gulliver slipped from his horse, seemingly oblivious that the castle hadn't changed since the last time he'd seen it. Gulliver was the one who had changed.

"Wait. This isn't going to work." Gulliver frowned at the adults, giving Hector an eye roll.

"What's wrong?" Brea looked around in confusion.

"It's you three, your clothes are too nice." Gulliver looked down at his own clothes. "Even mine are too new. The guards at the gates will never let us pass if they think you have coin to spare."

"He's right," Hector turned to examine them. "You need to rough up your clothes and get your hands dirty.

Griffin ran a weary hand through his hair. "We have to hurry, she's had too much of a head start."

"I'll be right back." Gulliver mounted his horse and took off down the road toward the nearest village. The one where most of the king's favorites lived with their servants.

Gulliver returned quickly, carrying a pile of garments he'd no doubt stolen right off some old village woman's clothesline. "Put these on over your clothes." Gulliver passed the heavily mended cloaks and robes to the others, stepping back to inspect them.

"Brea, drop your shoulders some," he instructed. "And maybe rub some dirt on your face. And Loch ... try not to look so much like a king."

"He can't." Brea fidgeted with her robes. "It's physically impossible."

"I *am* a king." Lochlan stood ramrod straight in his peasant garb, looking exactly like a king who wanted to blend into the crowd.

"Put your hood up and stay in the back," Gulliver ordered the King of Iskalt. "And don't speak. You sound too proper-like." Gulliver rubbed dirt on his face and ripped the neck of his tunic.

"You heard the man." Griffin smeared some dirt on his clothes and slumped his shoulders.

"All right. You'll do." Gulliver nodded, leading them down the ridge to the castle gates. Dark Fae streamed in and out of the gates, though their numbers were drastically diminished from what Griffin remembered of his last visits to Egan's fortress.

"Wait for my signal," Gulliver whispered as they approached the entrance. The adults followed Gulliver's lead, shifting through the crowd queuing up at the castle entrance. Some were there for work, others trying to get work and others were looking for a handout to keep their families from starving. Gulliver jerked his head toward the entrance. The guards didn't give them a second glance.

Once inside, Gulliver led them through the tents of the castle slums. Hector had worked hard to move the poorest souls to the nearby villages, but in his absence, the slums were once again bursting with the king's castoffs. Their numbers far outweighed what was left of the king's guard.

"It's like we did nothing," Hector muttered. Following Gulliver to the other side of the slums where they took the path around the back of the palace toward the kitchens and the fighting pits.

"This way." Gulliver waved them toward a smelly drain ditch that ran the length of the outer castle wall.

"This is just awful." Brea shook her head. "These poor people. Have they come to the castle from the villages?"

"No, Majesty." Gulliver shook his head. "The slums are always here. It's where Griff found me when I was three."

"Right near here, actually." Griffin winced as he remembered that day. "He was looking for water." He gestured at the stagnant drain water.

"We have to help these fae." Brea took Lochlan's hand.

"We have to find Riona first." Gulliver glanced over his shoulder and urged them all down into the steep ditch. "Keep your heads down."

"Gullie, how did you know this was here?" Griffin stooped down to help him move the grate from an opening in the ground.

Gulliver shrugged. "I pay attention." He bent to crawl inside. "It's not gross or anything, Brea. Just a little smelly till we get to the tunnels under the fighting pit." He disappeared into the drain, and they followed.

Griffin bent nearly in half as he shuffled down the tunnel a short distance where Gulliver moved another drainage grate aside. From there, they entered the wide tunnels where they could stand up straight and catch a whiff of fresher air now and then. But the tunnels spread out in every direction.

Griffin's heart nearly seized in his chest when he heard the sound of swords clashing, unaccompanied by the cheers of a crowd.

"You've done enough damage, Egan. You've lost." Riona's ghostly voice bounced off the stone walls, sounding as if it could have come from any direction.

"Where is she, Gullie?" Griffin reached for his son's hand.

Gulliver took a few steps in every direction before leading them to another tunnel, racing along in the darkness until they could hear Riona's struggle growing louder.

"You forget, my dear." Egan's laughter reached them. "I taught you to fight. You cannot hope to win against me, child. You don't have the experience. But if you surrender now, I can be convinced of your remorse ... in time."

"You will have to kill me first." Riona's weakening voice sent chills down Griffin's spine.

Riona

"Griffin O'Shea, if you think for one moment you came here to stop me, you can think again." Riona darted toward Egan across the sandy fighting arena she'd fought in countless times. Her sword arced wildly, crashing against his again.

Her arms felt like lead weights, but she would finish this. It was time, and Egan was hers to kill. He'd done her more harm than anyone else.

The sight of Griffin and Gulliver gave her strength. They were her family now. Even Hector, Brea and Lochlan were part of that family.

"You slaughtered my people." Riona charged Egan, barely registering the sensation of his knife slicing through the delicate flesh of her wings. She would feel it later, but right now the bright red blood splattering across the sand might as well have been his. It would be before she was finished toying with him.

"Riona!" Gulliver started toward her, but thankfully Griffin stopped him.

"Stay with Griff," Riona called over her shoulder. The kid had seen enough bloodshed to last him a lifetime, he would not see her death here today.

"I am your people, Riona." Egan's voice took on a kinder tone. The one he'd used with her to get his way. "Haven't I always been a father to you, my darling? And this is how you repay my kindness? I saved you from the extinction you would have succumbed to like the others of your village."

"Kindness?" Riona slashed with her dagger and grazed Egan's side, drawing blood. "You don't know the meaning of the word. Your fatherly affection always came with a price. You've manipulated and bribed me since the day you brought me to this crumbling ruin you call a castle. You handed out scraps and called them riches."

Egan's form faltered, and he showed the first signs of tiring. "How dare you scorn me now when I've given you everything!" Spittle flew from his mouth, and she took the opportunity to strike another blow, scraping her sword across his cheek. "I should have let you burn with your father."

"My father?" Riona stumbled back. "You told me my father was never around. He was of the sea. An Asrai. I was raised by my mother."

"Your father was Chieftain of your people, and he thought to rise above me." Egan parried her attack, but she drove him back across the cold dark arena. "He spoke of the prophesies your people carried in the form of their tattoos. That one of his people would rise up to name a new king of Myrkur. One who would be just and fair. I could not let others learn such magic existed within Myrkur. I had to kill them all."

"Except me." Riona parried his next blow, but gave him no ground, she had him nearly backed up against the high wall below his dais. "Why did you let me live?"

"The fighting was brutal and bloody. Your village burned,

and my soldiers found you hiding in a barn. They dragged you out. You were just a child. Hardly more than a babe, but you lashed out at my men, screaming and biting at them. I saw something in you that day. I knew you would be my greatest warrior and champion. So I let you live. And for a time, you were everything I could have wanted in a daughter of my own. Until you betrayed me." Egan pushed back in a sudden surge of energy and emotion. He was truly saddened by her betrayal. Hacking with his sword, he drove her back.

"You don't know what family is, Egan. You called me your favorite and treated me like a beloved daughter when it pleased you and ignored me when you had no use of me. That is not what love is!" Riona screamed, emotions dangerously close to the surface.

"You are not my blood, Riona. What would you have of me?" Egan shouted back. "I did right by you. You never needed anything."

"You made a mistake, Egan. A fatal error." Riona drew back, circling him. "When you sent me out into the world to be your eyes and ears, you allowed me to see everything I've missed. I've seen the love of a father for a boy who was not born of his blood. I've seen families who choose each other, not based on their blood ties, but through their bonds. You owned me once, Egan Bryne, but not anymore."

She charged him, swinging her sword with ruthless strength, driving him back against the wall. Caging him in, she leaned forward. "You failed the moment you let me live, my king. You saw me as a child, too worthless to be a threat." She drove her dagger into his gut and gave it a twist. Egan's eyes widened with shock.

"I have learned my true destiny while I've been away." She gave him a maniacal grin. "You see, I am that fae you feared the day you slaughtered my people. The one you so desperately needed to kill has been under your protection all this time. I will name a new ruler of Murkur, and she will be everything you are not." Riona stepped back, letting Egan slump forward as his blood stained the sandy ground beneath his feet.

"You lie," he spat.

"I already know who the rightful ruler of Myrkur is. An heir to the original kings your family murdered. I will raise her up and name her queen, and the people of Myr will know I speak the truth when they witness my destiny fulfilled. It is why my wings grow dark. My destiny is upon me." After reading the histories of her people in the library, Riona began to suspect that was what her darkening wings meant.

"She is right." Enis called from the dais far above the arena floor. "The book has told me as much." She held the book of power to her chest. "She was always meant to name a new ruler of the Dark Fae."

Egan clutched his wound as if to keep his guts from spilling on the ground.

"Then let us get on with it." Riona raised her sword and ran it through Egan's heart, letting him slide to the ground with his lifeless eyes staring at her.

"Riona?" Griffin ran to her side, taking the bloodied sword and dagger from her clutches. "It's over."

She nodded, too numb to speak.

Gulliver approached her, a wary look on his face. She draped her arm across his shoulders, leaning on him for strength. "I am all right." She squeezed his arm in reassurance.

"Riona, you were so brave." Brea gave her a regal nod.

Griffin still hadn't said anything, and when Riona lifted her eyes to him, she caught him staring at Egan's lifeless form. "He's dead."

A sob rose in her throat, but she held the emotion back.

Whatever Egan had been to her, in the end, he was just an enemy. Crossing to Griffin, she slid her hand into his.

He turned glassy eyes to her. "You did it. You ended this."

"It's not over yet." Gulliver gripped her other hand. The three of them had faced Egan's torment for so many years, it was hard to believe he was really gone, that all their suffering had meant something in the end.

It was a feeling Brea and Lochlan would never understand.

Hector cleared his throat, the sound echoing through the hollow arena. "What now?"

"Burn it." Riona's voice was a rasp in her throat.

"Burn it?" Lochlan frowned. "The arena?"

"All of it. The castle, the slums, the arena, everything. Get the fae out to the villages and then raze this awful place to the ground."

"I've had some experience with destroying palaces that hold bad memories." Brea nodded again. "It's therapeutic. We'll get right on it." She turned to Hector. "Can you issue the orders for everyone to evacuate the … er … castle?"

He looked from Griffin who hadn't moved away from Egan to Brea. "Yes, your Majesty." Hector left with Brea.

"My boys." Enis nearly skipped down the steps to the arena floor. "I am so pleased to see you." She came to stand before them, her arms wrapped around the book.

"Mother." Lochlan gave her a cold stare.

"Enis." Griffin's voice grew colder.

The Iskalt king and his brother had nothing but ice in their veins for their mother.

Riona pulled Gulliver aside, letting the O'Sheas have their privacy.

"I trust you have won your war with the Dark Fae?" Enis pasted on a smile that seemed fake even to Riona, a smile that didn't belong on such a dour day.

"No thanks to you," Lochlan said.

"My boys." She frowned. "The book—"

"The book is all you're here for, so why don't you just take it and go?" Griffin folded his arms across his chest, his voice resonating with a hard edge. "You are the keeper. It's your duty, is it not?"

"Yes. I—"

"You've made it clear, Mother." Lochlan towered over her. "Time after time, you've chosen the book and its power over us."

"Let's give her a final choice, brother." Griffin took a step toward their mother. "Give up the book. Let us place it somewhere safe where it can never be used again. Then you may rejoin your family. Get to know your sons and your grandchildren. Be there for us."

"Or," Lochlan interjected. "We will send you back to the human world with your book of power, and you can continue protecting it."

Enis lifted her chin. "You boys do not understand. As keeper of the book, it is my duty and my privilege to decide how the book is used and how it is protected. Grainee's descendants protected the book to the detriment of all magic. The book should be studied. Revered. It is the key to our future. You have access to the library. Surely by now you understand the wealth of knowledge stored there? The book is the key to the library. It can show the keeper things you will never find in a lifetime of research."

"Shall we create a portal for you?" Lochlan raised a brow.

Enis nodded. "You are grown men. You do not need your mother."

"That's not entirely true." Lochlan's icy blue magic swirled in his palm. "I am not ashamed to say I still need my mother. I value her counsel. My mother is Faolan, and Griffin's mother was Regan. You have never been a mother to either of us."

"Go." Griffin nodded toward the portal Lochlan created. "It is fine, Enis. I hope the book will love you and comfort you throughout what remains of your life."

Tears pooled in Enis' eyes as she took a step toward the portal. "One day I hope you will understand my choices. I always loved you both, and I always will." As she moved into the portal, she sang the song Griffin only vaguely remembered from his childhood before his family was ripped from him. It was a fitting farewell from the woman he would never truly understand.

She would keep the book, but the magic inside it could be controlled from the library. It wouldn't be able to hurt their world again.

And neither would she.

CHAPTER TWENTY-FIVE

Griffin

Fire.

It shouldn't have soothed Griffin's nerves, but it did. He continued to stare at the place where Lochlan's portal took his mother and the book to the human realm before closing her off from them forever.

A sob echoed behind him, and he turned to find Riona staring up at the flames bursting from the palace windows. Brea's magic kept the flames from reaching the slums until Hector evacuated every last fae, but it seemed she hadn't wanted to wait to begin.

Another sob escaped the always strong Riona, the woman who never shed a tear, who fought her sort-of father with a coldness that left them all chilled.

"I'm going to help Brea." Lochlan walked away, leaving Griffin to stare at Riona and Gulliver.

It was over.

Egan was dead.

He pulled Riona against him as he cleared her tears with a scorching kiss. He put everything they'd been through, every bit of pain and heartache, fear and doubt into that moment, letting it wash away.

Leaning his forehead against hers, he sucked in a breath. "You really did it," he whispered. "You killed him." And the people Griffin loved were still alive. It was an outcome he hadn't allowed himself to imagine, but now it was here.

"You came." Her eyes found his. "I left you—again—and you still came."

"Always." He wiped her tears away with his thumbs.

"I killed my father today."

Griffin pulled her into a hug, letting her bury her face in his shoulder. He knew what it meant to lose the one fae who'd always been there, but even he hadn't had to kill Regan. Brea took care of that. "Everything is going to be better now, Riona." He didn't know where they'd live or how they'd live. Lochlan and Brea both wanted them to move to Iskalt, but something about that didn't feel right. It wasn't home.

But wherever they went, they'd be together.

"Gullie," he called. "Stop staring at Egan like he's going to come back to life and get over here."

Gulliver stood from where he'd crouched next to the dead king and jumped over him.

Griffin pulled him into their hug.

"Griff," he complained. "Let me go."

"Never."

Something crashed nearby, a tower succumbing to the magical fire, stones and wood raining down. "We should probably go." Griffin urged Riona and Gulliver into a run.

They passed familiar crumbling structures, and Griffin wondered how they'd ever thought of it as more than it was—a symbol of oppression that no longer belonged in this world.

They found Brea and Lochlan, both using their power to control the flames, weakening the castle walls and freeing Myrkur of its dark past.

"Go help Hector," Brea grit out before mumbling a few Fargelsian words. Flames exploded from an untouched tower.

Griffin tore his eyes away and found the stream of fae carrying their few belongings through the gates, emptying the slums of the remaining indentured servants and soldiers of Egan's, the ones who hadn't joined his march into Eldur.

"Gullie." Griffin pushed him toward the gate. "Go get the horses."

"Griff—"

"No arguing. I have taken you into more danger than you should see in a lifetime, and you have proven yourself more capable than I could have imagined. Which is why I'm trusting you to bring our horses to the gate." If he knew Brea, there'd be a big finish once the slums were empty and a quick getaway was always a good idea.

Gulliver straightened his shoulders. "You trust me." He said it almost like an accusation, poking Griffin in the chest. "As much as Lochlan or Myles or anyone else."

"I wouldn't say I trust Myles," he grumbled, though he did. "Don't make a big deal about it, Gullie. Just go. Take Riona with you, she's barely able to stand."

Riona opened her mouth to protest, but closed it with a sigh as she turned to him. "Promise me you won't be long."

He pressed a kiss to her cheek. "I promise I'll come to you once this place has burned to the ground."

She wanted that more than anyone, but he knew the toll the fight with Egan took on her, and she seemed to realize her own weakness. With a nod, she followed Gulliver into the crowd fleeing the castle grounds.

Wasting no time, Griffin ran back to where Brea and Lochlan stood facing the flames.

"I told you to help Hector." Lochlan didn't look at him.

"I need to be the one to do this." He hadn't destroyed Regan's palace, and in the end, he'd tried to save her. Unlike Riona who'd had the courage to kill Egan. He hadn't gotten that moment.

But now... this place... he could make sure no fae ever again set foot inside.

Lochlan turned to him, pulling in his magic. He studied him for a long moment, and Griffin didn't know what he saw before nodding and running toward Hector.

"Come on then." Brea shot him a smile. "Let's destroy a castle."

It felt right, standing there with her. Everything that had happened began many years ago when he made the fateful decision to follow Regan's orders to abduct a girl from the human realm.

Now, they finished it together.

Flames ripped through the halls he'd walked as a prisoner, through the rooms his kids had been held against their will, the fighting pits where he'd first fought for his family and made the decision not to kill Riona.

Every part of this place held a memory, a hint of pain washed clean in the scorching heat of the fire.

The flow of fae from the slums slowed to a trickle until only four remained. Brea stepped back when Lochlan and Hector joined them, letting Griffin continue. He pulled on the flames, yanking stones from the walls as he did. When he turned, the fire spread along the high walls, speeding through the tents and hovels of the slums until they encircled the group.

Redemption was an odd thing. Griffin hadn't wanted it. He never searched for it or believed he deserved it. But as the flames erased this evil from Myrkur, they wiped it clean from his soul.

Maybe that wasn't redemption. He'd done so much bad, and nothing could make up for that. Forgiveness was a better term.

As Griffin let the heat of the flames wash over him, he forgave himself.

Forgetting wasn't the answer—Myrkur proved that. It only led to more pain, and Griffin didn't want to forget the things he'd done. The evil, though… it didn't define him, not anymore.

He hadn't realized Brea, Lochlan, and Hector all screamed his name as the flames closed in until their collective voices struck him.

"Griff!" Brea cried. "We need to get out of here."

"Time to go, brother." Lochlan tried to pull him back.

"You've done enough." Those were Hector's words, and they swirled through him. He'd done enough. Myrkur was free.

There was more work ahead, but with freedom, none of it seemed so daunting.

Turning, he realized Brea had to use her magic to keep the flames from overwhelming them. His eyes lifted to the burning castle, knowing it would be nothing but ash and soot stained ruins soon.

"Yes." He nodded. "We've done enough." Turning his back on it, he parted the flames even as his magic weakened. "Well, what are you waiting for?"

The four of them sprinted through the raging fires, nearing the crumbling gate. They burst through a wall of fire, all rolling to the ground on the other side.

Griffin's chest heaved as he looked up at the horses waiting for them, a smile curving his lips. He closed his eyes for a brief moment and opened them when a cheer wound through the darkness.

The fae who'd escaped the slums crowded together, lifting their voices in the kind of joyous sound that was foreign to Myrkur.

Pushing himself off the ground, Griffin watched as the fae who'd just lost the only home they had cheer for its destruction.

Riona rounded one of the horses and slid her arm through his, wiping black soot off his face. "I never knew it before, Griff, but this is Myrkur." She gestured to the fae who'd been little more than slaves and the villagers who'd come to help them. "Egan wasn't Myrkur. He was the one holding us back."

The inexhaustible Hector walked out among the people, a smile stretching his lips.

"Look!" Gulliver shouted, pointing into the distance.

Griffin strained his eyes to see the tiny bit of light streaking across the horizon, so different from the bright glow of the fire behind them. That was about desperation.

This... the dawn coming to Myrkur for the first time was hope.

"It worked." Gulliver bounced on his toes. "It's the light from the human realm."

The crowd of fae watched the brilliant pinks and oranges light up their dark world.

Gulliver turned to Griffin with a wry smile twisting his lips. "They're so going to need sunglasses."

"Aghadoon feels empty." Griffin lowered himself to the blanket Gulliver had spread in the village square.

Gulliver insisted they do this post-victory—his word—meeting outside instead of in the stuffy old library (also his word).

No one protested.

Throughout the morning, Hector worked to dispatch the Dark Fae soldiers who'd been staying in the village to aid those who'd escaped the slums, setting up temporary camps until some of the nearby villages could be improved to accommodate them.

Griffin had known Myrkur was a harsh place, but the sunlight streaked across the sky, illuminating the barren landscape in a way they'd never seen before. Yet, among the dying forests and shriveled crops, there was a beauty. In the distance, snowcapped mountains towered over the land with a majestic strength.

Lochlan lay sprawled on the blanket, soaking up the warmth. Both O'Shea brothers were happy to let their magic rest as it was meant to.

Tia and Toby had a thumb war. Griffin smiled at the memory of Brea teaching him the human game.

Brea joined them, kissing her husband before sitting with her kids.

They were only missing Riona. She walked toward them in her traditional dark clothing, but that wasn't what caught Griffin's eye. Her wings... the white was gone, leaving a thick inky blackness covering the surface.

She stopped before sitting down. "I know about the wings, okay? I don't need your comments. I'm choosing to believe not all darkness is bad. Maybe this is a good thing. Nihal had dark wings."

"He was also a liar who gave his life for a bad fae who might also be not bad? I don't really understand," Gulliver muttered.

Griffin pulled his tail. "Stop. Enis had a mission she wanted to devote her life to. End of story." Lifting his eyes to Riona, he arched one brow. "Finished? We have things to discuss."

Riona shut her mouth, crossed her arms, and took a spot next to Griffin.

Lochlan rubbed a hand over his face. "We had no choice but to let Enis leave with the book. She's the keeper. But, how do we control her now?"

Griffin met Tia's gaze. "This isn't about the book. Maybe it never has been."

Brea's brow furrowed. "What do you mean? My kids were taken. We fought a war over that thing."

"The book is dangerous because it has no conscience, nothing to decide whether showing someone a spell is right or wrong. If it thinks a fae needs a spell, it gives it—assuming that spell exists in the library. There is nothing good or evil about the book."

"Griff—"

"We already know how to control Enis and the magic. We've been doing it for months now. The book doesn't recognize evil, but we do. It doesn't control the library, the library controls the book."

"The fae can be its conscience," Riona said, her eyes widening.

Griffin nodded. "And now we have two realms to protect. The breach into the human realm can't be closed, so we must do what we can to control that as well. All of us."

"No." Toby's single word surprised them into silence. He shared a look with his sister. "Not all of us. You, Griff. You can protect it."

Tia unfolded her legs and stood, reaching a small hand down to Griffin. "We need to show you something."

"Now?" He looked to the others. "Tia... is it in the village? Because, honestly I'm exhausted and there's still so much to do to help the Dark Fae."

"This will help, Uncle Griff." Toby pushed to his feet. "We promise."

"Come on, Griff." Gulliver jumped up. "Don't be an old fae. It's not like you destroyed an entire palace last night or anything."

A tired laugh wound through Griffin, and he sighed. These kids were going to be the death of him. "Fine."

Tia smiled in triumph. "Good, because Papa definitely won't let us take the horses on our own."

Lochlan groaned, but the rest of them made no move to come. Traitors. Lazy, rotten traitors who'd rather sleep after everything they'd gone through than ride off with kids who had too much energy.

And yet, as the three kids surrounded him, they gave him life.

Wrapping an arm around Gulliver, he pulled him close. "Do you know what we're doing?"

Gulliver shrugged. "I trust Tia."

Griffin did too. Despite how young the twins were, they'd done well. They possessed more Fargelsian power than he thought possible.

The four of them rode the short distance to the ruins of Fela. As Griffin slid down, he realized it looked no different than it had before.

Walking through the rubble, he kicked over a pot, finding a tiny doll beneath it. With a sad shake of his head, he turned back to the kids. "Why are we here?"

Tia skipped forward, her hands clasped behind her back. "Do you know how Fargelsi was built?"

"Of course. I grew up there. The Fargelsian's grow their villages from the ground, calling forth treehouses and houses made of stone and sod. I've even heard about old villages grown right into the hills."

Toby kicked at a rock across the ground.

"We read all about it in the library." Tia nodded, the corners of her mouth twitching. "Lots of Gelsi villages sprout right from the forests, but we don't think that's necessary."

"I don't understand what any of this has to do with Fela." Or why it was so important it couldn't wait.

Tia and Toby shared a grin. Tia held out her palm, and Toby slapped his into it. They both closed their eyes, old Fargelsian words even he didn't understand falling from their lips.

"What are they doing?" Gulliver whispered.

Griffin was about to say he didn't know when the ground beneath his feet shook, the vibration traveling up his legs. Vines shot from the earth, twisting in the air, and Griffin yanked Gulliver out of their path, his eyes widening. He'd seen such magic in his youth, but seeing his own children wield it was startling.

All around them, a wind whipped through the destroyed village, clearing the debris as the ground shifted.

Griffin watched as several small buildings took shape from the stones beneath them, magic etched into their very core. Moss and vines grew up the walls just like in Fargelsi. Silvery black flowers sprouted from the vines, and their sweet fragrance chased away the pungent odors left from the fires that destroyed Fela.

Small cottages dotted the narrow roads, now paved with moss-covered stones still shifting into place. Rock fences closed in yards covered with fresh green grass and wildflowers in the darkest shades of red and purple bobbed in the breeze.

The village square shifted, and the ground churned as the twins called up more grass and sweet smelling clover to carpet the square. A thick, gnarled tree rose from the cracked, dry soil at the center of the village. Griffin watched in awe as it morphed into a gazebo with smooth bark covering every surface. Vines twisted around the gazebo, hanging heavy with purple fruit he didn't recognize.

Communal buildings took shape from new trees the twins called forth. And at the end of the cobble stone street, a large two-story house emerged from the cliff-side with shale shingles along the roof and big open windows. Ivy vines crept up the sides of the house and shrubs of night berries rose in the beds along the foundation.

With the village still morphing around them, Tia fell silent and released her brother's hand. Their chests heaved with a matching rhythm, but Griffin couldn't take his eyes from what they'd done.

Fela, looking like a quaint Fargelsian village, stood tall and proud. Cobblestone roads and paths wound between the structures. Griffin made note of everything there was to do to show his people the modern fae world. Crops to plant that would thrive in the sun, roads to pave, trade routes to create.

And it was all possible.

They could return.

Griffin was from Iskalt. He grew up in Fargelsi.

But Myrkur was home. These people were home.

"I know Papa wanted you to come home with us." Tia met his gaze. "But you don't belong there." She took his hand and led him down the street to the biggest house.

She was so young and yet saw so much.

No, he didn't belong in Lochlan's court. He never had.

"Plus." Toby took up Griffin's free hand "We're right by the tear into the human realm, and someone has to watch it."

He was right.

"Can I go inside?" Gulliver asked.

Griffin nodded, a tear sliding down his cheek.

Gulliver's shouts reached them from the second story. "It's

huge!" He stuck his head out of the window over the front door. Windows that would need glass in the coming months. "It's not a palace, it's way better." Gulliver's head disappeared from one window to appear in another. "Griff, I have my own room! And there are extras too."

Toby coughed. "That's... uh... for us when we come visit."

Tia smiled. "Do you like it, Uncle Griff?"

Wrapping one arm around each kid, he rested his chin on her head. "It's perfect. Absolutely perfect."

"We love you, Griff." She dropped the word uncle as she looked up at him, the truth in her gaze. Even if Lochlan would always be their father, it was okay for him to love them too.

"I love you too, kiddos. Now, what were you thinking putting a window in Gulliver's room? He's just going to sneak out all the time."

"Hey!" Gulliver appeared in the doorway. "Okay, that's probably true. But does it matter? Myrkur is safe now."

Griffin stepped past him into his forever home—the first he'd ever had—and shook his head. "Someday, Gullie, we'll discuss the difference between not under the control of an evil king, and safe to resume a life of thievery."

Griffin continued to argue with his son as he walked through the empty home. He couldn't wait to bring Riona here. And the others. He couldn't wait to fill the village with his family.

Riona

One month later

Riona stood beside Shauna, shielding her eyes from the sunlight shining across Fela, a sight she'd never expected to see in the land of perpetual darkness.

"I never get tired of looking at it." Shauna sighed, a blissful smile on her face. She'd arrived more than a week ago with the former Queen of Eldur. When Riona had first met Faolan, she'd seemed old and feeble, like she'd given up on life. But after Shauna's careful nursing, Faolan was a new woman.

It was amazing what love could do to a person.

"The sunlight or your beautiful queen?" Riona nudged her playfully.

"Can I say both?" Shauna laughed. "She's not a queen, though. Not anymore."

"I don't think you can ever take the queen out of a lady like Faolan."

Faolan walked with her grandchildren and their friends through the newly established berry patches, watching for signs of new growth.

New growth was everywhere in this part of Myr. Green grass and trees were just beginning to flourish under the sun. This close to the rift between worlds, the sunlight was at its brightest—though still not as bright as it was in the human realm or even Fargelsi. Riona's eyes were grateful for that.

Farther away, the light was dim, like a lingering sunset all day. And at the far reaches of Myrkur, it was still dark. The night realm had never known light, and for those Dark Fae who preferred it that way, they would always have a home that felt natural to them. But for those who relished the sun's rays, Fela and the villages growing up around it, had become a beacon of hope for a new life without the tyranny of a king who did not care for them.

That was why Shauna and Faolan had come to visit. Why Riona waited anxiously for the others to arrive. Nerves churned in her belly. It was time to choose a new ruler. Time to fulfill her destiny and name the true heir of Myrkur—should she choose to accept the role.

"I'll never get used to that." Shauna winced at the surge of magic sweeping through the center of town.

"Neither will I," Riona agreed. "Let's go greet our guests." Riona and Shauna set off across the grassy slopes leading down to the orchards. Griffin and Gulliver were already there with Hector.

The stone pillars appeared first—the markers of Aghadoon. The rest of the village emerged from an unnatural fog. Brea and Lochlan stood at the center of the magical village with their four children, and Alona and Finn walked up next to them with Logan and Darra.

Griffin waved frantically at the twins who were already running toward him and Gulliver.

Brandon emerged from the library with Myles and Neeve and their brood of little ones in tow.

"Riona!" Myles called as they all made their way down to the pillars. "We carpooled." He flashed the goofy grin Riona had come to expect from the lovable human.

"I am more than a little disturbed that I know what that means." Riona leaned in to give him a hug. "I've spent way too much time with this one." She smiled at Brea.

"He has a way of rubbing off on you, doesn't he?" Brea linked her arms through Shauna's and Riona's. "Now show us what you've been up to for the last month—besides mooning over your new loves."

"No one has been mooning over anything." Shauna frowned at the odd expression. "We have sunlight now."

Brea threw her head back and laughed. "You Myrkurians are a hoot, you know that."

Riona shrugged at that. There was no way she'd ever really understand this queen and her human ways.

"Brea!" Griffin called as he ran up the slope with Tia and Toby, wrapping her in his arms for a brief moment. "Lochlan, it's good to see you brother." He gripped his brother's hand.

"Daylight agrees with you and your new homeland." Lochlan slapped him on the back.

"It does." Griffin flashed a wink at Riona.

"Are you ready for this?" Brea asked as they made their way toward the center of Fela.

"As ready as I will ever be, I think." Riona sighed. It was a heavy burden, her destiny. "I would like to speak with you all privately first, if I may. Before we make anything official."

"We have a town hall now," Griffin said eagerly. "It's nothing fancy, but we love it." He guided their party of visiting royals to their modest building, looking as proud of it as he would if it were the finest castle anyone had ever seen. He and Hector had worked hard with some of the villagers to build it themselves.

The wooden structure opened to a great hall, a single room with high ceilings and exposed beams. One wall of windows faced the east, to catch the early morning light. Everyone filed into the hall, taking up their seats in a circle around the center fire pit. Griffin and Riona had laid the bricks themselves. It was a unique experience for Riona. Creating something meant to last. It was a simple building, but it had character. She imagined generations of villagers meeting here to discuss the town's communal system, and it made her feel like she was truly part of something greater than herself.

With an encouraging nod from Griffin, Riona stood to greet their guests. All the royals from the three Light Fae kingdoms, along with their children and the current leaders of Fela were here today to discuss the making of a queen. They just didn't know it yet.

"Thank you all for making the journey to Fela. We are so happy to have you here as our guests." Riona's voice shook for a moment. It wasn't like her to be so nervous. "Some of you know why we are here. I am the last of my kind. After much research, we've come to learn I am the last of the original Tuatha De Dannan. From us, all Dark Fae came. The Asrai, the Slyph, the land fae, even the Ogres owe their origins to those like me. Egan massacred the last of my people, a small village near the Black Sea. I was the only survivor."

Riona lifted her chin. "He killed my people because of a prophecy that said one of my village would rise up as a kingmaker to name the rightful ruler of Myrkur. Our tattoos hold the keys to our purposes in life. Egan knew one such as I could destroy his reign, and he sought to prevent that from coming to pass. He didn't know it, but when he chose to let me live, that prophecy survived the bloodshed of that day. He killed my mother and father, who was the village chieftain. But I have come today to fulfill my destiny. This heir to the last true royal family of Myrkur sits in this room today." Riona cast a glance around the Light and Dark Fae faces staring eagerly back at her.

"I think it is fitting that this heir is the child of both Light and Dark Fae." Murmuring spread across the room. "Shauna and Nessa could you please join me for a moment?" Riona reached her hand out to Nessa. She'd discussed this with the sisters the previous morning. She wanted to be certain they understood what she was asking of them.

Nessa smiled shyly and came to stand in front of Riona. Shauna stood uncertainly beside them.

"Shauna and Nessa's mother was Light Fae. The daughter of a convicted felon from Fargelsi. Shauna's father was also Light Fae, but he died when she was very young. Nessa's father was Dark Fae. A beloved man of Fela, but he also died when his daughter was just a baby. For most of their lives, Shauna and Nessa have only had each other. But Nessa's father was the great-great-great-grandson of the last king of Myrkur. A fact he likely didn't even realize. Nessa is the true heir to the throne."

Nessa beamed a beautiful smile at the room as everyone present fell into astonished whispers.

"I thought for sure it would be Riona," Brea said.

"You thought I would name myself queen?" Riona shook her head with a laugh.

"Well you deserve it. If it wasn't you, I thought it would be Griffin."

"No way." Griffin shook his head. "Our queen should represent the Dark Fae. Nessa hasn't come into her Dark Fae features yet, but she will. Our people need to see someone just like them on the throne."

"May I speak?" Nessa turned to Riona.

"Of course." Riona lifted her onto the edge of the cold fire pit so she could see everyone.

"I am young," Nessa said in her clear voice. "But what Riona says feels right inside here." She held a hand over her heart. "Maybe my ancestors were kings once upon a time. But that shouldn't make me a queen by default. I understand it is my right if I want to be queen. But ... this is a new world." Nessa's smile lit the room. "We should not look back to what was, but look to the future. To what Myrkur will be some day."

"Are you saying you don't want to be our queen, Ness?" Shauna asked carefully. "You may feel differently when you are older."

"I was never able to just be a child. Egan's Myrkur didn't allow for such lives. I have that chance now, and I want to take it. Before it is too late. Besides, I am a healer, like my mother and my sister, or at least, I wish to be. There are others here who would do a much better job at governing us." Nessa waved Riona over to her side and stood up on tip toes to whisper in Riona's ear.

Riona looked back, surprised. "You think so?"

Nessa nodded.

"You know, that's exactly what I was thinking too." Riona winked and took the young could-be queen by the hand as she jumped down from the fire pit and returned to her sister.

"I can choose another," Riona announced. "This magic that manifests as prophecy among my tattoos can guide me to whoever would fall next in line for the throne. But I'm not sure I believe that is the right course either." Riona looked to the circle around the fire pit, meeting each eye. "I believe Nessa has shown great wisdom today. We should look to the future.

But we can't ignore the past. Specifically the recent past. One among you has risen to the challenges of recent months. One of you has acted like a king." Riona stopped pacing and turned to the man standing beside Griffin.

"Hector. You have proven your worth. Since the moment this all began, you've worked tirelessly to help those in need. You've headed armies, bested Egan's finest soldiers, and fought for your freedom."

"I can't think of a better man for the job," Griffin said softly.

"Me?" Hector looked at them like they'd lost their minds. "I'm just a farmer."

"You're a leader, Hector." Griffin clapped him on the back.

"When Nessa declined, my purpose shifted." Riona glanced down at her swirling tattoos. They moved faster, the colors whirling together like paint in a bowl. "I believe you are the leader we need, Hector. And Nessa herself suggested it."

"It takes more than the right lineage to make a king." Lochlan moved to stand behind Hector. "You have what it takes to rule. I would be honored to call you my ally and fellow king."

"I—I can't be a king." Hector shook his head.

"That is precisely why you will make a good one, my friend." Griffin took a knee before him. "I have thirsted for power before, and I have seen others who have coveted crowns that did not belong to them. True kings and queens are humble. Like you, your Majesty."

"Get up, Griff," Hector pleaded.

"King Hector, ruler of Myrkur." Riona placed her hands on his trembling shoulders. "You will serve your people well." Riona's voice came out formal and tinged with a hint of ancient magic. Her tattoos stilled, growing dark as the color drained from them, like magic washed away once its purpose had been served.

Sadness echoed through her to see her markings go still and dark.

"Riona, your wings," Gulliver gasped. "They're beautiful."

As she'd fulfilled her purpose, the color from her tattoos faded away, switching places with the darkness of her wings that were once white—like a blank page—and had recently turned black. Now her tattoos were black and her wings swirled with the vibrant colors of her markings. She wrapped her wings around herself, overcome with the sheer beauty of such color.

It seemed over the last months as she moved closer and closer to fulfilling her destiny, her wings had grown dark in preparation for this moment.

"She's breathtaking," Griffin whispered in awe. For a moment, she stood before him, and all the others faded away. They had nothing but good things coming for them in the near future. A future of their own making.

Griffin

"I believe we have some unfinished business." Brea lowered herself to the ground beside Griffin.

Myrkur celebrated their new king with a bonfire in Fela's town square. Hector was a reluctant king, but he took to the role like a natural. He was a good man who would never let the power of ruling over others go to his head. He would be a benevolent and kind ruler.

"What business is that?" Griffin watched the young people of Myrkur dance and sing in the growing darkness.

Brea pulled something from her bag.

"Ahh, the marriage magic. I'd wondered when that would come back to haunt us again."

"I've studied this scroll with my sisters and Lochlan. We're all in agreement that this kind of magical bond is no longer necessary." Brea glanced down at the scroll in her lap. "More than ever, freewill is vital to our people and the future we are trying to build for our children. But still, a part of me—"

"Hates the idea of letting it go?" Griffin finished her sentence.

"Isn't that crazy?" Brea scoffed. "I shouldn't want or need magic to keep me in love with my husband. To keep me feeling close to you. I fear what will happen when it is gone. I know Lochlan and I will be fine. Most married couples will be just as strong without it. But I don't want to lose you, Griffin. You're not my husband, but you are family. You know that, right?"

Griffin reached out to take her hand. "I do, Brea. And part of me will always love you, but I need ... we both need to let our relationship evolve naturally. The fragments of magic holding us together will only hinder us. I think it's time we trust in ourselves and our relationships to keep us strong." Griffin's eyes searched through the crowd of revelers to find Riona. She was easy to spot with her brightly colored wings that seemed to suit her better than her white wings ever did. "Someone once said magic isn't the answer to everything. I feel those are wise words we should heed."

"She is a smart lady." Brea watched Riona dancing with Gulliver and Toby. She lifted the leather scroll holding one of the oldest bits of magic either of them had ever seen. "Would you do me the honor of finally divorcing me?"

Griffin stood and offered her his hand. "No human custom would please me more."

Together they walked through the crowd to the bonfire.

Griffin hesitated a moment. "Are we doing the right thing, Brea? This will affect everyone."

"It should be a choice, Griffin. Loving someone, creating a family with them. We owe it to our people to give them the freedom to choose."

"She's right, you know." Lochlan came up behind them.

"It's not about us anymore. We get to choose our family." He turned to watch the twins playing with the other royal children. "It's not about blood or magic. It's about love."

"Are we doing this?" Alona and Finn approached the fire with Neeve and Myles.

"This is going to change everything," Brea said, holding the scroll toward the flames.

"Do it." Myles took his wife's hand. "We'll find a new way forward."

"We always do," Alona agreed.

With a smile for her family, Brea dropped the scroll into the flames, and they all took a step back.

Griffin felt it the moment the last fragments of his bond with Brea shattered. It was like losing a thousand pound weight from his shoulders. It felt like freedom. For a man who'd spent so much of his life beholden to others, it was everything.

Fae's Rebellion is up next, but
Don't forget your bonus chapters.
That's right, there's more!
Get your bonus chapters here: michellelynnauthor.com/fpbonus

WHAT'S NEXT?
FAE'S REBELLION: QUEENS OF THE FAE BOOK 7

A powerful fae princess desperate to escape her future.

A broody prince holding her captive.

Tia O'Shea just wants to go home, back to the palace among snowy fields where her twin brother amplifies the power inside her, and her father tries to secure the future of the throne through her marriage.

A marriage she doesn't want and refuses to consider. As a future queen, Tia only wants a choice in this one part of her life.

On the night of the ball to introduce all possible suitors for her hand, she escapes to the human realm, planning to return after everyone has come to their senses. She never expected anyone to follow her, let alone her best friend and two of her suitors.

When the portal home goes awry, she finds herself separated from the others, without her magic, and stranded in a kingdom she knows nothing of, a kingdom torn apart by generations of war.

Tia has been through her fair share of war, she knows what

happens to those caught in the middle, but avoiding it might not be possible if she wants to find her friends.

To recover her missing magic and find a way back home across the treacherous fire plains, she might have to wade right into the fight.

But first, she has to escape the prince claiming her as prisoner.

Fae's Rebellion is the seventh book in the Queens of the Fae series. It begins the story of Tia O'Shea, a familiar face all grown up and struggling for independence in a world full of powerful magic and heightened expectations.

Prepare to lose yourself in this beautifully wicked epic fantasy world with masterful world building, dark and twisty secrets, lies, powerful magic—and devastatingly handsome fae princes.

WANT MORE FROM BREA'S WORLD?

Don't miss the FREE prequel,
Fae's Dilemma
BookHip.com/VJMXVGD

About Michelle

Michelle MacQueen is a USA Today bestselling author of love. Yes, love. Whether it be YA romance, NA romance, or fantasy romance (Under M. Lynn), she loves to make readers swoon.

The great loves of her life to this point are two tiny blond creatures who call her "aunt" and proclaim her books to be "boring books" for their lack of pictures. Yet, somehow, she still manages to love them more than chocolate.

When she's not sharing her inexhaustible wisdom with her niece and nephew, Michelle is usually lounging in her ridiculously large bean bag chair creating worlds and characters that remind her to smile every day - even when a feisty five-year-old is telling her just how much she doesn't know.

See more from M. Lynn and sign up to receive updates and deals!

www.michellelynnauthor.com

ALSO BY M. LYNN

Queens of the Fae

Fae's Deception | *Fae's Defiance* | *Fae's Destruction* | *Fae's Prisoner* | *Fae's Power* | *Fae's Promise* | *Fae's Rebellion* | *Fae's Refuge* | *Fae's Return* | *Fae's Envoy* | *Fae's Enemy* | *Fae's End*

The Hidden Warrior

Dragon Rising | *Dragon Rebellion*

Fantasy and Fairytales

Golden Curse | *Golden Chains* | *Golden Crown*

Glass Kingdom | *Glass Princess*

Noble Thief | *Cursed Beauty*

Legacy of Light

A War For Magic | *A War For Truth* | *A War For Love*

About Melissa

Melissa A. Craven is an Amazon best-selling author of YA Contemporary Fiction and YA Fantasy (Contemporary fans will know her as Ann Maree Craven). Her books feature strong female protagonists who aren't always perfect, but find their inner strength along the way. Melissa believes in stories that make you think and she loves foreshadowing, leaving clues and hints for the careful reader.

Melissa draws inspiration from her background in architecture and interior design to help her with the small details in world building and scene settings. She is a diehard introvert with a wicked sense of humor and a tendency for hermit-like behavior. (Seriously, she gets cranky if she has to put on anything other than yoga pants and t-shirts!)

Melissa enjoys editing almost as much as she enjoys writing, which makes her an absolute weirdo among her peers. Her favorite pastime is sitting on her porch when the weather is nice with her two dogs, Fynlee and Nahla, reading from her massive TBR pile and dreaming up new stories.

Visit Melissa at Melissaacraven.com for more information about her newest series and discover exclusive content.

ALSO BY MELISSA A. CRAVEN

Queens of the Fae

Fae's Deception | *Fae's Defiance* | *Fae's Destruction* | *Fae's Prisoner* | *Fae's Power* | *Fae's Promise* | *Fae's Rebellion* | *Fae's Refuge* | *Fae's Return* | *Fae's Envoy* | *Fae's Enemy* | *Fae's End*

Immortals of Indriell

Emerge (Book 1) | *Edge* (Book 0) | *Catalyst* (Short Story)

Judgment (Book 2) | *Scholar* (Series Companion) |

Volunteer (Short Story) | *Captive* (Book 3)

Assignment (Novella) | *Heir* (Book 4) | *Betrayal* (Book 5)

Runaway (Book 6) | *Proving* (Book 7)

Ascension of the Nine Realms

The Reluctant Queen | *The Rejected Queen* | *The Rebel Queen* | *The Ruthless Queen*

www.ingramcontent.com/pod-product-compliance
Lightning Source LLC
Chambersburg PA
CBHW030526310726
48979CB00010B/1820/J

* 9 7 8 1 9 7 0 0 5 2 2 5 1 *